Banana Hammock

A "Write Your Own Damn Story"
Harry McGlade Adventure

by JA Konrath

Author's Warning

This ebook is filled with raunchy humor, and has something to offend everyone. If you believe there are taboo things that shouldn't be laughed at or made fun of, stop reading right now and pick up one of my other, less-offensive books. But if you like roasting sacred cows, read on. You'll probably laugh.

Author's Note

This is not a single, linear ebook, and should not be read in order.
I repeat: DON'T READ THIS PAGE BY PAGE.
This ebook is meant to be read out of order, depending on the path you, the reader, choose.
Harry McGlade is a continuing character in the Jacqueline "Jack" Daniels series. At the end of each section, you decide where Harry goes, and what he does. By following different paths, you can arrive at many different endings. There are literally hundreds of variations.
You control the character. You control the fun.
Join Harry and a cast of characters pulled from JA Konrath's and Jack Kilborn's stories, and push ebook technology to the boundaries of reading enjoyment, or something like that.

Banana Hammock Drink Recipe

2 oz. light rum
1 oz. 99 Bananas Schnapps
1 oz. amaretto
1/2 oz. lime juice
1/2 oz. sweet and sour mix
Shake with ice.
Strain into a chilled cocktail glass.
Garnish with two maraschino cherries and half a peeled banana.

And so it begins…

I was on my Facebook page, racking up some major points in Combville—a game where you used a virtual comb to comb a virtual head of hair, over and over and over again until time and life lost all meaning and you questioned the reason for your birth. Then she walked into my office.

This woman had it all. Legs. Eyes. Elbows. A big head of blond hair that for some reason I wanted to comb. She wore a plain blue dress, and had a white bonnet on her head, which was unusual for Chicago. Actually, it was unusual for pretty much everywhere.

"Are you Harry McGlade? The private investigator?"

I nodded, still tapping the COMB button on my screen. Fifty-six thousand more strokes and I'd get a virtual gold coin. When I earned ten coins, I'd be able to buy a different color comb.

"My name is Lula. Lula Coleslaw. I need your help."

"Have a seat, Ms. Coleslaw," I said, pointing to the chair opposite my desk. Then I tore myself away from Facebook. Or at least I pretended to, and kept pressing the button.

She sat down and crossed her legs, in that way women do, with one leg over the other. Her perfume smelled like Crunchberries. She pulled a Kleenex out of her Gucci and dabbed at her Cover Girl eyes, asking me if I could give her a Diet Coke.

"Just get to the point," I said, indicating the book on my desk, Fair Use of Trademarked Brand Names.

"It's my husband, Mr. McGlade. I believe he's having an affair."

"I see. And you want me to find the floozy and scar her face with acid, make her unappealing to him?"

"What? No! That's barbaric."

"Should I scar his face with acid so she won't love him anymore?"

"I don't want any acid thrown in anyone's face. I just want you to follow him and tell me who he's sleeping with."

I nodded, closing my desk drawer, the one filled with all the acid bottles. "I charge five hundred a day, plus expenses. Expenses include tolls and parking meters, brunch, Xbox Live games, and air mattresses."

"Why do I have to pay for air mattresses?"

I shrugged. "Inflation."

"That's a lot of money for me, Mr. McGlade. You see, I'm Amish."

That probably explained the bonnet. And the Kiss Me I'm Amish button she wore. Which was odd, because I thought the Amish didn't wear buttons.

"Forgive me if this sounds insulting, you loony whackjob, but I wasn't aware of any Amish settlements in the Chicago metropolitan area."

"I'm from Indiana. We have a farming community near Gary. I'm a milkmaid."

I glanced at her hands, trying to imagine her strong, firm, insistent grip, and wondering how she managed to keep her fake nails from falling off.

"A milkmaid? Can you prove it to me? Maybe pretend I have udders?"

"No, I can't. But did you know that a cow has four stomachs?"

"That's a lot of tripe," I declared.

"Yes, it is."

"If I were to take this case," I said, "I'd want to be paid in actual cash money. Not three chickens and a handsomely made maplewood dresser."

"But it's a really nice dresser. Dovetail joints. Corner blocks."

I raised an eyebrow. "Mortise and tenon drawer frames?"

"Of course. And lacquered until it shines like a welfare baby's neglected wet bottom."

I clucked my tongue. But though I was a sucker for old world craftsmanship, you can't pay the rent with dovetail joints and a cherrywood inlay. Or can you? I never tried before. I did once try to pay my rent in spareribs, but got in trouble for pushing them under my landlord's door.

"It's a tempting offer, sugar lumps. But I'm afraid I only take cold, hard, stiff cash."

"How about credit cards?" she asked.

"The major ones, and some of the minor ones."

"Which minor ones?"

"You know. Angler's Club. The Bank of Murray. Velveesa."

She whipped out an Angler's Club card, a big picture of a walleye on it. Something about this was kind of fishy.

"Hold on a second, babydoll," I said, holding up my palm. "I haven't actually taken the case yet. Let me think about this while I comb."

Should Harry take the case? If so, go to page 5.

If he should keep playing Combville, go to page 6.

We walked out of my office, onto the city street. It was buzzing with electricity, and ComEd was there with a group of technicians and paramedics, trying to protect people from getting shocks and third-degree burns. As we rounded the corner, Lulu gasped at the sight of her horse and buggy being towed away. I soon saw why it had happened—she'd tried to pay the parking meter with two fresh eggs and a jar of marmalade.

"Amos is going to thrash me for this," Lulu pouted.

"Amos is your husband?"

She nodded. "I have welts on my bare bottom where he's beaten me with a switch."

"I may need to look at those later," I said. "For evidence, or something."

Lulu began to sob, her mascara running. "He's a horrible man, Mr. McGlade. A plain, God-fearing, horrible man. He beats me for the smallest of offenses. Burning down our home. Letting our son drown. Flarching…"

"Flarching?"

"That's farting during sex."

I stared at her. "I don't think that's a real word."

"Give it a month. Someone will upload it to UrbanDictionary.com."

Hmm. Perhaps the Amish were more progressive than I thought.

"So what should we do, Mr. McGlade? Go to the auto pound and pay to get my horse? Or just forget it and get on with this dumb story?"

To get the horse, go to page 9.

To get on with the story, go to page 10.

To return to the previous section, go to page 8.

"Will you help me, Mr. McGlade?"

"Hmm?"

Combville had once again captured my attention. Damn these repetitive, boring, addictive Facebook games. Why did I even bother with Facebook? And why did I only have five Facebook friends? And why were they all jerks?

I kept combing.

"Will you help me?" she asked, apparently still in my office.

"What? Oh. No. No I won't. I've got too much to do right now. But check back in a few days."

Sadness fell across her face and she stood up, turning to leave.

"Wait," I said. "Are you on Facebook?"

"No. We shun modern technology, Mr. McGlade. My ereader doesn't even have 3G."

"You mean it's only WiFi?"

She nodded, sadly. I felt for her, but I had to be firm on this. "Sorry, tastycakes. I'm really busy."

"Please, Mr. McGlade. I really need your help."

"Let me think about it again."

Should Harry take the case? If so, go to page 5.

If he should keep playing Combville, go to page 7.

"Will you help me, Mr. McGlade?"

"Hmm? Who are you?"

I'd gotten into a rhythm, tapping the Combville button in time with my heartbeat. It was almost as much fun as combing hair in real life, without all the hard work. Like having to actually lift a real comb.

I've always loved hair. Years ago, in a school play, I took the role of Macbeth's toupee. But it was a bad part.

(Please press the rimshot button on your ereader.)

"I'm Lulu Coleslaw. I—"

"You said that already. I thought you were leaving."

She turned to leave, giving me a sexy peek at her bloomers as her fifty pound dress twirled.

"Wait," I said.

"Yes?"

"Are you on Facebook?"

"You asked me that already."

"What did you say?"

"I said—"

"Nevermind. This is getting repetitive."

"Please. Will you help me?"

"I haven't decided yet. Let me think it over."

Should Harry take the case? If so, go to page 5.

If he should keep playing Combville, go to page 8.

"Mr. McGlade?"

"Hmm? Do I know you?"

"How many times are we going to keep doing this?"

"Doing what?" I asked.

Comb, comb, comb, comb, comb…

"Will you take my case or not?"

"Yes, I've got to make a decision, don't I? You seem to be getting annoyed, doing the same thing again and again. Personally, I think it's pretty funny."

"So will you?"

"Will I what?"

"Will you help me, Mr. McGlade?"

"Who are you again?"

"Lulu. Lulu Coleslaw."

"I think I knew a stripper named Coleslaw. Are you her?"

"Of course not. I'm Amish."

"Yep, I've known a lot of strippers with bad names."

"Are you going to help me?"

"I don't know. I'll have to think this through."

Should Harry take the case? If so, go to page 5.

If you want to read a list of bad stripper names, go to page 46.

If you believe that you have the power to change fate, go to page 6.

"Hell no, I don't want to get your damn horse," I said. "I'm an important man, with important stuff to do, probably."

I had my iPhone out and was accessing the Combville app.

"But Amos will starve! There's nothing to eat in an auto pound."

"Your horse is named Amos?"

She nodded.

"Isn't your husband named Amos as well?"

"Yes."

"You don't think that's odd?" I asked.

"Not at all. But my brother Amos finds it strange."

"I promise we'll get the horse later," I lied. "Right now we need to go to the costume shop."

"For what?" Lulu asked.

"For one of those plain black suits and an Abe Lincoln beard." I winked. "I'm going undercover as an Amish guy."

To go to the costume shop, go to page 10.

To skip to the end of the story, go to page 6.

To return to the previous section, go to page 5.

Clandestine Weston's Costume Shoppe was located two blocks from my office. It took forty minutes to find a cab. We arrived around four o'clock, which was perfect. Any later and we would have gotten caught in the after-work costume rush. I hated crowds. Especially crowds of people.

Weston, the owner, was dressed as a pirate, complete with an eye patch and a plastic hook for a hand. He wore a Show Me Your Booty button.

"Hello again, Jessica. Returning the costume so soon?" he asked Lulu.

"Don't mind her, Weston," I told him. "I need you to make me look like Harrison Ford's most famous character."

"The retard from Regarding Henry?"

"No. His other famous character."

"Ah. The Amish cop from Witness."

"Nailed it in two, Weston."

Weston walked past a Star Wars display and over to the Mennonite aisle. Lulu grabbed my shoulders and began to shake me, urgently.

"We need to get out of here," she said. "Right away."

"Stop it," I told her. "I thought you were Amish, not a Shaker."

I grinned at my clever pun, but Lulu didn't see the humor.

"I am Amish," she said. "Why would I lie about that? Do you think I'm lying? What good would it do me to lie?"

"Ease off the throttle, Goldilocks. You're too high strung. Let me rent this costume, and I'll blend into your quaint, idyllic community without anyone noticing, and find out who Amos is snogging."

A moment later, Weston had returned with full Amish regalia for me.

"Pay for it, tootsiepop," I told Lulu. Then I went into the dressing room, to get dressed. But halfway into putting on my pants, the magic of Combville ensnared me, and half an hour later someone was knocking on the door.

"Mr. McGlade?"

"Call me Sexybeast," I said. "That was my childhood nickname."

Actually, my childhood nickname was Bitch Tits. But that made me cry. "Are you okay in there?"

I finished dressing and opened the door. "I'm fine, baby. I've been dressing myself since high school."

She let out a deep sigh. "I was worried. I thought you figured out I was faking this Amish thing, and had taken off."

"I figured out no such thing. We ready to rock?"

Lulu nodded. Weston came up to us, grinning. "You look terrific, Harry. Here's one final touch.

He pinned a button to my coat. It said Amish is as Good as a Mile. Now my disguise was perfect. No one would ever know I was an imposter, living among the God-fearing.

But did I truly know enough about this mysterious and elusive race of prehistoric proto-humans known as the Amish? Was I ready to delve into their strange cult where they worshipped some imaginary savior named Jesus? Perhaps I needed to do some research before diving in.

Should Harry research the Amish? If so, go to page 12.
Should Harry just delve right into the case? If so, go to page 13.

I Googled "Amish" on my iPhone and wound up surfing several Amish porn sites, where I learned that their culture dates back to 1693, they're pacifists, and that threeways—mostly girl-girl-guy—were common.

After two minutes of exhaustive research, I gave up. Don't get me wrong. I like pornography as much as the next guy, if the next guy watches porn sixteen hours a day. But I was on a case, and nothing was going to deter me from finding out if Amos Coleslaw was cheating on his wife. So after a brief, forty-minute Combville session, Lulu and I hopped in my car and headed to Indiana.

To continue with the case, go to page 13.

To instead read *Pride and Prejudice with Sexy Vampires*, go to page 16.

The ride to Indiana was uneventful, except for those strange lights in the sky that we saw but really don't remember too well, and somehow we lost six hours and my butt hurts and I've got weird dreamlike memories about being strapped to a table and probed by skinny gray guys with huge black eyes. But other than that, nothing noteworthy happened.

When we arrived in the Amish settlement of Plaintown, I parked next to a Cadillac, put on my straw hat, and went with Lulu to find her husband. The day was sunny, and everywhere I looked there were crops and people tending crops. It seemed like a really croppy way to live.

"So, which one is Amos?" I asked Lulu.

"That's Amos over there." She pointed to a plain looking guy with a beard. I nodded, rolling up my sleeves. I'd been working this case for long enough. It was time to get some answers. Amos would tell me what I wanted to know, even if I had to beat on that pacifist all night and into tomorrow.

"You're sure these guys are pacifists, right?" I asked Lulu.

She shrugged, checking the messages on her cell phone. "I guess. Hit one a few times and see."

I stormed over. Seeing all of this peaceful cooperation and brotherly love was pushing my anger to an all-time high. I walked through the wheat, or the corn, or whatever it was, fists clenched and jaw set.

"Hey! You! With the beard!"

Eight men looked at me.

"I meant the one named Amos!"

"We're all named Amos," one of the Amoses said.

"No," I clarified, "the one wearing black!"

Since they all wore black, they looked at each other, confused.

"The one with the beard wearing black and the straw hat!"

More shrugs and confusion.

"The one pooping in the field!"

My victim said, "That's me." After wiping with a nearby plant, he pulled up his black pants and offered his hand. I didn't take it, because it had crop all over it.

"Can, I help you, Brother?" he asked, polite and peacefullike.

"You and your non-violent stance make me sick," I said. "Who do you think you are, going around, not hitting anybody? Tell me something, braniac, how would we defend this great country of ours if the whole world suddenly turned into pacifists?"

"Your beard is coming off."

"Don't sass me," I said, slapping that non-threatening look right off his face. I braced myself, waiting for him to hit me back. He didn't. But even if he tried to, I wasn't worried. The guy had to be at least ninety years old.

I slapped him again.

"That's for beating your wife, you peaceful old man. Shame on you for picking on someone who can't defend themselves."

"My wife is dead, Brother."

This made my fury even furiouser. "You killed her? You heartless, God-fearing man of the earth!"

"Say, Brother, what's going on here?"

I looked around, and saw the Amish had surrounded me. I don't scare easily, except during scary movies and lightning storms and being in rooms with too many minorities. Diversity was another way of saying put your wallet in your front pocket. But being surrounded by pacifists made my heart turn into ice.

Well, actually, my heart didn't really turn into ice. If it did, I'd be dead. Then I couldn't be telling you this story in the first person.

"Back off! Everyone! This man here cheated on his dead wife, who hired me."

I pointed at Lulu, but she'd vanished.

"What did you do with her body, you gray-bearded bastard!" I slapped him again.

"See here, Brother," said one of the younger, healthier-looking Amish. He seemed about my age and height, so I backed away from him.

"Keep your distance," I warned him. "I'm not looking for a fair fight."

"There must be some misunderstanding. Why don't we go inside and discuss this over some apple pie?"

I laughed. "You think you can bribe me with three slices of pie with homemade ice cream on top? Who do you think I am? Some sort of pie lover?"

Should Harry accept the pie? If so, go to page 38.
Should Harry keep beating defenseless Amish ass? If so, go to page 41.

It is a truth universally acknowledged, that a single man in possession of a good fortune, must be in want of a wife.

A sexy vampire wife!

However little known the feelings or views of such a man may be on his first entering a neighborhood, this truth is so well fixed in the minds of the surrounding families, that he is considered the rightful property of some one or other of their daughters.

"My dear Mr. Bennet," said his lady to him one day, "have you heard that Netherfield Park is let at last?"

Mr. Bennet—who was a SEXY VAMPIRE!—bit her on the neck and bled that nosy bitch dry. Then she became a vampire, and they had hot vampire sex, sucking each other in ways that made them both go, "Oooooo, that's nice." They even installed a mirror above the bed. But that didn't really do much.

Then the sun came up and they both caught on fire turned to dust.

The End

To go back to the Harry McGlade story, go to page 13.

To read *The Ugly Duckling Does Meth*, go to page 17.

It was so beautiful out on the country, it was summer—the wheat fields were golden, the oats were green, and down among the green meadows the hay was stacked, and so was the farmer's daughter, Roxy, whose breasts were the size of country hams, but without the brown sugar glaze. There Roxy sulked about in her shiny pleather jacket and torn black fishnets, scowling a lot, fiddling with one of the five piercings in her right eyebrow. Roxy was a Goth, and had so many piercings that magnets would leap off the refrigerator and stick to her face when she walked past, which made her scowl even more. Yes, it was indeed lovely out there in the country, but to Roxy it might as well have been a diaper landfill, judging by the unhappy expression on her face.

Roxy was a meth dealer.

In the midst of the sunshine there stood an old manor house that had a deep moat around it. From the walls of the manor right down to the water's edge great burdock leaves grew, and there were some so tall that little children could stand upright beneath the biggest of them, though none of them knew what the word "burdock" meant and had to look it up in the ereader dictionary, just like you're about to do. In this wilderness of leaves, which was as dense as the forests itself, denser even than a Mongoloid child dropped down a flight of stairs, a duck sat on her nest, hatching her ducklings. She was becoming somewhat weary, because the welfare check hadn't come yet, and she needed a snort of ice soon or she was going to chew off her own face.

Then, Roxy hooked her up, and so began a downward spiral that soon had her giving handjobs for fifty cents down at the old folks' home, losing her teeth, and eventually overdosing and dying in an alley, rotting in a pool of her own feces. Seventeen elderly men came to her funeral, which was actually quite nice. They served little cakes.

The End

To go back to the Harry McGlade story, go to page 13.
To read *Huckleberry Finn: The Director's Cut*, go to page 19.

You don't know about me without you have read a book by the name of The Adventures of Tom Sawyer; but that ain't no matter. That book was made by Mr. Mark Twain, and he told the truth, mainly. There was things which he stretched, but mainly he told the truth. That is nothing. I never seen anybody but lied one time or another, without it was Aunt Polly, or the widow, or maybe Mary. Aunt Polly—Tom's Aunt Polly, she is—and Mary, and the Widow Douglas is all told about in that book, which is mostly a true book, with some stretchers, as I said before.

Now the way that the book winds up is this: Tom and me found the money that the robbers hid in the cave. Then we got rip-roarin' drunk and blew the cash on whores. Tom's was so old her hips crackled like fried pig skins, and mine had sores on her feminine parts that smelled like rotten chicken feet. Now I got me some sores too, 'ceptin' they're on my slappin' stick, which bleeds when I pee. Hurts, too. Like someone is shoving a maple branch up the piss hole and twistin' it hard.

Then some men came and hung Miss Watson's slave, Jim.

Also, my Pap raped me in the bum.

The End

To go back to the Harry McGlade story, go to page 13.
To read the *Book of Genesis with Zombies*, go to page 20.

In the beginning God created the heaven and the earth. And the earth was without form, and void; and darkness was upon the face of the deep. And the Spirit of God moved upon the face of the waters. And God said, Let there be zombies: and there were zombies. And the zombies spread across the land, riding around on dinosaurs, eating people and turning them into more zombies. And then the dinosaurs also became zombies. And then Cain slew Able, and ate him, and they both ate Moses, which angered the Lord, because there was no eating on the Sabbath.

And on the seventh day, God rested. And He hasn't been back to work since.

Then the Jews killed Jesus, and seized control of the media and the banks.

Also, the earth is only five thousand years old.

To go back to the Harry McGlade story, go to page 13.

To file a formal complaint about this ebook, go to page 6.

To quit this case and have Harry take a different case about private schools, go to page 21.

Bored with the Amish, I put that case on hold and went back to my office to take a new case.

"Cute kid," I said.

The kid looked like a large pink watermelon with buck teeth and bug eyes. If I hadn't already known it was a girl, I couldn't have guessed from the picture. What was that medical name for children with a overdeveloped heads? Balloonheadism? Bigheaditis? Melonoma? Freak?

"She takes after her mother."

Yeeech. My fertile mind produced an image of a naked Mrs. Potatohead, unhooking her bra. I shook away the thought and handed the picture back to the proud Papa.

"Where is Mom, by the way?"

Mr. Morribund leaned close enough for me to smell his lunch—tuna fish on rye with a side order of whiskey. He was a thin guy with big eyes who wore an off-the-rack suit with a gold Save The Dolphins tie tack.

"Emily doesn't know I'm here, Mr. McGlade. She's at home with little Rosemary. Since we received the news she's been… upset."

"I sympathize. Getting into the right pre-school can mean the difference between summa cum laude at Harvard and offering mouth sex in back alley Dumpsters for crack money. I should know. I've seen it."

"You've seen mouth sex in back alley Dumpsters?"

I nodded my head in what I hoped what looked like a sad way. "It isn't pretty, Mr. Morribund. Not to look at, or to smell. But I don't understand how you expect me to get little Rotisserie—"

"It's Rosemary."

"—little Rosemary into this school if they already turned down your application. Are you looking for strong-arm work?"

"No, nothing like that."

I frowned. I liked strong-arm work. It was one of the perks of being a private eye. That and breaking and entering.

"What then? Breaking and entering? Some stealing, maybe?"

I liked stealing.

Morribund swallowed, his Adam's apple wiggling in his thin neck. If he were any skinnier he wouldn't have a profile.

"The Salieri Academy is the premier pre-school in the nation, Mr. McGlade. They have a waiting list of thousands, and to even have a chance at attending you have to fill out the application five years before your child is conceived."

"That's a long time to wait for nookie." But then, if I were married to Mrs. Potatohead, I wouldn't mind the wait.

"It's the reason we took so long to have Rosemary. We paid the application fee, and were all but assured entrance. But three days after Rosemary was born, our application was denied."

"Did they give a reason?" Other than the fact that your kid looks like an albino warthog who has been snacking on an air compressor?

"No. The application says they reserve the right to deny admittance at their discretion, and still keep the fee."

"How much was the fee?"

"Ten thousand dollars."

Ouch. You could rent a lot of naughty videos for that kind of money. And you'd need to, because those things get boring after the third or fourth viewing.

"So what's the deal? You want me to shake the guy down for the money."

He shook his head. "Nothing of the sort. I'm not a violent man."

"Spell it out, Mr. Morribund. What exactly do you want me to do? Burn down the school?"

I liked arson.

"Goodness, no. The Salieri School is run by a man named Michael Sousse."

"And you want me to kidnap his pet dog and take pictures of me throwing it off a tall building, using my zoom lens to capture its final barks of terror as it takes the express lane to Pancakeville? Because that's where I draw the line, Mr. Morribund. I may be a thug, a thief, and an arsonist, but I won't harm any innocent animals unless there's a bonus involved."

Morribund raised an eyebrow. "You'd do that to a dog? The Internet said you love animals."

"I do love animals. Grilled, fried, and broiled. Or stuffed with cheese. I'd eat any animal if it had enough cheese on top. It wouldn't even have to be dead first."

"Oh."

Morribund made a face, and I could tell he was thinking through things. I glanced again at his Save the Dolphins tie tack and realized I might have been a little hasty with my meat-lovers rant.

"I had a dog once," I said.

"Really?"

"Never tried to eat him. Not once."

I mimed crossing my heart. Morribund stared at me.

"This all seems terribly familiar," he said.

"Did you read Jack Daniels Stories by J.A. Konrath? This was one of the many hilarious cases in that excellent collection. Only $2.99 at Smashwords. Do you have an ereader? All smart, attractive, successful people have ereaders. So perhaps you don't have one."

"You sound like a shill for Smashwords."

I picked up my Leonard Riggio Rocks My World coffee mug and took a sip of cold joe. "I don't shill for any corporations. Even corporations as efficient, inexpensive, and customer friendly as BarnesAndNoble.com. You can get seventeen J.A. Konrath ebooks for under three bucks each. But we're getting a bit off track here."

When Morribund spoke again, his voice was lower, softer.

"Headmaster Sousse, he's a terrible man. A hunter. Gets his jollies shooting poor little innocent animals. His office is strewn with so-called hunting trophies. It's disgusting."

"Sounds awful," I said, stifling a yawn.

"Mr. McGlade," he leaned in closer, giving me more tuna and bourbon. "I want you to find out something about Sousse. Something that I could use to convince him to accept our application."

I scratched my unshaven chin. Or maybe it was my unshaved chin. I get those words confused.

"I understand. You want me to dig up some dirt. Something you can use to blackmail Sousse and get Rheumatism—"

"Rosemary."

"—into his school. Well, you're in luck, Mr. Morribund, because I'm very good at this kind of thing. And even if I don't find anything incriminating in his past, I can make stuff up."

"What do you mean?"

"I can take pictures of him in the shower, and then Photoshop in the Vienna Boy's Choir washing his back. Or I can make it look like he's pooping on the floor of the White House. Or being intimate with a camel. Or eating a nun. Or…"

"I don't want the sordid details, Mr. McGlade. I simply want some kind of leverage. How much will something like that cost?"

I leaned back in my chair and put my hands behind my head, showing off my shoulder holster beneath my jacket. I always let them see the gun before I discussed my fees. It dissuaded haggling.

"I get four hundred a day. Three days minimum, in advance. Plus expenses. I may need to bring in a computer expert to do the Photoshop stuff. He's really good."

I took a pic out of my desk drawer and tossed it to him. Morribund flinched. I smiled at his reaction.

"Looks real, doesn't it?"

"This is fake?"

"Not a single baby harp seal was harmed."

"Really?"

"Well actually, they were all clubbed to death and skinned. But the laughing guy in the parka wasn't really there. We Photoshopped him into the scene. That's the beauty and magic of jpeg manipulation. Look at this one." I threw another photo onto his lap. "Check out that bloody discharge. And those pustules. Don't they look real? It's like they're going to burst all over your hands."

Morribund frowned. "I've seen enough."

"Want to see one with my head on Brad Pitt's body with Ron Jeremy's junk?"

"I really don't."

"How about one of a raccoon driving a motorcycle? He's wearing sunglasses and flipping the bird."

Morribund stood up.

"I'm sure you'll come up with something satisfactory. When can you get started?"

I fished an appointment book out of my top drawer. It was from 1996, and only contained doodles of naked butts. I pretended to scrutinize it.

"You're in luck," I said, pulling out a pen. I drew another butt. A big one, that took up the entire third week of September. "I can start as soon as your check clears."

"I don't trust checks."

"Credit card?"

"I dislike the high interest rates. How about cash?"

"Cash works for me."

After he handed it over I got his phone number, he found his own way to the door, and I did the Money Dance around my office, making happy noises and shaking my booty.

Things had been slow around the agency lately, due to my lack of renewing my Yellow Pages ad. I didn't get many referrals, because I charged too much and wasn't good at my job. Luckily, Morribund had found me through my Internet site. The same computer geek who did my Photoshop work was also the webmaster of my homepage. Google "Chicago cheating spouse sex pictures" and I was the fourth listing. If you Google "naked rhino make-over" I was number two. I still didn't understand the whole keyword thing. That's probably why Morribund thought I was an animal lover.

A quick check of my watch told me I wasn't wearing one, so I looked at the display on my cell phone. Almost two in the afternoon. Time to get started.

I booted up the computer to search for the Salieri School and Christopher Sousse. But instead, I wound up on YouTube, and watched videos of a monkey in a funny hat, a fat woman falling down the stairs, and a Charlie Brown cartoon that someone dubbed over with the voice track to Goodfellas.

After wasting almost an hour, I went to MySpace and read all of my messages from all of my friends, all of whom seemed to work in the paid escort industry.

After that, I checked my eBay bids, my Hotmail account, and added a new entry to my blog about the high cost of parking in the city.

After that, porn.

Finally, I located the Salieri School's website, found their phone number, and dialed.

"Salieri Academy for Exceptionally Gifted Four-Year-Olds, where children are our future and should be heavily invested in, this is Miss Janice, may I help you?"

Miss Janice had a voice like a hot oil massage, deep and sensual and full of petroleum.

"My name is McGlade. Harrison Harold McGlade. I'd like to enroll my son Stimey into your school."

"I'm sorry sir, there's a minimum five year waiting period to get accepted into the Salieri academy. How old is your son now?"

"He's seven."

"We only accept four-year-olds."

"He's got the mind of a four-year-old. Retard. Mom dropped him down an escalator, he fell for forty minutes. Very sad. All someone had to do was hit the off switch."

"I don't understand."

"Why? You a retard too?"

"Mr. McGlade…"

"I'm willing to pay money, Miss Janice. Big money. I'll triple your enrollment fee."

"I'm sorry."

"Okay, I'll double it."

"I don't think that…"

"Look, honey, is Mikey there? He assured me I'd be treated better than this."

"You know Mr. Sousse?"

"Yeah. We played water polo together in college. I saved his horse from drowning."

"Perhaps I should put you through to him."

"Don't bother. I'll be there in an hour with a suitcase full of cash. I won't bring Stimey, because he's with his tutor tonight, learning how to chew. Keep the light on for me."

I hung up, feeling smug. I hadn't shared this with Morribung, but this case really hit home for me. Years ago, when I was a toddler, I'd been forced to drop out of pre-school because I kept biting and hitting the other children. The unfairness of it, being discriminated against because I was a bully, still haunted me to this day.

I hit the computer again and prowled the Internet for dirt on Sousse. Nothing jumped out at me, other than a minor news article a few weeks back about one of his teachers being dismissed for reasons unknown. According to the story, Sousse was deeply embarrassed by the incident and refused to comment.

Then I surfed for Morribund and his wife and kid, and found zilch.

Then I surfed for naked pictures of Catherine Zeta Jones until it was time for me to keep my appointment.

But first, I needed to gear up.

I wound my spy tie around my neck, careful with the wires. Concealed in the tie clip was a digital camera, a unidirectional microphone, and a 20 gigabyte mp3 player loaded with bootleg Tori Amos concerts. It weighed about two pounds, and hurt my back to wear. But it would be my best chance at clandestinely snapping a few photos of Mr. Sousse during our meeting—photos I could later retouch so it looked like he was molesting a pile of dirty laundry.

People would pay a lot of money to keep their dirty laundry out of the news.

Forty minutes later I was pulling into a handicapped parking spot in front of the Salieri Academy on Irving Park Road. Last year, I'd bought a handicapped parking sticker from a one-legged man in line at the DMV. It only cost me ten dollars. He had demanded five hundred, but I simply grabbed the sticker and strolled away at a leisurely pace. Guy shouldn't be driving with only one leg anyway.

The Academy was a large, ivy-covered brick building, four stories high, in the middle of a residential area. As I was reaching for the front door it began to open. A woman exited, holding the hand of a small boy. She was smartly dressed in skirt and blazer, high heels, long brown hair, maybe in her mid-thirties. The boy looked like a honey-baked ham stuffed into a school uniform, right down to the bright pink face and greasy complexion. When God was dishing out the ugly, this kid got seconds.

I played it smooth. "Wouldn't let you in, huh?"

"Excuse me?"

I pointed my chin at the child.

"Wilbur, here. All he's missing is the curly tail. The Academy won't take fatties, right?"

The boy squinted up at me.

"Mother, is this stupid man insinuating that I have piggish attributes?"

I made a face. "Who are you calling stupid? And what does insinuating mean?"

"Just ignore him, Jasper. We can't be bothered by plebeians."

"Hey lady, I'm 100% American."

"You're 100% ignoramus."

"What do dinosaurs have to do with this?"

She ushered the little porker past me—no doubt off to build a house of straw—and I slipped through the doorway and into the lobby. There were busts of dead white guys on marble pedestals all around the room, and the artwork adorning the walls was so ugly it had to be expensive. I crossed the carpeted floor to the welcoming desk, set on a riser so the secretary looked down on everyone. This particular secretary was smoking hot, with big sensuous lips and a top drawer pulled all the way out. Also, large breasts.

"May I help you, Sir?"

Her voice was sultry, but her smile hinted that help was the last thing she wanted to give me. I got that look a lot, from people who thought they were superior somehow due to their looks, education, wealth, or upbringing. It never failed to unimpress me.

"I called earlier, Miss Janice. I'm here to see Mikey."

Her smile dropped a fraction. "I informed Mr. Sousse that you were coming, and he regrets to inform you that—"

"Cork up that gas leak, sweetheart. I'm really a private detective. I'd like a chance to talk with Mr. Sousse about some embarrassing facts I've uncovered about one of your teachers here," I said, referring to that incident I'd Googled. "Of course, if he doesn't want to talk with me, he can hear about it on the ten o'clock news. But I doubt it will do much for enrollment, especially after that last unfortunate episode."

Miss Janice played it coy. "Whom on our staff are you referring to?"

"Are you Mr. Sousse? I can avert my eyes if you want to lift your skirt and check."

She blushed, then picked up the phone. I gave her a placating smile similar to the one she greeted me with.

"Do you have ID?" she asked, still holding the receiver.

I flashed my PI license. She did some whispering, then hung up.

"Mr. Sousse will see you now."

"How lucky for me."

She stared. I stared back.

"You gonna tell me where his office is, or should I just wander around, yelling his name?"

She frowned. "Room 315. The elevator is down the hall, on the left."

I hated to leave with an attractive woman annoyed with me, so I decided to disarm her with wit.

"You know, my father was an elevator operator. His career had a lot of ups and downs."

Miss Janice kept frowning.

"He hated how people used to push his buttons," I said.

No response at all.

"Then, one day, he got the shaft."

She crossed her arms. "That's not funny."

"You're telling me. He fell six floors to his death."

Her frown deepened.

"Tell me, do they have heat on your planet?" I asked.

"Mr. Sousse is expecting you."

I nodded, my work here done. Then it was into the elevator and up to the third floor.

Sousse's office was decorated in 1960's Norman Bates, with low lighting that threw shadows on the stuffed owls and bear heads and antlers hanging on the walls. Sousse, a stern-looking man with glasses and a bald head, sat behind a desk the size of a small car shaped like a desk, and he was sneering at me when I entered.

"Miss Janice said you're a private investigator." His nostrils flared. "I don't care for that profession."

"Don't take it literally. I'm not here to investigate your privates. I just need to ask you a few questions."

A stuffed duck—of all things—was propped on his desktop, making it impossible for me to get a clear shot of his face with my cleverly concealed camera tie. I moved a few steps to the left.

"Which of my staff are you inquiring about?"

"That's confidential."

"If you can't tell me who we're discussing, why is it you wanted to see me?"

"That's confidential too."

I shifted right, touched the tie bar, heard the shutter click. But the lighting was pretty low.

"I don't understand how I'm supposed to—"

"Does this office have better lights?" I interrupted. "I'm having trouble seeing you. I'm getting older, and got cadillacs in my eyes."

"Cadillacs?"

I squinted. "Who said that?"

"Do you mean cataracts?"

"I don't like your tone," I said, intentionally pointing at a moose head.

Sousse sighed, all drama queen, and switched on the overhead track lighting.

Click click went my little camera.

"Did you hear something?" he asked.

I snapped a few more pics, getting him with his mouth open. My tech geek should be able to Photoshop that into something particularly rude.

"Does your tie have a camera in it?" he asked.

I reflexively covered up the tie and hit the button for the mp3 player. Tori Amos began to sing about her mother being a cornflake girl in that whiney, petulant way that made her a superstar. I fussed with the controls, and only succeeded in turning up the volume.

Sousse folded his arms.

"I think this interview is over."

"Fine," I said, loud to be heard over Tori. "But you'll be hearing from me and Morribund again."

"Who?"

"Don't play coy. People like you disgust me, Mr. Sousse. Sure, I'm a carnivore. But I don't get my jollies hunting down ducks and mooses and deers and squirrels." I pointed to a squirrel hanging on the wall, dressed up in a little cowboy outfit. "What kind of maniac hunts squirrels?"

"I'm not a hunter, you idiot. I abhor hunting. I'm a taxidermist."

"Well, then I'm sure the IRS would love to hear about your little operation. You better hope you have a good accountant and that your taxidermist is in perfect order."

I spun on my heels and got out of there.

Mission accomplished. I should have felt happy, but something was nagging at me. Several somethings, in fact.

On my way through the lobby, I stopped by Miss Janice's desk again.

"When Sousse fired that teacher a few weeks ago, what was the reason?"

"That's none of your business, Mr. McGlade."

"Some sex thing?"

"Certainly not!"

"Inappropriate behavior?"

"I won't say another word."

"Fine. If you want me to pick you up later and take you to dinner, stay silent."

"I'd rather be burned alive."

"We can do that after we've eaten."

"No. I think you're annoying and repulsive."

"How about a few drinks? The more you drink, the less repulsive I get."

She folded her arms and her voice went from sultry to frosty. "Employees of the Salieri Academy don't drink, Mr. McGlade."

"I understand. How about we take a handful of pills and smoke a bowl?"

"I'm calling security."

"No need. I'm outtie. Catch you later, sweetheart."

I winked, then headed back to my office. When I arrived, I spend a good half hour on the Internet, digging deeper into the Salieri story, using a reverse phone directory to track a number, and looking up the words insinuating, plebian, ignoramous, and taxidermist. Then I gave Morribund a call and told him I had something for him.

An hour later he showed up, looking expectant to the point of jubilation. Jubilation is another word I looked up.

"Did you get the pictures, Mr. McGlade?"

"I got them."

"You're fast."

"I know. Ask my last girlfriend."

We stared at each other for a few seconds.

"So, are you going to give them to me?"

"No, Mr. Morribund. I'm not."

He leaned in closer, the whiskey coming off him like cologne. "Why? You want more money?"

"I'll take all the money you give me, but I'm not going to give you the photos."

"Why not?"

I smiled. It was time for the big revealing expositional moment.

"There are a lot of things I hate, Mr. Morribund. Like public toilets. And the Red Sox. And massage girls who make you pay extra for happy endings. But the thing I hate the most is being lied to by a client."

"Me? Lie to you? What are you talking about?"

"You don't want to get your daughter into the Salieri Academy. You don't even have a daughter."

His eyes narrowed.

"You're insane. Why would you think such a thing?"

"When I went to the Academy, I ran into some kid in a Salieri uniform, and he was uglier than a hatful of dingle-berries with hair on them. If he got in, then the school had no restrictions according to looks. Isn't that right, Mr. Morribund? Or should I use your real name... Nathan Tribble?"

He sighed, knowing he was beaten. "How did you figure it out?"

"You didn't pay me with a check or credit card, because you didn't have any in the name you gave me. But you did give me your real phone number, and I looked it up in the Internet. I also found out you once worked at the Salieri Academy. Fired a few weeks ago. For drinking, I assume."

"It never affected my job! I was the best instructor that stupid school ever had!"

I didn't care about debating him, because I wasn't done with my brilliant explanation yet.

"You came to me because you found me on the Internet and thought I liked dogs. That's why you wore that Save the Dolphins tie tack. You said Sousse was a hunter, to make me dislike him so I'd go along with your blackmail scheme."

"Enough. We've established I was lying."

But I still had more exposing to expose, so I went on.

"Sousse isn't a hunter, Tribble. He's a taxidermist. And you're no animal lover either. You can't be pro-dolphin and also eat tuna. Tuna fisherman catch and kill dolphins all the time. But your breath smelled of tuna during our last meeting."

"Why are you telling me things I already know?"

"Because that's what I do, Tribble. I figure out puzzles by putting together all the little pieces until they all fit together and form a full picture, made of the little puzzle pieces I've fit together. Or something."

"You're a low-life, McGlade. All you do is take dirty pictures of people. Or you make up dirty pictures when there are none to take."

"I may be a low-life. And a thief. And a voyeur. And an arsonist. And a leg-breaker. But I'm not a liar. You're the liar, Tribble. And you made a big mistake. You lied to me."

Tribble snorted. "So? Big deal. I got fired, and I wanted to take revenge. I figured you wouldn't do it if I asked, so I made up the story about the daughter, and added the pro-animal garbage to get you hooked. What does it matter? Just give me the damn pictures and you can go play Agatha Christie by yourself in the shower."

I stood up.

"Get out of my office, Tribble. I'm going to make two calls. The first, to Sousse, to tell him what you've got planned. I bet he can make sure you'll never get a teaching job in this town again. The second call will be to a buddy of mine at the Chicago Police Department. She'll love to learn about your little blackmail scheme."

Tribble looked like I just peed in his oatmeal.

"What about the money I gave you?"

"No give-backsies."

He balled his fists, made a face, then stormed out of my office.

I grinned. It had been a productive day. I'd made a cool twelve hundred bucks for only a few hours of work, and that was only the beginning of the money train.

I got on the phone to my tech geek, and told him I was forwarding a photo I needed him to doctor. I think Sousse would look perfect Photshopped into a KKK rally, wearing a Nazi armband and goose-stepping. Also, raping a manatee.

Sure, I wasn't a liar. But I was a sucker for a good blackmail scheme.

Not bad for a pre-school drop-out.

The End

To go back to the other Harry story, go to page 13.

To read an exclusive X-rated manatee sex scene, go to page 6.

If you've reached this page, you did so by cheating. Because this page isn't actually connected to any other pages.

Don't you know that cheaters never win?

Except in this case.

In this case, cheaters win… immortality!

That's right! Because you decided not to follow the rules, and go through this ebook page by page instead of skipping around like you were supposed to, the Magic Smashwords Fairy* has granted you the gift of eternal life.

You are now an immortal!**

So go out there and do all those things you always dreamed of doing. Like setting yourself on fire. Or jumping off of a high building. Or tying a big rock to your neck and dropping it into a lake.

Yes, the fun you can have with immortality is practically limitless.

So what are you waiting for? Commit suicide and test your immortality today!

*Yes, Smashwords is indeed magic. Marc Coker also cures cancer.†

**Some restrictions may apply. Immortality may include side effects such as boredom, boring other people, disgust with the lack of quality programming on television, itching, diarrhea, and instant death if you do anything stupid, like the examples noted above. Void where prohibited, and in the state of Maryland.

† Marc Coker doesn't really cure cancer. But he does cure unhappiness.

"Mmmm-mmm. This is some fine pie, Amos."

I wiped off my mouth on his wife's dress and gave the little filly a playful slap on the ass.

"I'm glad you enjoyed them, Brother McGlade. I'd offer you more, but you've eaten all six."

It was just as well. I needed to lose some weight. I know this because I've got a recent picture of me hanging on the wall, and it keeps falling off.

"Just bring over that tub of lard and that bag of brown sugar," I said. "That'll be fine."

I dipped my finger in the lard, then the sugar, and licked it clean. I could certainly see the appeal of living like this, eating organic, with no harsh chemical additives like guar gum, or yellow number 5, or H2O. I hated harmful additives so much that I've completely given up soda pop, which was bad for you. These days I drink only straight corn syrup.

"So you say a woman named Lulu hired you?" Amos asked.

"Did I?" I was on my second lard-finger, sucking up the health benefits.

"The worry is, Brother McGlade, we've been having some trouble lately. A construction company keeps trying to buy our land. They've sent in their heavies to beat us, day and night. Our children, too. Little Amos there has two freshly broken legs."

I glanced at some child on crutches, his eyes red from crying.

"Yeah, that's a real tragedy," I said. "Now hobble over to the cupboard for me, Little Amos, and get Brother Harry that pound of butter."

Like a good little Ahmlet, he listened to his elder.

"And keep the moaning down," I said. "I'm eating here."

"We've even gone to the local authorities," Amos continued, apparently thinking I cared. "But the construction company paid them off. They dragged old Amos out into the field the other day, and kicked him between the legs so many times his procreation parts swelled up to the size of a suckling piglet."

I dipped my finger in the butter, then the sugar, then the lard, and took a big lick. Downhome goodness. "I don't care about your quaint local customs, Amos. I'm here to find out who Lulu's husband is screwing."

"Please, Brother McGlade." Amos's wife clasped her hands over Little Amos's ears, so hard she knocked away his crutches. "Language."

"Oops. My bad. Let me rephrase it for the sensitive viewers. All I care about is finding the... lady... that Amos is... making babies with."

"Thank you," Mrs. Amos said.

I nodded. "Of course, it isn't really making babies if they're sucking each other off, or if he's drilling her up the shit chute."

"Mother, you and Little Amos go into the bedroom," Amos told them. They hurried away, as fast as his painful little broken legs could carry him.

"Brother McGlade, I don't mean to be hospitable..."

"Then don't," I grinned, giving him a friendly tug on his beard.

"Brother McGlade..."

"Look," I said, sticking the jar of lard under my arm. "I'm very busy, and you plainly aren't helping. Get it? Plainly?"

"Brother McGlade..."

"How many of you moronites are in this little settlement?"

"It's Mennonites."

"Aren't those the things in the ocean, like coral?"

"You're thinking of anemones."

"So how many of you anemones are in this little settlement?"

"Our settlement has two hundred and eighteen folk here."

"Holy shit! That many? How many families is that?"

"Seventeen."

"Damn! And your women are so damn plain!"

Amos nodded humbly. "The Lord said to multiply."

"Maybe he was talking about being good at math. Man, haven't any of you heard of condoms? Maybe you should grow those, instead of corn. I'll be leaving now."

I took the pot of sugar under my other arm, then left.

But where was I to go next?

Should Harry interview other Amish in town? If so, go to page 44.

Should Harry try to find Lulu? If so, go to page 45.

Should Harry quit this case and take another one about assassination? If so, go to page 141.

To return to the previous section, go to page 13.

There I was, surrounded by Amish. But I wasn't going to allow myself to get intimidated by a bunch of tolerant, God-fearing pacifists. Not in my America, the land of Chuck Norris, who is so tough that he wipes his ass with Arnold Schwartzenegger.

I moved in on the nearest one, the old guy I'd been slapping around, and hit him so hard it knocked out his entire family's teeth. Then I spun around, kicking another Amos in the chest, knocking him back into the corn where no doubt some creepy Stephen King children would sacrifice him to an unholy monster, maybe.

The Amish knew the best offense was a good defense, so they fled into the field, hoping to overpower me by retreating. I followed, pushing corn out of my way, coming to a round clearing in the middle of the field. All of the crops were neatly broken, in a giant circle.

How odd. One might even call it alien.

"Hey! Anyone there?"

Whoever wasn't there didn't answer.

I shivered. It was getting dark out. Dark and spooky. I realized that a lot of nocturnal animals came out at night. Some were very scary, like panthers. And piranha.

Then I saw a bright flash of eerie, green light from above. I squinted up at it. Was it God? Or just some asshole in a helicopter with a search light?

But I didn't hear helicopter propellers. Just a strange, otherworldly humming sound.

Was I having a religious experience in the middle of this cornfield? Maybe God was mad because I'd broken all of his commandments, except that false idol one, but only because I had no idea what it meant. Did people in old times actual pray to idols? What morons. Didn't they know it was much smarter to pray to an imaginary, ethereal being?

Then, somehow, through some supernatural miracle, God beamed me up and I was suddenly in heaven, surrounded by angels. Except that heaven looked a lot like a high tech space laboratory, and the angles were little green people with big, bald heads and ray guns.

"So," I said, "which one of you ugly guys is Jesus?"

Then one of the angels zapped me with some sort of heavenly stun laser, paralyzing me.

"Puny earth human," he said, "we are Reptiloids from the planet Reptilon in the Reptilish Galaxy. We will first probe you with our uncomfortable butt devices, then force you to fight in intergalactic gladiator games for the amusement of a live, television audience."

I squinted at him. "Look, I know I missed church on a few Sundays. Like all of them. But there's no need to be a dick about it."

The little green angels surrounded me, strapped me face-first to a table, and then violated me in ways that I normally paid $39.95 for at my local massage parlor. But there was no happy ending this time. Instead, I was dressed in some sort of cheap, plastic armor and dropped in the middle of a stainless steel coliseum, the rafters filled with thousands of ugly green dudes waving banners that said, "Death to Earthlings" and "This Isn't Heaven You Dumb Ass."

"Enough!" I yelled, my voice all echoey in the arena. "I demand to speak to St. Peter. First of all, I don't even remember dying. Second of all, I actually don't believe in God. The whole Intelligent Design argument is moronic. An intelligent designer would have eliminated the need for flossing. And toilet paper. And what's with kidney stones? What kind of all knowing, all powerful being would…"

My words trailed off when I saw a gate open and a tyrannosaurus rex stomp out.

A tyrannosaurus rex ridden by a zombie.

Acting quickly, I panicked. Panic soon became frantic running around in tight circles while screaming and waving my hands.

Suddenly, by the power of grayskull, two items materialized in the sand right in front of me.

One was a steel broadsword, of the King Arthur type.

The other was a book of matches and a can of aerosol hairspray.

Should Harry take the sword? If so, go to page 100.

Should Harry take the matches and can of hairspray? If so go to page 102.

To return to the previous section go to page 13.

I knew the only way to get to the bottom of things was to actually do some work. This was unfortunate, as I preferred to take the easy way out. But since I was getting paid, I figured I might as well make at least a token effort.

Unfortunately, Lulu was nowhere to be found. I should have gotten her cell phone number. I also should have gotten her address, having absolutely no idea where she lived. Planning ahead was one of those skills I hadn't mastered yet.

So I walked down the quaint dirt road to another plain house. I stepped onto the quant, plain porch and knocked on the quaint, plain door. A bearded man entered.

"Are you Amos Coleslaw?"

"No, I'm Amos Johannsen. What can I help you with, Brother?"

"I'm looking for Coleslaw."

"I wish I could help you. How about potato salad instead?"

"Not the food. The person. Where does Amos Coleslaw live?"

"I don't know anyone by that name. I'm sorry. There's no one in Plaintown named Coleslaw. I'd be surprised if there is anyone in the country named Coleslaw. It sounds made up."

And then it hit me. It was so obvious I should have realized it sooner.

This guy was obviously Amos Coleslaw, and lying about it.

I shoved him backward and shut the door behind me. I was sick of all this Amish treachery. I swore I'd get the truth out of this man even if I had to beat him so hard he automatically confessed to everything I accused him of.

"It's all over, Coleslaw. I know everything. And I'm willing to smack you around until you admit to my outlandish whims. Tell me about Lulu."

"Who?"

"Wrong answer. You had your chance. Now we do it my way."

If Harry should beat him into confessing, go to page 193.

If Harry should use reason and common sense, go to page 196.

To return to the previous section, go to page 38.

I had to find Lulu. But there had to be seventeen houses in this Amish settlement, which could take me the better part of the night.

Of course, it's easy to dwell on the negative. That's why I do it, because it's easy. I deal with so many negatives, I oughta go into photography.

Hey, don't get mad at me. You're the one who paid $2.99 for this.

Frankly, I was getting pretty sick of this adventure. And since this is an ebook, I saw no reason why I had to stay in this story, when there are other perfectly good stories available on Snashwords.

In fact, you and I could go check one out, if you prefer. Or, we can keep schlepping through this one and hope it ends soon. It's your choice.

To continue with this adventure, go to page 44.

To skip into another ebook, go to page 104.

To return to the previous section, go to page go to page 38.

Harry's List of Bad Stripper Names

We all know strippers named Candi and Princess and Chesty. Here are a few with unfortunate nicknames:

Beans

Clitorectomy

Bulemia

Iron Lung

Wife

Fisty

Dingle Berry

Melanoma

Barbara Bush

Queefmaster

Sloppy Eighths

Tranny

Mom

The Yeaster Bunny

Open Sore

Jesus

Red Stain

OD

Crying Mail Order Bride

Third Trimester

Molested By Daddy

Earl

Spastic Colon

Son

Skid Marks

Leaky

Gramps

To return to Harry's Amish adventure, go to page 5.

To read another Harry adventure, where he battles zombies, go to page 48.

Bored with people named Amos, I went back to my office and took another case.

Chapter 1

"It's my husband, Mr. McGlade. He thinks he can raise the dead."

The woman sitting in front of my desk was named Norma Cauldridge. She had the figure of a Barlett pear and so many freckles that she was more beige than Caucasian. She also came equipped with a severe overbite, a lazy eye, and a mole on her cheek. Not a Cindy Crawford type of mole, either. This one looked like she glued the end of a hotdog to her face. A hairy hotdog.

Plus, she smelled like sweaty feet.

Any man married to her would certainly have to raise the dead every time she wanted sex. But I didn't become a private investigator to meet femme fatales. Well, actually I did. But mostly I did it for the money. And hers was green just like anyone else's.

I took a can of Lysol aerosol deodorizer from my desk and gave the air a spritz. Now it smelled like sweaty feet and pine trees. With a hint of lavender.

"I get four hundred a day, plus expenses," I told her.

I put away the air freshener and tried to sneak a look behind her large round Charlie Brownish head. When she walked into my office a minute ago, I'd been watching the National Cheerleading Finals on cable. The TV was still on, but I had muted the sound to be polite.

"I didn't tell you what I want you to do yet."

She was a whiner too. Nasally and high-pitched. It's like God took a dare to make the most unattractive woman possible.

"You want me to take pictures of him acting crazy, so you can use them in the divorce."

On television a group of nubile young twenty-somethings did synchronized cartwheels and landed in splits. I love cable.

"How did you know?" Norma asked.

I glanced at Norma. The only splits she ever did were banana.

"It's my job to know, ma'am. I'll need your address, his place of work, and the first three days' pay in advance."

Norma's face pinched.

"I still love him, Mr. McGlade. But he's not the same man I married. He's…obsessed."

Her shoulders slumped, and the tears came. I nudged over the box of Kleenex I kept on the desk for when I surfed certain internet sites.

"It's not your fault, Mrs. Drawbridge."

"Cauldridge."

"A man is talking, sweetie. Don't interrupt."

"Sorry."

"The fact is, Nora, some men aren't meant to marry. They feel trapped, tied down, so they seek out different venues."

She sniffled. "Necromancy?"

"I've seen all sorts of perversions in my business. One day he's a good husband. The next day, he's a card-carrying necrosexual. Happens all the time."

More tears. I made a mental note to look up "necromancy" in the dictionary. Then I made another mental note to buy a dictionary. Then I made a third mental note to buy a pencil, because I always forgot my mental notes. Then I watched the cheerleaders do high kicks.

When Norma finally calmed down, she asked, "Do you take Visa?"

I nodded, wondering if I could buy used cheerleading floormats on eBay. Preferably ones with stains.

Chapter 2

Ebay didn't have any.

Instead I bid on a set of used pom-pons and a coach's whistle. I also bid on some old Doobie Brothers records. That led to placing a bid on a record player, since mine was busted. Then I bid on a carton of copier toner, because it was so cheap, and then I had to bid on a copier because I didn't have one. But after thinking about it a bit, I realized I didn't really need a copier, and those Doobie Brothers albums were probably available on CD for less than the cost of a record player.

I tried to cancel my bids, but those eBay jerks wouldn't let me. The jerks.

I buried my anger in online pornography. Three minutes later, I headed out the door, slightly winded and ready to get some work done.

Chapter 3

This chapter is even shorter than the last one.

Chapter 4

George Drawbridge worked as a teller for Oak Tree Bank. At a branch office. It was only three o'clock, and his wife told me he normally stayed until five, so I had plenty of time to grab a few beers first. Chicago is famous for its stuffed crust pizza, and I indulged in a small pie at a nearby joint and entertained myself by asking everyone who worked there if they made a lot of dough.

An hour later, after they asked me to leave, I sat on the sidewalk across the street from the bank, hiding in plain sight by pretending I was homeless. This involved untucking my shirt and pockets, messing up my hair, and holding up a sign that said *"I'm homeless"* written on the back of the pizza box.

Other possibilities had been, *"Will do your taxes for food"* and *"I'm just plain lazy"* and my favorite *"this is a piece of cardboard."* But I went with brevity because I still didn't have a pencil and had to write it in sauce.

I sat there for a little over and hour before George Drawbridge appeared.

He looked like the picture his wife gave me, which wasn't a surprise because it was a picture of him. Balding, thin, pinkish complexion, with a nose so big it probably caused back problems. After exiting the bank he immediately went right, moving like he was in a huge hurry. I almost lost him, because it took over a minute to pick up the eighty-nine cents people had thrown onto the sidewalk next to me. But I managed to catch up just as he boarded a northbound bus to Wrigleyville.

Unfortunately, the only seat left on the bus was next to George. So that's where I parked my butt, because I sure as hell wasn't going to stand if I didn't have to.

I gave him a small nod as I sat down.

"I'm not following you," I told him.

George didn't answer. He didn't even look at me. His eyes were distant, out there. And up close I noticed his rosy skin tone wasn't natural—he was sunburned. Only on the left side of his face too, like Richard Dreyfuss in that Spielberg movie about aliens. The one where he got sunburned on only the left side of his face. I think it was *Star Wars*.

Unlike his wife, George didn't smell like sweaty feet. He smelled more like ham. Honey baked ham. So much so that I wondered if he had any ham on him. I've been known to stuff my pockets with ham whenever I visited an all-you-can-eat buffet. After all, ham is pricey.

I restrained myself from asking if he indeed had any pocket ham, but couldn't help humming the Elton John song *"Rocketman"* and changing the lyrics in my head.

"Pocket ham… And I think I'm gonna eat a long, long time…"

I didn't know the rest of the song, so I kept think-singing that line over and over. After a few stops George stood up and left the bus. I followed him, keeping my distance so I didn't make him nervous. But after walking for a block I realized I could stand on the guy's shoulders and piss on his head and he still wouldn't notice me. George Drawbridge was seriously preoccupied.

We went into an Ace Hardware Store, and George bought twenty feet of nylon clothesline He also bought something called a magnetron. I knew that there was something I needed to buy, but I couldn't remember what it was, and I hadn't written it down because I needed to buy a pencil. So I got one of those super large cans of mega energy drink. It contained three times the recommended daily allowance of taurine, whatever the hell taurine was.

After the hardware store it was back to the bus stop. We were the only two people there. George didn't pay any attention to me, but I was worried all of this close contact might get him a little suspicious. So I made sure I stood behind him, where he couldn't see me. Then I popped open my mega can and took a sip.

The flavor on the can said "Super Berry Mix." The berries must have been mixed with battery acid and diarrhea juice, but with a slightly worse taste. It burned my nose drinking it, to the point where I may have lost some nostril hair. Plus it was a shade of blue only found in nature as part of neon beer signs. I could barely choke down the last forty-six ounces.

The bus came. Again, the only seat available was next to George. I took it, and pulled my shirt up over my mouth and nose to disguise myself.

"Goddamn germs on public transportation," I said, loud enough for most of the bus to hear. This provided a clever reason for my conspicuous face-hiding behavior. I said it seven more times, just to be sure.

We took the bus to Jefferson Park, a northwest side neighborhood named after that famous politico, Thomas Park. George exited on Foster. I followed, tailing him up Pulaski and into the Montrose Cemetery, my mind racing like a race car on a race track, driven by a race car driver, named Race.

I never liked cemeteries. Not because I'm afraid of ghosts, even though when I was a child all the kids used to tease me because they thought I was. They would dress up like ghosts and try to scare me by visiting my house at night and threatening to hang us all because my family didn't go to church. They usually left after burning a cross on our lawn. Damn ghosts.

No, I hated graveyards for much more realistic reasons. When a person died they shouldn't be kept around, like leftovers. People had a freshness date. Death meant *discard*, not preserve in a box. What ghoul thought that one up? Fifty thousand years ago, did some caveman plant Grandma in the ground hoping to grow a Grandma Tree? What fruit did *that* bear? Saggy wrinkly breasts that hung to the ground and smelled like Ben Gay and pee-pee? And what's with neckties? Why are men forced to wear a strip of cloth around their necks good for absolutely nothing except getting caught in things like doors and soup?

As my computer-like mind pondered these imponderables, George cleverly gave me the slip by walking someplace I could no longer see him. That left me with three options.

1. Wait at the entrance for him to come out.

2. Search for him.

3. Drain the lizard. Those eighty ounces of Super Berry Taurine had expanded my bladder to the size of a morbidly obese child, named Race.

I opted for number 3, and chose *Mary Agnes Morrison, Loving Wife and Mother*, to sprinkle. Maybe the taurine would liven up her eternity.

I soaked her pretty good, and had enough left over for the rest of the Morrison family, including the *Loving Husband and Father*, the *Beloved Uncle*, and the *Slutty Skank Daughter*.

I made that last tombstone up, but it would sure be cool if it was real, wouldn't it? And wouldn't it be cool if someone made a flying car? One that gave you head while you drove? I'd buy one.

I shook twice, corralled the one-eyed stallion, and began to look for George. An autumn breeze cooled the sweat on my face, neck, ears, hair, armpits, back, legs, and hands, which made me aware that I was sweating. I put a hand to my heart and discovered it was beating faster than Joe Pesci in a Scorsese flick. Because he beats people in those flicks. Beats them fast.

Why was I so edgy? Had my subconscious tapped into some sort of collective, primal fear? Did my distant ancestors, with their reptile brains and their bronze weapons made of stone, leave some sort of genetic marker in my

DNA that made me sensitive to lurking danger?

I did a 360, looking for pointy-headed ghosts with gas cans. All I saw were tombstones, stretching on for as far as I could see. Hundreds. Thousands. Maybe even billions.

"Easy, McGlade. Nothing to be afraid of. It's not like you desecrated their graves or anything."

Noise, to my left. I had my Magnum in my hand so fast that it probably looked like it magically appeared there to anyone watching, even though I didn't think anyone was watching.

Anyone *alive*.

My eyes drifted up an old, scary-looking tree, which had branches that looked like scary branch-shaped fingers, but with six fingers instead of the usual five, which made it even scarier. The sun was going down behind the tree, silhouetting some sort of nest-shaped mass on an extended limb that I guessed was a nest.

"Chirp," went the nest.

My first shot blew the nest in half, and two more severed the branch from the tree.

"Dammit, McGlade. Stay cool. You just assassinated a bird."

Which saddened me greatly. Magnum rounds were a buck-fifty each. Plus, I didn't have any extras on me. I needed to stay cool.

"Chirp," went the nest.

BLAM! BLAM!

By heroic effort I didn't shoot the nest a sixth time, instead walking briskly in the opposite direction. I was in a state that might be called "hyper-awareness," which was a lot like being the lone antelope at the watering hole. I could feel the stares of flying insects, and hear the grass growing. It was freaking me out a little bit, so I began to run, tripping over something on the ground, skidding face-first against a tombstone. A damp tombstone.

Mary Agnes Morrison.

I scurried away, palms and knees wet, and saw the bright red object that caused me to fall.

The empty can of Super Berry Mix energy drink.

So my paranoia wasn't really paranoia after all. It was just an unhealthy amount of caffeine in my veins. Which would have been kind of funny if I wasn't soaked with my own piss. Along with the taurine, the drink apparently contained a full day's supply of irony.

I stood up and shook out my pants legs.

"Get a grip, McGlade. And stop talking to yourself. You always know what you're going to say anyway."

I took three or ten deep breaths, holstered my weapon, and then set out looking for George.

I had no idea that in just two minutes I was going to die.

Chapter 5

I didn't actually die. I'm lying to make the story more exciting, because this part is sort of slow.

It starts to pick up in Chapter 8. Trust me, it's worth the wait. There's sodomy.

Chapter 6

It was a fruitless search, but that didn't matter—I wasn't looking for fruit. After a few minutes, I'd found him. He'd given me the slip by cleverly disguising himself as a group of three bawling women. Closer inspection, and some grab ass, revealed they really were women after all. I did my "pretend to be blind and deaf" act and stumbled away before any of them called the police or their lawyers.

Luckily, I caught sight of an undisguised George heading into the mausoleum. I never liked mausoleums. Burying the dead was bad enough. Putting them in the walls was just begging for mice to move in. And not the kind of mice who wear red pants and open up amusement parks. I'm talking about dirty, vicious, baby-face-eating mice, the size of rats.

Actually, I'm talking about rats.

Speaking of non-sequiturs, I really needed to take another leak. The mausoleum was decent-sized, with a few hundred vaults stacked four high. Well lit, temperature controlled, silk plants next to marble benches every twenty feet. It was the kind of place that would have a bathroom, I thought, while pissing on one of the silk plants. The pot it was in wasn't any realer than the plant, because all of my piss leaked out the bottom. I stepped over the puddle and commenced the search.

One of the techniques they teach you in private eye school is how to conduct a search, I bet. I have no idea, because I didn't go to private eye school. I wasn't even sure that private eye school actually existed. But it did in my fantasies. All the teachers were naked women, and wrong answers were punished with spankings. And the water fountains were actually beer fountains. If they had a school like that, I'd go for sure.

George wasn't down the first aisle. He wasn't down the second aisle either. Or the first aisle, which I checked again because I got confused.

"You do this?"

I spun around, wondering who spoke. It was some little old caretaker guy, clutching a mop. He pointed at the puddle on the floor.

"It was that other guy," I said, thinking fast. "You see him anywhere?"

"I only seen you, buddy. Did you go to the bathroom on my floor? There's a bathroom right there behind you. What kind of man does a thing like this?"

"That's what happens when you don't go to college."

"You piss on the floor?"

"You get a job cleaning up piss on the floor."

I left the guy to his menial labor and peeked down the second aisle again. Still no George. That led me down the third aisle, and I caught a glimpse of George crawling into a hole in the wall.

Closer inspection revealed it wasn't a hole. It was a vault. He'd crawled into someone's open tomb. I didn't even want to think why he'd do that, but my mind thought of it anyway, and then started thinking of it in enough detail that made me nauseous, yet oddly disgusted. Maybe a necromancer was someone who got his freak on with corpses. It was certainly a cheap date—only a few bucks for Lysol and Vaseline—and unless your game was really weak you'd pretty much always score. Still, I liked my women partially awake, and aware enough to be able to fight me off and tell me no. Because *no* means try harder.

I crouched down, peering into the blackness, and saw nothing but the aforementioned blackness. I fished out my keys, which had a mini flashlight attached to the ring, and illuminated the situation.

This wasn't a grave after all. In the hole was a slide, like you'd find in a children's playground, if the playground was in a mausoleum, and the children were all dead. Probably wouldn't be a lot of kids begging to go to a park like that. Not the dead ones, anyway.

I gritted my teeth. There was only one way to find out where this slide went.

"Hey, old caretaker guy!" I yelled. "Where does this slide go?"

"Go to hell!"

"I told you, it wasn't me. I had asparagus on my pizza. Does it smell like asparagus?"

"Go to hell!"

I rubbed my chin. Maybe old caretaker guy was trying to tell me that this slide went straight to hell. I didn't really believe him. First of all, I didn't see any flames, and there wasn't any smoke or brimstone or screams of the damned. Second, hell doesn't really exist. It's a fairy tale taught by parents to make their kids behave. Like Santa Claus. And the death penalty.

Still, going down a pitch black slide in a mausoleum wasn't on my list of things to do before I died. My list was mostly centered around Angelina Jolie.

"This *does* smell like asparagus, you bastard!"

A glanced over my shoulder. Old caretaker guy was hobbling toward me, his drippy asparagus mop raised back like a baseball bat—a stinky, wet baseball bat that you wouldn't want to use in a baseball game, because you wouldn't get any hits, and because it was soaked with urine and stinked.

I decided, then and there, I wasn't going to play ball with old caretaker guy. Which left me no choice. I took a deep breath and dove face-first down the slide.

Chapter 7

When I was ten years old, my strange uncle who lived in the country took me into his barn and showed me a strange game called *milk the cow*. The game involved a strong grip, and used a combination of squeezing and stroking until the milk came. I remember it was weird, and hurt my arm, but kind of fun nonetheless.

Afterward, we fed the cow some hay and used the fresh milk to make pancakes. When we finished breakfast, we watched a little television. It was a portable, with a tiny ten-inch screen.

Many years later, my strange uncle got arrested, for tax evasion. So I have no idea why I'm bringing any of this up.

The slide was a straight-shot down, no twists or curve. The dive jostled my grip and my key light winked out, shrouding me in darkness, like a shroud. I had no idea how fast I was going or how far I traveled. Time lost all meaning, but time really didn't matter much anyway since I'd bought a TiVo. Minutes blurred into weeks, which blurred into seconds, which blurred into more seconds. When I finally reached the bottom, I tucked and rolled and athletically sprang to my butt, one hand somewhere near my holster, the other cupped around my boys to protect them, not to fondle them, even though that's what it might have looked like.

I listened, my highly attuned sense of hearing sensing a whimpering sound very near, which I will die before admitting came from me, even though it did.

I'd landed on my keys. Hard.

When I stood, they remained stuck in me, hanging from my inner left cheek like I'd been stabbed by some ass-stabbing key maniac. I bit my lower lip, reached back, and tugged them out, which made the whimpering sound get louder. It hurt so bad I didn't even find it amusing that I now had a second hole in my ass, and perhaps could even perform carnival tricks, like pooping the letter X. That's a carnival I'd pay extra to see.

I found the key light and flashed the beam around, reorienting my orientation. I was in some sort of secret lower level beneath the mausoleum. Dirt walls, with wooden beams holding up the ceiling, coal mine style. To my left, a large wooden crate with the cryptic words TAKE ONE painted on the side. I refused. Why did I need a large wooden crate?

Noise, from behind. I spun around, reaching for my gun, and a dark shape tumbled off the slide, ramming into me and causing my keys to go flying, blanketing me in a blanket of darkness.

The ensuing struggle was viscous and deadly, but my years of mastering Drunken Jeet Kune Do Fu from watching old Chinese karate movies paid off. Just as I was about to deliver the Mad Crazy Hamster Fist killing blow, my attacker got some sort of weapon between us and smacked me in the face. The blow staggered me, and I reached up and felt the extensive damage, my whole head bathed in warm, sticky liquid that smelled a lot like asparagus.

Then a light blinded me. A real flashlight, not the dinky one I had on my keys. I squinted against the glare, and saw him. Old caretaker guy. A light in one hand. His mop in the other.

I spat, then spat again. My mouth had been open when he hit me.

"I'm a private detective. My name is McGlade. I'm on a case."

"Does your case involve pissing on my floor?"

I spat again. I could taste the asparagus. And the piss. It tasted like I always guessed piss would taste like. Pissy.

"Listen, buddy, you're violating federal marshal law by interfering with my investigation. Climb back up the slide and go call 911. Tell them there's a 10-69 in progress, with, uh, malice aforethought and misdemeanor prejudicial something, rampart."

My knowledge of cop lingo didn't galvanize him into action.

"Climb up the slide? How?"

"Hands and knees, old man."

"I'll get all dirty."

"You're a janitor."

"I'm a caretaker."

"You clean up in a cemetery. Dirt shouldn't bother you."

The flashlight moved off of my face and swept the area.

"What is this place? Some sort of secret lower level under the mausoleum?"

I spat again. "No duh."

"Look, there's a crate."

Old caretaker guy waddled over to the wooden TAKE ONE box, opened the top, and pulled out a brown robe.

"I guess we're supposed to take the robes."

"Obviously."

I walked over, grabbing a robe for myself. It was made out of felt, and had a large hood. A monk's robe. Or rather, a store-bought Halloween monk's costume.

Old caretaker guy put his on, and as he was tugging it over his head I gave him a Crazy Hamster Elbow to the chin. He went down, hopefully in need of some facial reconstructive surgery. I scooped up his flashlight, located my keys, and limped down the tunnel.

I followed the path a few dozen yards into the darkness, ducking overhead beams when they appeared overhead, keeping an eye peeled for rats, and giant spiders, and that guy I was supposed to be following, I think his name was Fred or George or something common and only one syllable. Maybe Tom. Yeah, Tom.

No, it was Fred.

The air down here was cool and heavy and smelled like asparagus piss, but for the most part it was clean. That meant ventilation, either in the form of an exit, or an air osmosis recirculator, and I'm pretty sure that osmosis thing didn't exist because I just made it up.

The tunnel ended at a large metal door, the kind with a slot at eye-level that opened up so some moron could ask you for a password. Which is exactly what happened. The slot opened, and a pair of eyes stared out at me, and whoever belonged to those eyes asked for a password.

"Tom sent me," I said.

"That's not the password."

"Tom didn't say there was a password."

"Tom who?"

"Tom," I improvised, "from Accounting."

"How is Tom?"

"Good. Just got over a cold, still kind of congested."

"It's great you know Tom, but I'm not supposed to let you in without a password."

I was tempted to give him a Three Stooges eye poke through the slot.

"Look," I reasoned, "why else would I be down here?"

"I have no idea. Maybe you got lost."

"I'm wearing the robe." I did a little sashay to emphasize the fact.

"Maybe you're a cop."

"I'm not a cop."

"How do I know that?"

"Because I don't have a badge. You want to frisk me to check?"

"No. You smell like pee-pee."

I set my jaw. "Doesn't anyone ever forget the password?"

The eyes shrugged. "Sure. Happens all the time."

"So what happens then?"

"I ask them for the back-up password."

I drew my Magnum, jammed it in the slot.

"Is the back-up password *open the fucking door or I'll blow your head off?*"

"Yep that's the password."

He opened the door. I considered smacking password boy in the head, and it seemed like a good idea, so I gave him a little love tap with the butt of my pistol. When he fell over, I gave him another little love tap in the stomach, with my foot. This made my ass hurt even more, so I kicked him again, which hurt even more, so I kicked him again for causing me pain, and again, and again until the pain got so bad I had to stop, but I didn't, I kicked him once more.

Then I wandered through a short hallway and into a large open area, roughly the size of a woman's basketball court, which is the same size as a men's basketball court, but a woman's court has bouncing boobs. I noticed little details like that. Unfortunately, this room didn't have bouncing boobs. It had a dozen-plus boneheads in robes, all carrying flashlights, standing around and chanting something monkish.

I wormed my way into the group and considered the camera in my pocket. Mrs. Drawbridge had hired me to take pictures of her husband acting nutty. This qualified, but it was too dark to make out any details, and a flash might cause attention. Plus, these jamokes all had their hoods on, making positive ID pretty impossible.

I scanned the room, seeing if I could find Tom. I spotted him through my clever detective technique of looking around, and noticed his bag from the hardware store, still clenched in his hand. Maybe I could get up close, shove the camera in his face, get a quick snapshot, then run away.

"Attention, everyone!"

The chanting stopped. One of the wannabe monks had his hands up over his head, his knuckles brushing the dirt ceiling. Everyone stared at him.

"Let us form the sacred pentagon, and pray to Anubis, god of the dead, to bless the ceremony this evening. All hail, Anubis!"

"All hail, Anubis!" the monks chanted in reply.

Then we all arranged ourselves in a five-sided square around something in the center of the room. As I probably should have guessed—but didn't because I was too busy rubbing my painful throbbing ass—in the center of the room was a coffin.

The head monk shouted, "Who shall be the first to partake in the carnal pleasures of beyond the grave?"

I looked around, wondering what idiot would be stupid enough to bone a corpse, then found myself shoved into the center of the circle.

"My friend will go!"

I spun around, aiming the flashlight. It was old caretaker guy, a big grin creasing his face.

"the first has been chosen!" head monk bellowed. Two other monks— big ones—grabbed my arms and escorted me to the coffin.

"Guys, I'm new here. I'd sort of prefer to wait until next time before violating any dead people."

I tried to pull away, but these monks had supernatural strength. The weight of the situation began to weigh on me. Sex with a cadaver wasn't on the list of things I wanted to do before I died, unless the cadaver was Angelina Jolie.

Then I stopped struggling, because I realized this had to be some kind of joke. Like a hazing prank, and when the coffin opened a stripper would pop out and blow me. That made a lot more sense than a society of necrophiliacs meeting secretly under one of Chicago's largest cemeteries. Right?

I smiled, hoping the stripper had big tits, not even protesting when I was depantsed by one of the hulky monk guys. They also took my gun. I figured that was okay—I only needed one type of gun to handle a hot stripper. You know what I mean.

My penis. I'm talking about my penis.

"Okay." I clapped my hands together. "Let's do this."

Another monk opened the coffin, and I stared in grinning expectation at a naked dead man.

"That's a guy," I said.

Head monk came in close and whispered. "Couldn't find girl this time. It doesn't matter. Death is death. It's all a turn-on. You're here to get laid, right?"

I eyed the body. A chubby bald white guy, late fifties. The Y cut across his chest indicated he was autopsied. Death was probably a heart attack, based on the size of his gut.

"I'm actually not really feeling it right now," I said.

"We can flip him over, if that helps."

"I don't think it will help."

"How fresh is it?" someone in the crowd yelled.

"Planted eight days ago," head monk answered.

The crowd cheered.

"I got sloppy seconds!"

"I got thirds!"

"I want to go last, when he's so full he's leaking out of his nose!"

I tried to step away, but the inhumanly muscular monks held me firm.

"I'm really not horny right now," I insisted. "In fact, I may never be horny again."

"My friend is shy!" That damn old caretaker guy again. "He doesn't like to pitch! He prefers catching!"

"No problem. Fetch the bicycle pump!"

Someone brought over a bike pump, complete with needle tip. The head monk fussed around with the poor dead guy's junk, then pushed the needle into the pee hole at the shriveled tip. I had an anti-erection, my dick actually retreating into my body as I watched.

He began to pump. And, incredibly, the corpse's johnson responded by filling out in length and width, until it stuck up like a tent pole. The monk kept pumping, and then the scrotum inflated. First apple-sized. Then grapefruit. Then soccer ball. I winced, waiting for the *POP*, but he quit before it got to medicine ball proportions. Which is a good thing, because balls that big would be bad medicine indeed.

"This is wrong on so many levels," I said.

Someone stuck a tube of KY into my hand, the head monk said, "Have fun," and then I was tossed onto the corpse, the coffin lid slamming closed above me with devastating finality.

Chapter 8

I lied. There isn't any sodomy in this chapter. Instead, there was a good minute of mindless screaming panic, followed by a minute of mindless yelling terror, and another two minutes of unmanly begging.

"We're not opening up until you finish," head monk spoke through the coffin lid.

"I'm finished." I hoped I sounded sincere. "It was fantastic. Best dead sex I ever had."

He wasn't buying. "The only way you're getting out of there is by embracing your necrophilia. That's why you came, isn't it? That's why we're all here. To make our fantasies come true. To taste the forbidden."

"I tasted it. It's like rotten meat, and disappointingly unresponsive."

"We can stay here all night if we have to."

I collected my thoughts, the sum total of which were *Get me the fuck out of here.* Then I calmed down a little. Then I started screaming again. Then calm. Then more screaming. Then even more screaming.

Finally, I took a deep breath, and really started screaming.

Being hysterical is pretty exhausting, so I took a time-out and tried to rationalize what to do next, other than scream.

Unfortunately, clearing my head made me even more aware of my current situation, and how disgustingly horrible it was. I was trapped in a coffin, lying on top of a naked dead guy with nuts the size of a basketball. A curly-haired basketball with a bratwurst glued onto the top. It pressed against my pelvis in a way that could only be described as awful.

My upper half wasn't any happier, with my face inches away from a dead man's. He didn't really smell like rotting meat. Not exactly. It was more like meat that was about to go bad, but dunked in formaldehyde first. His flesh was waxy, sort of stiff, and cold in a way that only dead people get. I moved my hands up across his nude, hairy chest, fighting the urge to vomit, and then pressed my elbows into his gut to force some distance between us.

It was a mistake. His autopsy meant his ribs had been cut away, and no ribs meant no internal support. My elbows ripped through the stitches and my arms disappeared into his still-moist body cavity.

I felt things. Horrible things. Squishy things. To prevent the organs from leaking, the clever embalmer had placed them in plastic bags, like some sort of lunch snacks from hell. I thanked the darkness that it was dark and I couldn't see anything, because I had no light. But I screamed anyway.

When the screaming finally stopped, I screamed a little more, and then realized the only way I was going to get out of here is to do what women have been probably doing with me ever since I'd been sexually active.

I'd have to fake it.

Unfortunately, the only way to fake a sexual movement is to perform a sexual movement. So I locked my knees on either side of his hips, his giant scrotum tucked beneath my legs like a fleshy bicycle seat, and began the humping motion. I also began to cry.

The coffin went with the rhythm, back and forth and back and forth, and it was a high end model which meant springs in the cushion which meant this felt even more like the real thing. Even though I couldn't see I squeezed my eyes shut and invented gods in my imagination so I could pray to them to make this end. I tried to think back on happy times, but too many of my happy times involved sex and that didn't help me block out the unhappy fact that I was fake dry-humping a corpse. I tried thinking about happy times when I was a kid, and unwillingly focused on the time I was six years old and my mother bought me a Hoppity Horse for my birthday, and how I used to love bouncing up and down the neighborhood and, oh goddamn it...

I threw up in my mouth. Energy drink and pizza mixed with stomach acid. I swallowed it because adding puke to this situation was possibly the only thing that could make it worse.

Scratch that last thought. My pelvic gyrations had loosened up some trapped air in the nether regions of the cadaver, prompting extreme flatulence. He ripped one so loud it sounded like a trumpet. But is sure as hell didn't smell like one. You think you know stink? Dead guy farts are number one on the stinkmeter. It was so bad, I'm sure if I could see I would have seen green gas.

"Do it! Give it to him!"

I wasn't sure who the head monk was cheering on, me or the dead guy. But I knew in order to properly fake it, I had to add some vocals to the rhythm.

"Oh, daddy!" I moaned, trying not to breathe. "Oh, yes, daddy!"

Someone slapped on the top of the coffin, urging me on. There was more corpse farting, more crying, more humping, and finally I couldn't handle this anymore without a complete nervous breakdown and I cried out "Oh, god!" and then went still.

Eventually, miraculously, the coffin lid opened. I made it. I was alive. Amazingly, wonderfully alive. Now I needed to find my gun and eat a bullet.

The strongarm monks pulled me out of the coffin, my arms slupping from the dead man's chest cavity, glistening with guck.

"Congrats!" head monk said, giving me an *attaboy* slap on the back. "You really rocked his dead world!"

I wiped my hands on his fake robe.

The rest of the perverts queued up for their shot at playing Megaball, and I managed to stumble into my pants. I even got my gun back. I cocked the hammer and stared deep into the blessed release promised by the inside of the barrel, and then remembered I only had one bullet left, and if anyone should die, it was old caretaker guy.

I looked around for the bike pump, flitting with the idea of filling his nads up with air before sending him to hell. Or maybe I would just pump him up and let him live. Live out the remainder of his pathetic life with unusually large testicles. The humiliation he'd suffer. The stares. The laughter. Plus, it would be impossible to find pants.

Regrettably, the bike pump was nowhere to be found. Neither was old caretaker guy. And I'd apparently won the loser trifecta, because Bill, the man I'd been hired to follow, was also MIA.

Some pinhead hopped into the coffin with Frankengroin, and I picked up the flashlight and made my way to the exit before the groaning began. I needed some fresh air. I also needed a hatchet and some steel wool, so I could access and scour the last half an hour from my brain.

Conveniently, the exit was a large door marked EXIT, which opened up to some concrete steps. I took them up, and they ended in a maintenance closet, which opened up into the mausoleum. It was an easier—and faster— entrance than the nightmare slide, but lacked the dramatic effect.

I pulled out my gun, did a quick search for old caretaker guy, scared the hell out of some grieving old man, mourning his dead wife or some similar maudlin bullshit, and then made my way through the cemetery, across the street, and into the first place that sold liquor.

Three shots and two beers later, I called the police.

Chapter 9

The cop I called was a somewhat tasty little morsel named Lieutenant Jackie "Jack" Daniels. So-so face, great legs, nice rack, especially for an older broad. I knew her back in the day, when we were partners in blue, and she continued to have a crush on me almost two decades later.

"I don't owe you shit, McGlade. And if you bother me again I'm going to send some uniforms over to trash your apartment and beat you with phone books for so long you'll have area codes embedded in your skin."

"Pay attention, Jackie. I'm offering you a prime bust here. As we speak, there's a group of perverts running a train on a dead guy with gonads the size of a Thanksgiving turkey."

"Let me guess. Is it a *Butterball*?"

"They have to be stopped. Would you want some loonies digging you up and poking your cooter after you've been laid to eternal rest?"

"Sex with a corpse, disgusting as it is, isn't a crime, Harry. Didn't you read *Bloody Mary* by JA Konrath? There was a character in there, did the same thing."

"I listened to part of the audiobook. The author thinks he's funny, but he's not."

"It's a he? I thought a woman wrote those books."

I tried to make my voice sound soothing, a tough trick because I had screamed myself raw.

"Jackie, partner, be a good cop and send a team over to the cemetery. You'll get brownie points from the Captain, a little TV spotlight, and the satisfaction knowing that you got a bunch of lunatic perverts off the street."

"What do I charge them with, McGlade? Public indecency? You want me to waste manpower on a minor misdemeanor?"

"Aggravated sexual assault. Trust me. It was aggravating."

"Who's going to press charges? The cadaver? You want to bring a corpse to trial? The cross examination would be riveting, I bet."

I clenched my fist. "Dammit, Jackie! I was violated in ways you can't even begin to understand. I'll never be the same. My sex life might very well be ruined, and I won't be able to ever watch basketball on TV again. And I love basketball. If you don't arrest these assholes I'm going to go on a killing spree and when they bring me in I'll tell them you could have stopped it just by doing your job."

She sighed big, but I knew I'd won. "Cut the melodrama, McGlade. I'll send a few uniforms over to check it out."

"If you arrest a creepy old caretaker guy, call me. I'm going to impale him on his mop and make him clean all the floors in Union Station."

"I got extra tickets to the Bulls game tomorrow. Want them?"

"You can really be a mean bitch sometimes, Jackie."

I hung up, ordered another tequila, drank it, ordered another, drank it, then called a taxi to take me back to my condo to really start drinking.

Chapter 10

My plan had been to drink so much I didn't dream. And when I peeled my eyes open, I thought it worked. I couldn't remember a single nocturnal image, let alone any nightmares.

Then I realized I was lying naked on the kitchen floor, straddling a head of lettuce.

"Oh hell no."

Like any freaked-out person, I needed answers. So I searched Google, using the terms "post dramatic stress disorder sex with corpses and giant testicles" which linked me to a bunch of unhelpful porn sites. I dutifully surfed them anyway, but there were no answers there.

Then I went to eBay, and I was still the top bidder on everything. Lousy eBastards. I decided I just wouldn't pay if I won, but then I'd get negative feedback, and negative feedback was permanent. I'm proud of my 99.4% positive score. My only bad mark came from some jerk who didn't read the whole product description, only the header. I sold him a mint Babe Ruth baseball card for $260. The card had some tears and a few bends, but I'd stapled some mint leaves to it. Which I mentioned, in two point font, at the bottom of the listing. Some guys can't take a joke.

Next I checked my email, where I discovered I'd won the Irish lottery, inherited eighty million dollars from an unknown relative, and was asked to shuffle funds into my bank account from the President of Rwanda. They all got my standard response: enthusiastic replies with an attachment supposedly containing my routing number. The attachment really contained an email bomb, which once opened would bombard their computers with tens of thousands of naked pictures of actress Bea Arthur. I called it the Maude Virus.

I had a bit of a hangover, my ass still hurt from where I'd fallen on my keys, and I was hungry. But the only food I had in the condo was that head of lettuce, which I wasn't going to eat even if I were starving to death, so I changed into a slightly less dirty suit and hit the corner convenience store for an overpriced cup of joe, a dose of Advil, and a prepackaged cheese Danish.

It was a gorgeous Chicago day, the sun shining, the lakeshore breeze blowing, the pigeons singing their lovely song. I leaned against the storefront window and called my client.

"Hello?"

"Is this Maxine Drawbridge?"

"It's Norma Cauldridge."

I rubbed my nose. "Hi, Maxine. It's Harry McGlade. I need more money."

"Did you find something out, Mr. McGlade?"

"I did. And it's ugly. Real ugly. Plus, I was gravely injured during my surveillance." I smiled at my unintentional pun, which was actually intentional. "I'm not going near him again without more cash."

"I've already paid you twelve hundred dollars."

My nose still itched, so I scratched it. On the inside.

"I want double that. Think of it as an investment. When the lawyers see the dirt I've got on old Roy, you'll take the freak for every dime he has."

I removed my finger, noted something gray and waxy stuck to the end I'd been picking my nose for years, and this was the strangest booger I'd ever seen.

"Who's Roy?"

"Whatever the hell his name is."

I took a closer look. Sniffed. It smelled familiar.

"Do you have pictures?"

"I will. Send the money to my PayPal account. My email is... oh god..."

The odor was rotten meat and formaldehyde. Somehow, while I was in the coffin, I'd gotten a hunk of dead flesh up my nose. Dead flesh covered in boogers. And a nose hair.

I leaned over and puked up the coffee, Danish, and Advil. Eighteen bucks and change, shot to hell.

"Mr. McGlade? Are you there?"

I wiped a toe through the puke, looking for the Advil. They were probably still good. Instead, I saw something that made me want to quit eating forever.

Part of a human ear.

I got closer, sure it had to be some coincidentally-shaped chunk of chewed Danish.

No, it was an ear. The upper, cartilagey part. I often nibbled women's ears when we were fooling around. I must have got caught up in the role-playing and bitten off a hunk.

"Mr. McGlade?"

"Scratch that. I want triple."

"That's outrageous."

"Lady, I went to third base with a dead guy last night, all because of your husband. Pay me, or find some other schmuck to do your dirty work."

"You did what with a dead guy?"

"Don't believe me? You want to talk to him?"

I held my cell phone over the ear. Then I realized I was acting a bit hysterical. Maybe I was still asleep, and this was just a dream.

I felt my backside, wondering if the pain in my ass was truly from sitting on my keys, or from something that was *still up there...*

I stuck my hand inside my pants, reaching down the plumber's crack...

It's a dream, it has to be a dream...

A pigeon waddled over, pecked up the ear, and ran off. My fingers crept closer...

"Mr. McGlade?"

A dream, all a dream, just a harmless dream...

And then I touched the severed end of something that shouldn't be there. Something that felt like a Pepperidge Farm County Style Breakfast Sausage Link.

"Please!" I cried out. "If there's any decency left in this cruel world, let this be a dream!"

Chapter 11

It was a dream. I woke up in bed next to an empty bottle of tequila. Blessedly, there was no head of lettuce between my legs. And the puddle of puke on my pillow didn't contain anything resembling human flesh. I did a nose check and an ass check, and they were both free and clear.

So much for drinking away the nightmares.

I rolled out of bed, padded to the can, showered, dressed in a slightly less dirty suit than yesterday, and visited the local convenience store for a coffee, Danish, and some Advil. That should have been my tip off I'd been dreaming—paying eighteen bucks for those three items. I forked over the real-life money—twenty-six bucks—then called Mrs. Drawbridge and demanded quadruple my rate. She reluctantly agreed, and mentioned her husband was in bed, still asleep. I decided to stakeout her house and tail him. And this time, I'd be taking some sophisticated equipment.

I returned to the condo and entered my Crime Lab. It was actually an extra bedroom that I converted into a crime lab by stocking it with spy stuff and writing *Crime Lab* on the door. The modern private detective had to stay current with modern gadgetry, so I bought all of the latest high-tech stuff. Phone tappers. Listening devices. Infra red things. A remote control tank with a miniature video camera hooked up to the turret. Cell phone jammers. A set of brass knuckles with a microchip inside that played Pat Benatar when I socked somebody. All the essentials.

I popped the SanDisk memory card out of the tank and plugged it into my computer, to check the footage I'd recorded during my practice run. The video was a little choppy, but more than acceptable.

The first scene was of a dog in Grant Park, urinating.

Cut to the same dog, pooping.

Cut to another dog, pooping.

Cut to the first dog, eating the second dog's poop.

Cut to a third dog, trying to hump the first dog, who was still munching on the poop.

Cut to the poop, which didn't look like it warranted being eaten.

Cut to some gangbanger punk, running off with my tank.

Cut to me explaining to the cop why I fired my gun in a populated area, and then me getting arrested.

With some editing, and the right soundtrack, the footage could be the backbone of a really good documentary about urban crime, and the amusing social lives of dogs.

I opened up a fresh SanDisk card, put that in the tank, and loaded everything into in a gym bag, along with a digital camera that could shoot night-vision, a Bionic Ear listening cannon, and a little wind-up nun that shot sparks out of her eyes. Thusly equipped, I high-tailed it over to the long term garage, jumped in my stakeout car—an inconspicuous green Chevy El Camino with yellow racing stripes on the hood—and drove to Jim Drawbridge's house.

The key to any successful stakeout is three-fold: Food, tunes, and a pot to piss in. The food should consist of chips and snack cakes. Sugar and carbohydrates jack up the insulin level, which leads to a heighten sense of awareness, probably. The music should be high energy, like heavy metal, but don't include the power ballads. The piss pot can be an old milk jug or thermos. Try to avoid cellophane potato chip bags, as I've learned from experience they tend to leak.

Since I never knew when I'd have to go on a stakeout, I kept my car stocked with everything I needed. But once I found a suitable vantage point—on the street directly in front of Jim's house—I realized I was less stocked than I should have been. I was way low on sugary snacks, but had a surplus of urine in an old apple juice bottle. Unless it was, perhaps, actually apple juice. A quick sniff would tell me.

It was urine. And I needed to stop eating asparagus.

I took a moment to muse about the gratuitous amount of bodily fluids that seem to have come up in this case, and cracked open the door and dumped the piss onto the street, where it made a foamy little river down the curb and to the sewer drain.

Then I cranked up the Led Zeppelin, licked the crust out of some old Twinkie wrappers, and waited for Jim to show up.

After half an hour, the coffee needed to be set free, so I filled up half the apple juice bottle. The secret to zero splatter is aiming for the inside edge, and then squeezing dry rather than shaking.

After an hour, Mrs. Drawbridge came out of the house and knocked on my window.

"George left before you got here."

"Do you have any snacks?"

"No."

I noticed she had some orange powder in the corner of her unattractive mouth.

"You have cheese curls," I said.

"No I don't."

"Bring me the cheese curls."

She folded her arms. "I don't have any."

"You have Cheetos dust on your lips."

"I was eating carrots."

"Were they powdered carrots?"

"Maybe."

"Bring me the goddamn Cheetos, or I'm off the case."

She frowned and waddled off. I called after her, "And anything Hostess or Dolly Madison!"

I air guitared in perfect synchronization with Jimmy Page until the ugly wife returned with my treats. The Cheetos bag only had a few left in the bottom, and Mrs. Drawbridge's cheeks were puffed out chipmunk-style. She also brought me half a raspberry Zinger.

"You ate them," I said, stating the obvious.

She shook her head. "Mmphmtmummuffff."

"Don't lie. You did. You're still chewing."

"Ummurrfumamamm."

"Are too."

She swallowed, and I watched the large lump slide down her throat.

"I think my husband went to his parent's house," she said after smacking her lips.

"What am I supposed to do with half a Zinger? It's like the size of my thumb."

"I said I think my husband went to his parent's house."

"Who?"

"My husband. After his parents died, he refused to sell it. I'm not allowed to go over there. He's got all kinds of locks and security devices. I think he may be hiding something."

I scarfed down the rest of the cheese curls, then washed them down with the remaining half a Zinger. It wasn't even half. Maybe a third, at best.

"I'm the detective, lady. I'll decide if he's hiding anything. Gimme the address."

She gave it to me. It was in the neighborhood of Streeterville, less than a mile away.

"I'll call you in exactly two hours. If you don't hear from me, I want you to call Lt. Jacqueline Daniels in District 26 and tell her where I am. Tell her it's an emergency. Did you get that?"

"Yeah. Is that apple juice?"

I glanced at my pee bottle.

"Yeah. But it's warm."

"I have ice in the house."

"Help yourself."

She took the piss, and I started the car and drove off. Little did I know I was about to face the darkest moment of my entire career. A moment so dark, that had I known it was coming, I would have done something else instead, like see a movie, or go to the zoo and bang on the windows in the monkey house. But I didn't know what was going to happen, because I couldn't predict the future, because if I could I would have predicted the lottery numbers and been super-rich and never would have needed the money that caused me to go to that house in Streeterville, which was the darkest moment of my entire career. So that's where I went. Unbeknownst to me.

In hindsight, I really shouldn't have gone.

Chapter 12

aka The Darkest Moment Of My Career

So I had no idea I was heading into the darkest moment of my career, but I went anyway.

Before going there, however, I stopped for red hots at Fat Louie's Red Hots on Clark and got a dog with the works. It was terrible, and I have really low standards. In my humble opinion, hot dogs shouldn't have veins. Or anything resembling a foreskin. I could barely choke the third one down.

Uncomfortably sated, I pressed onward to Phil's parent's house. The house was unassuming enough. Split-level, single family, red brick exterior. There was an oak tree out front, and a chainlink fence partitioning off the tiny backyard. I parked on the street, then took out my remote control surveillance tank. After double-checking the batteries, servos, memory card, remote sensor, camera focus, tread alignment, and wireless frequency, I gingerly set the tank down in the street and a taxi ran it over.

Damn taxi jerks. I decided to charge it to Mrs. Drawbridge's bill.

My next course of action was to figure out my next course of action. I played a little more air guitar, broke an air string, put on a new one and spent a minute air tuning it, and then decided on my approach.

I could put on my ghillie suit—a mesh shirt and pants with real and fake grass and shubbery sewn into it that I ordered from PsychoSniper.com—and then slowly belly-crawl across the lawn, traverse the fence using a carbide steel bolt cutter, inch my way into the backyard, creep up the porch in slow increments stopping often to pretend to be a potted plant, trick his surveillance system by recording a loop from his outdoor camera and feeding the playback into the main line, drill into his door frame using a cordless screwdriver to disable the burglar alarm alarm sensor, pick the pick-proof Schlage deadbolt, and sneak inside his house using my Invisible Voyeur NightVision Goggles, which I bought at CautiousStalker.org.

Or I could knock on the front door and ask what's up.

"What's up?" I asked when the front door opened.

Since I'd seen him yesterday, Ken had gone from half a sunburned face to a full sunburned face. The smell coming from his house was real bacon, which sure beat the smell of fake bacon, which my mother used to make out of soy and library paste and brown Crayons.

"Who are you?"

"Housing inspector." I flashed him my PI badge, too fast for him to read it. "I'm here to check for gas leaks. Are you leaking any gases?"

"No. Can I see that badge again?"

"I smell something. Are you cooking in there?"

"No, I'm not."

"Is it bacon?" I smacked my lips. "I love bacon. I read somewhere that you could shave with bacon. Rub it on your face raw, and it lubricates better than shaving cream. Have you ever heard of that?"

"No."

"I tried it once. Closest shave I ever had. But I got an E. Coli infection and they had to remove eight yards of my large intestine. Can I come in?"

"No. Hey, you look kind of familiar."

I flashed an *aw shucks* grin. "I get that a lot. I've made a few videos. You might know my screen name, *Sir Dix-A-Lot.*"

"I don't think that's it."

"Ever see *Snow White and the Seven Blowjobs*?"

"No."

"*Robin Hood, Prince of Anal*?"

"I don't think so."

"*The Empire Strikes Scat*?"

"Maybe you should come in. I may have some gases for you to check on."

I nodded, stepping into his humble abode. It was no surprise he let me in. Fast talking is one of my special skills. That and being able to swallow pills. If I had a super power, it would be the ability to swallow a whole handful of pills at once. Big pills too. None of that baby aspirin crap for babies. I secretly hoped that one day I'd get cancer, and the doctor would prescribe me a lot of pills, and he'd tell me to space them out throughout the day because there were so many, but I'd tell him no need to and grab the whole handful and swallow them up right there while he watched, amazed.

That's what I was thinking about when Phil hit me in the head with the hammer.

Chapter 13

I awoke from a terrible dream that I was trapped in a coffin with an inhumanly large-testicled man, to the terrible reality of being tied to a chair in some freak's basement.

Said freak was standing over me, staring.

"You're awake," he said.

"No I'm not."

I shook my head, which caused a spike of pain. My left eye stung, and I looked down my nose and saw some dried blood on my cheek. The freak still held the hammer. He waved it in front of my face in a way I'm sure he thought was menacing, which actually was pretty menacing.

"Yes you are! And I know what you want! That whore hired you!"

"Which whore? I know a lot of whores."

He poked me in the chest with the hammer. "She hired you to spy on me! To find out what secrets I had hidden in my parent's house! Well, now you'll be privy to those secrets, Mr. Private Eye! Because I'm going to show them to you!"

I checked my bonds, noted he had used the same clothesline he'd purchased at the hardware store. The knots were tight, expert. My legs were bound as well, tied to the steel chair legs of the steel chair, which was made of steel. The basement was unfurnished, concrete floor, I-beams and joists exposed in the ceiling, menacing curtains sectioning off the area we were in.

"Got any aspirin?" I asked. "Some asshole hit me with a hammer."

"Silence!"

"And can you please stop shouting? I'm right here. It's not like I'm in another part of the house and you're calling me for dinner."

The freak chuckled, the nostrils on his large nose flaring out.

"Oh, funny you should mention dinner. Because the main course…" He cackled.

"Yeah?" I asked.

"The main course…" More cackling.

"What's the main course, Emeril?"

"The… main course… is…" Hysterical laughter now.

I interrupted him. "I got it. The main course is me. You're going to eat me. Scary. What a scary guy you are."

"Not me, Mr. McGlade. You're going to be a snack," cackle cackle, "for my… zombie wife!"

I waited for the giggles to die down before I said, "Dude, your wife isn't a zombie."

"Yes she is."

"She's not even dead. I just saw her like an hour ago."

"Not that hag. I mean my first wife. The love of my life, tragically taken from me after only one year of marriage."

"So what about that ugly chick back at your house?"

"Her? I married her for the money."

I smiled. "Thank god. I thought you were totally nuts there for a minute."

"No kidding. She's a real heifer, isn't she?"

"I said in the first chapter that it was like God took a dare to make the most unattractive woman possible."

"Yes, that's Norma."

"Who?"

"My second wife! But now it's time for you to meet my first wife! And to feed her! Do you know what a necromancer is, Mr. McGlade?"

I shrugged. Not an easy task when tied up. "I meant to look it up."

"It's someone who has the power to raise the dead. Since Roberta died..."

"Who?"

"My first wife."

"This is a lot of names to keep straight. Can you write them down on a sticky pad for me?"

He didn't take the bait. I'd hoped he would have gone off in search of a sticky pad, which would have given my time to scoot my chair over to the menacing curtains hanging from the ceiling and hide behind them. He'd never think to look for me there, and would probably go watch TV or something.

But he was too smart to be tricked.

"Since Roberta died, I've been searching for a way to bring her back. Now, through a combination of magic and science—something I call sci-magic—I have finally gained mastery over death! Behold, Mr. McGlade, the living dead!"

He cast aside the menacing curtain. Hanging from the ceiling was a dead body.

"Is that her?" I asked.

"That, indeed, is Roberta, my Zombie Wife!"

He spread out his hands, as if waiting for applause. Even if I wasn't tied up, I wouldn't have applauded.

"That's not a zombie," I said. "That's a dead chick hanging on a rope."

"Really, Mr. McGlade? Really?"

"Yeah. Really."

"Well, watch this then." He turned to face the corpse. "Roberta, my love, come to me!"

Phil grabbed an overhead rope, and Roberta swung forward using a system of weights and pulleys. He made her wave at me.

"You're butt nuts," I said.

"She lives, Mr. McGlade! And she thirsts for your flesh! For nothing else can quell the hunger of the living dead! Isn't that right, Roberta?"

He tugged another rope, and she nodded. Actually, it was more of a sideways flop then a nod.

"Look, buddy, this has all been tremendously entertaining, but what do you say we untie me, I go to the cops, and you get put in a nice room with soft rubber walls so you don't hurt yourself?"

"I'm not crazy! Roberta is one of the walking dead!"

"More like the swaying dead."

He got in my face. "Admit she's undead!"

"No."

"But she moves! See!"

He made her do a little dance.

"You're making her move using pulleys and ropes, like some strange sad puppet."

He raised the hammer, aiming for the same spot where he hit me before. "Say she's a zombie!"

"She a zombie," I said quickly. "You're a genius who has conquered death. I'm in awe of your brilliance."

He stared at me hard, and then spun and yanked the dead chick closer. I realized she was naked, and her boobs were missing. I always notice little things like that. Her skin had become dark brown and wrinkly, like a giant raisin. Whack job had also cut some blue eyes from a magazine or poster, and stapled them over her eye sockets. Her teeth were bared, the corners of her mouth turned up. Twist ties, to make it look like she was smiling.

It was kind of endearing, in a raving psychotic way.

"Roberta does seem sort of tired today." He caressed what was left of her cheek. "Perhaps she needs another treatment. I shall fetch the Rejuvenation Ray!"

He scuttled insanely off, and I wondered what time it was, and if his butt ugly whore of a second wife had remembered to call Lieutenant Jackie when I failed to check in. Then I remembered I'd given her a bottle full of piss and told her it was apple juice, so I probably couldn't count on that particular horse to come in.

Like it had happened so many times before, the burden of saving my own skin rested on my own skin. I needed to figure out some sort of ingenious plan to escape. If I could only do that, then I'd be free.

Freak boy returned, pushing a wheeled wine cart stacked with electronic equipment. He shoved it in front of his living undead zombie wife who was really just a putrefying corpse.

"Behold the Rejuvenation Ray, Mr. McGlade!"

"How do you know my name, anyway?"

"Your wallet."

"I had eight bucks in there. It better still be in there."

"I didn't take your money."

"And a Blockbuster Video card. They charge you five bucks if you lose that."

"Silence! Through magnetron technology, I have harnessed the life-giving properties of ordinary microwaves, coaxing the spirit back into the body!"

"That's a big microwave?"

"Behold!"

He hit a switch, and the stack of electronics hummed and whirred, throwing off an huge amount of heat. Most of it was directed at Roberta, the undead living zombie wife. Some of it came my way, and it hurt like a bad sunburn.

Then the smell hit me. Honey baked ham and bacon strips. I watched through squinty eyes as Roberta sizzled and popped and exuded a scent that was downright mouth-watering.

Now it all made sense. Phil's sunburn. Why he smelled like ham. Why his first wife's skin was so brown and wrinkly. Why his second wife smelled like sweaty feet.

Actually, this didn't explain why his second wife smelled like sweaty feet. But I guessed that to be a hygiene thing.

Blofeld finally turned off the microwave stack, then embraced his hanging wife. The embrace became a kiss. The kiss became a nibble. The nibble became a corn-on-the-cob chow-down, and I realized what had happened to the zombie's breasts.

"And now!" He wiped the grease off his mouth with his sleeve. "Now it is time for Roberta to feast!"

Fred reached under the cart, pulled out a meat cleaver. Didn't see too many meat cleavers, outside of a butcher shop.

"What shall we start with, Roberta? The leg? Yes, I agree. The leg looks delicious. Do you prefer the left one or the right one, dear? Yes, the left one."

He raised the cleaver. There are few things more terrifying than being tied to a chair about to be hacked up by a lunatic so he could feed the pieces to his dead wife who he thinks is actually a zombie and is hanging from the ceiling using an admittedly clever series of weights and pulleys.

"Stop!" I yelled.

Incredibly, he stopped.

"What?"

"Your parents!" I said, speaking quickly. "What would your parents think?"

"Why don't we... ask them!"

He stepped over to the menacing curtain, and with a flourish drew it back. Mom and Dad were hanging there, roped together so it looked like Dad was giving it to Mom, doggy-style.

"Oops!" Fred said, tugging on ropes and making his parents bump uglies. "Daddy! Why are you hurting Mommy?"

He pulled the cord again and again, Dad's hips rising and falling. A shrink would have a field day with this guy. Field days were fun. I liked dodge ball best.

"Say that again, Daddy? You're wrestling? What wrestling move is that?"

It looked, to my untrained eye, like a sodomyplex. I tore my eyes away and pointed at something with my chin. "What's that hanging next to them?"

"Fluffy. My cat."

"And those tiny things?"

"My goldfish, BA and Hannibal. Fluffy loves to chase them around. Don't you, Fluffy?"

More manic pulling of ropes, and the three dead animals knocked into each other. While he was preoccupied, I called out in my best falsetto, "Honey, it's Roberta!"

John turned his attention back to Roberta the zombie living bacon wife.

"Dearest? Did you say something?"

"I said," I said, "We should let Mr. McGlade go. I'm not hungry right now."

Nut job was buying it. He wrapped his arms around her, nuzzling against her tasty ribs.

"But you need to eat, honey. You're getting thinner and thinner."

"Tack a couple of tomatoes to my chest. I'll look a lot better."

Bert began to laugh. A chilling laugh that chilled me. He spun, pointing the cleaver at my nose.

"You idiot! Do you think I'm that stupid?"

"Yes."

"What good husband doesn't know the sound of my wife's own voice?"

"You, I was hoping."

"Enough of this tomfoolery! This ends now!"

He launched himself at me, screaming and drooling insanely, his probably very sharp cleaver raised for the killing blow.

Then Lieutenant Jackie Daniels shot him in the head.

Chapter 14

"You're an idiot, McGlade," Jackie said, using the cleaver to cut away the ropes.

Carl was dead on the floor. He was finally with his wife. Because she was dead on the floor too. Jack had made me sit there until the Crime Scene Unit arrived, taking pictures and gathering evidence. They cut the bodies down before they freed me.

"So how did you know I was here?" I asked.

Jack wore a short skirt and heels that probably cost a fortune but still looked kind of slutty, just how I liked them.

"Norma Cauldridge," she said.

"Who?"

"George Cauldridge's wife."

"Who?"

"She called me, wanted me to arrest you for trying to poison her. I asked where you were, and she said probably here. After we nabbed those necrophiliacs at the cemetery last night, I needed to find you anyway to get your statement. Lucky I heard your girlish screams which gave me probable cause to bust in here without a warrant."

I wasn't listening, because it sounded like a boring infodump.

"Can I give you my statement tomorrow?" I asked. "I gotta take a monster dump. I had some hot dogs earlier that are going to look better coming out than going in."

Jackie leaned in close. I braced myself for the kiss. It didn't come.

"Did you give Norma a bottle full of your urine and tell her it was apple juice?"

"Maybe. Did she drink any?"

"She said the second glass went down rough. She's going to sue you, McGlade."

"She can take a number. Seriously. I've got one of those number things. I swiped it from the deli." I grinned. "You can come over later, and watch me cut the cheese. You know you want to."

"I'd rather gouge out my own eyes with forks."

"Don't be coy. This could be a way to pay back what you owe me."

She cocked her hips, hot and sexy. "Excuse me? I just saved your ass, McGlade."

"Are you kidding? This is front page news. You'll probably get a promotion. There's no need to thank me. It's all part of the service I perform."

"I really think I hate you."

"Really, Jackie?" I raised an eyebrow. "Really?"

She nodded. "Yeah, really. Be in my office tomorrow morning for your statement. And try to stay of trouble until then."

I stood up, stretched, and gave her one of my famous Harry McGlade smiles.

"I'll try. But trouble is my business." I winked. "And business is good."

The End

To go back to the beginning, go to page 2.

To return to the Amish adventure, go to page 5.

I chose the blade, because only a complete moron would try to battle a T-rex with some matches and hairspray.

Taking the vorpal sword in hand, I bravely wet my pants and cried like a little Amish boy whose bunny just died. The dinosaur was big. We're talking dinosaur big. It had a head the size of a pickup truck. Not a full-sized truck, like a Dodge Ram or a Chevy Silverado. But a bit larger than a mid-sized, like a Nissan Frontier or a Toyota Tacoma. But it didn't have doors. Or wheels. Or an engine.

"Don't cry. I won't hurt you."

I stopped peeing myself long enough to realize the dinosaur was talking to me. It was only a few feet away, and had breath like car exhaust. Not an eight cylinder car, like a Ford Mustang or a BMW M3. But more like a hybrid car, like a Toyota Prius, or a—

"I said I won't hurt you," said the dinosaur. "We can both live through this if we work together. We just have to put on a show for the aliens."

"A show?" I asked.

"Yeah. I'll roar and snap at you. You wave your sword and run around. We do that for a little bit, then we make a break for it."

"There's a zombie on your back."

"Yeah. He was dying to ride me. But don't worry, he won't hurt you either."

"You really promise not to hurt me?"

"I'd cross my heart, but I've got these tiny little arms and can't reach."

"I believe you," I said.

Then I raised my sword and jabbed it into the monster's throat. The crowd of angels thundered into applause as the ghastly monster choked on its own blood and fell over. Then I disemboweled the creature, running my blade down its belly, its guts spilling out like a dinosaur being disemboweled.

The zombie, who was pinned under the beast, was making a *time-out* signal with his hands, which I then chopped off.

"Dude! Don't kill me! I'm unarmed!"

"You're also defeated," I said. Then I cut off his feet.

Finally, I delivered the final blow, and sliced off the zombie's head. Because I always wanted to get ahead in life.

The crowd went crazy, and a little green angel ran out onto the field with a microphone and said, "Reptiloids of Reptilon, I give you your new champion! His name is..." He cast a sidelong glance at me. "What's your name, buddy?"

This was my chance to come up with some super-cool badass name, like Mister Killer, or Captain Pain, or Psychoticus Maximus. anything but Bitch Tits.

"I present your champion, Bitch Tits!"

Shit. They must be able to read minds in heaven.

"We can read minds. And this isn't heaven."

Still, the crowd applauded like the fatties at Super Buffet when they brought out another tray of chicken wings. I raised my sword up and posed mightily like the mighty gladiator I was.

"To the victor, the spoils!" said the green angel. "What do you wish to do? Mate with another earthling in front of this crowd of adoring fans? Or eat some bananas?"

"Huh?" I said. I had been thinking about Amtrak, and lost my train of thought.

"Sex or bananas? Which shall it be?"

Should Harry have sex in front of the crowd? If so, go to page 171.

Should Harry eat some bananas? If so, go to page 173.

To return to the previous section, go to page 41.

Moving quickly, I snatched up the hairspray and matches as the zombie rider steered the dinosaur straight at me.

I had barely enough time to light a cigarette and then give my hair one final styling before the tyrannosaurus rex bit me in half.

Nice job, moron. You killed me. Way to go.

To start the adventure over, go to page 2.

To grab the sword, go to page 103.

To return to the previous section, go to page 41.

I reached for the sword, grasping it in both hands. But I couldn't raise it because I WAS ALREADY BITTEN IN HALF DUE TO YOUR STUPIDITY! My guts were strewn about the arena like Christmas decorations, and I was bleeding from eighteen different arteries. What good would a sword do me?

Boy, you're an idiot.

To return to the beginning, go to page 2.

To get really confused, go to page 102.

To return to the previous section, go to page 41.

"Jesus, McGlade. Do you ever clean up?" Jack said.

I wondered how Lieutenant Jacqueline "Jack" Daniels got into my apartment. In fact, I wondered how *I* got into my apartment. A second ago I was in Indiana in an Amish cornfield.

Then I remembered. This was a *Write Your Own Damn Story* ebook, and you, the reader, made me come here instead. Thanks a lot for that.

This particular scene I was now involved in was during one of Jack's cases, the one where I helped her immeasurably.

But then, that's pretty much all of Jack's cases.

"Nah," I told her. "I pay a girl to come in once a week. But every time she comes over we just hump the whole time and she never has a chance to clean anything. Want to go into the kitchen, have a seat?"

"I'm afraid I'd stick to something and never be able to leave."

"No need to be rude," I said. Then I belched, and watched Jack look at my aquarium. Moldering fish corpses and chunks of multicolored rotting things bubbled around in the brown water, buoyed by the tank aerator. She stared as a corn dog floated by.

"Some kind of fish disease wiped out my whole gang within twenty-four hours," I explained.

"There's a shocker."

"I like it more now. There's always something new growing, and I save a bundle on fish food."

Jack pulled her eyes away. "I'm here to talk about Theresa Metcalf. She was a client of yours. Back in April."

"Got a picture? I can't place the name."

She handed me one. Yuck. Ugly.

"Yuck. Ugly," I said.

"She's dead."

"Then she'd smell bad too."

"Do you remember her?"

"Not offhand. No. But then I have a hard time remembering last week. How long has it been, Jackie?"

"Not long enough."

I raised an eyebrow. "You're not still mad at me, are you?"

A while ago Jack and I had a misunderstanding. Since she was a bit bitchy, she had trouble learning how to forgive. Nice boobs, though.

"If you don't feel like cooperating…" Jack said.

"You'll drag me in. Can't it wait? I was watching the new *Snow White* DVD, the director's version with the extra footage. The gang-bang scene is next."

It featured the eighth dwarf, Sodomy. He played a big part in the end.

Man, I'm funny.

"Do you keep files?" Jack asked.

"Sure. At the office."

Jack walked to my right, stepping on all my stuff that I was storing on the floor.

"Hey, watch out for the pizza, Jack. I'm not done with it."

"Get dressed," she said. "We're going to your office."

"Kiss my piles. It's my day off. I'm not going anywhere."

"Then you're under arrest."

"For what?"

"For being an asshole."

"You can't do that. I've got an Asshole License."

"Okay. How about for assaulting an officer?"

"I haven't laid a hand on you," I said.

"Seeing you in your underwear qualifies as assault."

"Look," I told her. "We've already done this exact same song and dance in a previous book. Can't we do some new material?"

Jack squinted at me, her nose wrinkling up. "What the hell are you talking about, McGlade?"

"*Whiskey Sour* by J.A. Konrath. The first published Jack Daniels thriller. Remember it? This scene was from the middle of the book. Then, several chapters later, we wind up in the sewers and—"

"Shut up!" Jack said. "God, you're such a dick."

"How am I a dick?"

"What if someone hasn't read *Whiskey Sour* yet? You want to spoil the ending for them?"

"Yes, I do," I said smiling. "At the end of *Whiskey Sour* I—"

Do you want Harry to spoil the ending? If so, go to page 287.

To go back to the beginning, go to page 2.

To return to the previous section, go to page 45.

Deb decided against taking a bath. She'd get up early, deal with it then. Right now, she just wanted to sleep and try to forget this day ever happened. She took off her fanny pack, placed it on the sink, and pulled out her toothbrush and toothpaste. The water was rusty colored, but she made do. Afterward, she picked up a hand towel and left the bathroom. Then she sat on the edge of the bed and undressed down to her underwear.

I really hate this part.

Deb hit the release valves on her prosthetics, breaking the suction. She eased them off and set the Cheetah artificial legs on the floor, next to the bed. Then she rolled down the gel sock, sheathing the vestige of her left calf. A day's worth of accumulated sweat dripped onto the floor. Deb wiped the sheath with the towel and gave it a tentative sniff.

Not too funky. I can get another wear out of it.

She pulled the silicone end pad out of the bottom, dried it off, and repeated the process with the other side, setting the sheaths on the night stand. Then Deb finally looked at her legs.

The amputations were transtibial; below the knee. Her left leg was three inches longer than her right, and both came to tapered ends. Deb hated that they were uneven—it made her feel even more deformed. To make the complete package reach *eleven* on the hideous scale, each leg had raised, ugly scars, from her surgery, and from her cougar injuries. On top of all that, she needed to shave.

Yuck, Deb thought. *I'm a monster.*

She always thought that when she looked at her stumps.

Her skin below each knee was pruned and red. The gel sheet provided cushioning, but Deb sweat so much she got heat rash. The alternative was to wear stump socks, which would wick away sweat just like regular socks did. Unfortunately, the suction of the prosthetics weren't as tight when she wore socks, and Deb didn't want to risk having a leg fall off while in motion. Still, she'd eventually have to come up with some sort of compromise. Even the strongest antiperspirants didn't do much to help.

She draped the towel over her legs, then began to dry her stumps, massaging the muscles. Then she yawned, and flicked off the light switch next to the bed. The room went dark, and Deb buried her face in the Roosevelt pillowcase, letting her mind blank out.

Less than a minute later, she heard something creak.

Like someone is walking toward the bed.

Deb's eyelids snapped open, and she fumbled for the light switch.

The room was empty.

She waited, riding out the adrenaline, her heart dancing a rhumba. But there were no more noises. No one around.

Okay. Old houses creak. No need to get paranoid about it. The door is locked. I'm alone. I need to go back to sleep.

She hit the switch, adjusted the pillow, and rested her head.

Creak, creak, creak.

Closer this time.

The light on once again, Deb sat up in bed. No one was in the room. She wondered if there was some reasonable explanation for this. Maybe the creaks were coming from the floor below. Or next door. Or maybe she was hearing something else that she mistook for footsteps.

But it didn't sound *nearby*. It sounded like it was coming from in the room.

She waited longer this time. Waited for the creaking to come back.

There was only silence.

Deb put her head back down, but she left the light on. If there was another creaking noise, she wanted to be able to see what was causing it.

Is someone messing with me?

Who? I'm alone in here.

After another long minute, she closed her eyes. She let her mind wander, and it found its way back to Mal. Cute guy. Obviously interested. All Deb needed to do was get out of her own way, and let things develop. If she stopped second-guessing everything, stopped thinking ten steps ahead, maybe she could actually—

Creak.

Deb opened her eyes, wide.

The creak came from right under my bed.

Moving slowly, she peeked over the edge, half-expecting to see some masked psychopath lying on the floor, waiting to spring.

She saw nothing. And that scared the living hell out of her.

My prosthetics are gone.

Deb left them alongside the bed. She was sure of it. She checked the nightstand, saw the gel sheaths were still there.

Maybe I'm brain dead. Maybe I put them on the other side.

Rolling over, Deb peered over the other end of the mattress.

All she saw was bare floor.

Someone took my legs.

Then the bed moved. Just a bit, but enough for Deb to realize what was happening.

The person who took my legs is under the bed.

Deb stared at the closet. She had her cosmetic legs in her case. If she could get to them, strap them on, she'd at least have a chance at getting away.

But how? Ease onto the floor and crawl there? That's at least five yards away. I'll never get there in time.

The bed jerked again. Harder this time. Whoever was under there lifted up the box spring and let it drop.

Then she heard him chuckle. Soft and low.

The fear that overtook Deb was the worst thing she ever felt. Worse than when she was falling off the mountain. Worse than when she was being stalked by the cougar.

This isn't a mistake. This isn't mother nature.

This is a human being deliberately intending to do me harm.

Her mind flashed back to the blowout. Maybe Mal had been right. Maybe someone had shot out the tire, to make sure they couldn't get away.

And maybe that someone was under her bed right now.

What am I supposed to do? Any other person would be able to run away.

Maybe I can talk to him

Deb's voice was shaking when she said, "Who's there?"

After a terrible silence, a voice directly beneath Deb said, *"I'm Harry."*

It hit Deb like a slap to the face. She was so frightened she began to shiver. He was *right* beneath her.

"What... what do you want, Harry?"

No answer.

"Harry...?"

"I think I'm stuck. Could use a little help here."

A moment later some chick with no legs was pulling me out from under the bed.

"How did you get under there?" she demanded.

I brushed off some dust bunnies and shrugged. "Whoever is reading this is playing ereader roulette," I said. "Any idea what ebook this is?"

"It's *Endurance* by Jack Kilborn."

"A horror novel, huh?"

Deb nodded.

"Isn't Kilborn really J.A. Konrath?" I asked.

"Yeah."

"Why'd he use a pen name?"

Deb shrugged. "I dunno. He said different genres have different fans, or something stupid like that."

"What's this one about?" I asked, not really caring.

"Inbred mutants in a spooky bed and breakfast in West Virginia. I thought one of them was under my bed."

"You really went out on a limb, there."

Deb's forehead furrowed. "Was that some kind of crack?"

"What do you mean?"

"I have no legs, and you used the word *limb*."

"No offense intended. I love crippled broads. Want to hear some amputee jokes?"

"Want me to knock your teeth out?"

"Easy, sister. I'm your kind of people. See?" I raised my right hand, showing her my prosthetic. "I lost this in the Konrath book *Rusty Nail*. He apparently likes cutting off body parts."

"Wait... *Rusty Nail*? Are you Harry McGlade?"

"In the flesh."

Deb chewed her lower lip. "I've read all the Jack Daniels books. You're my favorite character. I loved the one where you and Jack were in the truck, hauling all those explosives."

"*Dirty Martini*," I said. "One of my many shining moments."

"You're funny." Deb trailed a finger across my chest. "I dig funny guys."

"Cool," I said. "Wanna fool around?"

"Sure."

After a few minutes of trying to shove Deb back onto the bed, we opted for floor sex. But I'd barely gotten my pants off when some freaky inbred asshole with two noses broke into our room and chopped off my head with an axe.

What a shitty ending. I hope *Endurance* was a lot better than that.

The End

To restart the adventure, go to page 2.

To read Harry's favorite amputee jokes, go to page 199.

To return to the previous section, go to page 134.

Harry's List of Rejected Dr. Seuss Book Titles

HOW THE GRINCH STOLE MY WIFE

HORTON HATCHES A TERRORIST PLOT

ON BEYOND DONKEY PUNCH

MARVIN K MOONEY WILL YOU GO TO HELL

ARCHER THE FLARCHER

THE CAT IN THE HAT GETS FELINE AIDS

GREEN EGGS AND E COLI

THIDWICK THE BIG HEARTED PIMP

MR. BROWN CAN MOO, AND THEY PUT HIM AWAY

THERE'S A WOCKET IN MY POCKET, AND I BLAME VIAGRA

BOOMER THE TUMOR

CRAP ON POP

THE 500 FISTINGS OF BARTHOLOMEW CUBBINS

IF I RAN THE CRACK HOUSE

I CAN LICK THIRTY HOOKERS TODAY!

OH, THE PLACES YOU'LL PUKE

SHIT-HEAD MAYZIE

To return to the previous section, go to page 134.

To start over, go to page 2.

To read an entirely different Harry adventure about dogs, go to page 114.

Bored with that Amish story, and desperate to have single, linear narrative without bouncing around all over the place, I found myself back at my office, awaiting my next client. I was halfway through a meatball sandwich when a man came into my office and offered me money to steal a dog.

A lot of money.

"Are you an animal lover, Mr. McGlade?"

"Depends on the animal. And call me Harry."

He offered his hand. I stuck out mine, and watched him frown when he noticed the marinara stains. He abruptly pulled back, reaching instead into the inner pocket of his blazer. The suit he wore was tailored and looked expensive, and his skin was tanned to a shade only money can buy.

"This is Marcus." His hand extended again, holding a photograph. "He's a Shar-pei."

Marcus was one of those unfortunate Chinese wrinkle dogs, the kind that look like a great big raisin with fur. He was light brown, and his face had so many folds of skin that his eyes were completely covered.

I bet the poor pooch walked into a lot of walls.

"Cute," I said, because the man wanted to hire me.

"Marcus is a champion show dog. He's won four AKC competitions. Several judges have commented that he's the finest example of the breed they've ever seen."

I wanted to say something about Marcus needing a good starch and press, but instead inquired about the dog's worth.

"With the winnings, and stud fees, he's worth upwards of ten thousand dollars."

I whistled. The dog was worth more than I was.

"So, what's the deal, Mr…"

"Thorpe. Vincent Thorpe. I'm willing to double your usual fee if you can get him back."

I took another bite of meatball, wiped my mouth on my sleeve, and leaned back in my swivel chair. The chair groaned in disapproval.

"Tell me a little about Marcus, Mr. Thorpe. Curly fries?"

"Pardon me?"

I gestured to the bag on my desk. "Did you want any curly fries? Potatoes make me bloaty."

He shook his head. I snatched a fry, bloating be damned.

"I've, um, raised Marcus since he was a pup. He has one of the best pedigrees in the sport. Since Samson passed away, there has quite literally been no competition."

"Samson?"

"Another Shar-pei. Came from the same littler as Marcus, owned by a man named Glen Ricketts. Magnificent dog. We went neck and neck several times."

"Hold on, a second. I'd like to take notes."

I pulled out my notepad and a pencil. On the first piece of paper, I wrote, "Dog."

"Do you know who has Marcus now?"

"Another breeder named Abigail Cummings. She borrowed Marcus to service her Shar-pei, Julia. When I went to pick him up, she insisted she didn't have him, and claimed she didn't know what I was talking about."

I jotted this down. My fingers made a grease spot on the page.

"Did you try the police?"

"Yes. They searched her house, but didn't find Marcus. She's insisting I made a mistake."

"Did Abigail give you money to borrow Marcus? Sign any contracts?"

"No. I lent him to her as a favor. And she kept him."

"How do you know her?"

"Casually, from the American Kennel Club. Her Shar-pei, Julia, is a truly magnificent bitch. You should see her haunches."

I let that one go.

"Why did you lend out Marcus if you only knew her casually?"

"She called me a few days ago, promised me the pick of the litter if I lent her Marcus. I never should have done it. I should have just given her a straw."

"A straw?"

"Of Marcus's semen. I milk him by…"

I held up my palm and scribbled out the word 'straw.' It was more info than I wanted. "Let's move on."

Thorpe pressed his lips together so tightly they lost color. His eyes got sticky.

"Please, Harry. Marcus is more than just a dog to me. He's my best friend."

I didn't doubt it. You don't milk a casual acquaintance.

"Maybe you could hire an attorney."

"That takes too long. If I go through legal channels, it could be months before my case is called. And even then, I'd need some kind of proof that she had him, so I'd have to hire a private investigator anyway."

I scraped away a coffee stain on my desk with my thumbnail.

"I'm sorry for your loss, Mr. Thorpe. But hiring me to bust into someone's home and steal a dog…I'm guessing that breaks all sorts of laws. I could have my license revoked, I could go to jail—"

"I'll triple your fee."

"I take cash, checks, or major credit cards."

Night Vision Goggles use a microprocessor to magnify ambient light and allow a user to see in almost total blackness.

They're also pricey as hell, so I had to make due with a flashlight and some old binoculars.

It was a little past eleven in the evening, and I was sitting in the bough of a tree, staring into the backyard of Abigail Cummings. I'd been there for almost two hours. The night was typical for July in Chicago; hot, sticky, and humid. The black ski mask I wore was so damp with sweat it threatened to drown me.

Plus, I was bloaty.

I let the binocs hang around my neck and flashed the light at my notepad to review my stake-out report.

9:14pm—Climbed tree.

9:40pm—Drank two sodas.

10:15pm—Foot fell asleep.

Not too exciting so far. I took out my pencil and added, "11:04pm— really regret drinking those sodas."

To keep my mind off of my bladder, I spent a few minutes trying to balance the pencil on the tip of my finger. It worked, until I dropped the pencil.

I checked my watch. 11:09. I attempted to write "dropped my pencil" on my notepad, but you can guess how that turned out.

I was all set to call it a night, when I saw movement in the backyard.

It was a woman, sixty-something, her short white hair glowing in the porch light.

Next to her, on a leash, was Marcus.

"Is someone in my tree?"

I fought panic, and through Herculean effort managed to keep my pants dry.

"No," I answered.

She wasn't fooled.

"I'm calling the police!"

"Wait!" My voice must have sounded desperate, because she paused in her race back to the house.

"I'm from the US Department of Foliage. I was taking samples of your tree. It seems to be infested with the Japanese Saganaki Beetle."

"Why are you wearing that mask?"

"Uh...so they don't recognize me. Hold on, I need to ask you a few sapling questions."

I eased down, careful to avoid straining myself. When I reached ground, the dog trotted over and amiably sniffed at my pants.

"I'm afraid I don't know much about agriculture."

From the tree, Ms. Cummings was nothing to look at. Up close, she made me wish I was still in the tree.

The woman was almost as wrinkly as the dog. But unlike her canine companion, she had tried to fill in those wrinkles with make-up. From the amount, she must have used a paint roller. The eye shadow alone was thick enough to stop a bullet. Add to that a voice like raking gravel, and she was quite the catch.

I tried to think of something to ask her, to keep the beetle ploy going. But this was getting too complicated, so I just took out my gun.

"The dog."

Her mouth dropped open.

"The what?"

"That thing on your leash that's wagging its tail. Hand it over."

"Why do you want my dog?"

"Does it matter?"

"Of course it does. I don't want you to shoot me, but I also don't want to hand over my dog to a homicidal maniac."

"I'm not a homicidal maniac."

"You're wearing a ski mask in ninety degree weather, hopping from one foot to the other like some kind of monkey."

"I had too much soda. Give me the damn leash."

She handed me the damn leash. So far so good.

"Okay. You just stand right here, and count to a thousand before you go back inside, or else I'll shoot you."

"Aren't you leaving?"

"Yeah."

"Not to second-guess you, Mr. Dognapper, but how can you shoot me, if you've already gone?"

Know-it-all.

"I think you need a bit more blush on your cheeks. There are some folks in Wisconsin who can't see it from there."

Her lips down turned. With all the lipstick, they looked like two cartoon hot dogs.

"This is Max Factor."

"I won't tell Max if you don't. Now start counting."

I was out of there before she got to six.

After I got back to my office, I took care of some personal business, washed my hands, and called the client. He agreed to come right over.

"Mr. McGlade, I can't tell you how…oh, yuck."

"Watch where you're stepping. Marcus decided to mark his territory."

Thorpe made an unhappy face, then he took off his shoe and left it by the door.

"Mr. McGlade, thank you for…yuck."

"He's marked a couple spots. I told you to watch out."

He removed the other shoe.

"Did you bring the money?"

"I did, and I—wait a second!"

"You might as well just throw away the sock, because those stains…"

"That's not Marcus!"

I looked at the dog, who was sniffing around my desk, searching for another place to make a deposit.

"Of course it's your dog. Look at that face. He's a poster boy for Retin-A."

"That's not a he. It's a she."

"Really?" I peeked under the dog's tail and frowned. "I'll be damned."

"You took the wrong dog, Mr. McGlade. This is Abigail's bitch, Julia."

"It's an honest mistake, Mr. Thorpe. Anyone could have made it."

"No, not anyone, Mr. McGlade. Most semi-literate adults know the difference between boys and girls. Would you like me to draw you a picture?"

"Ease up, Thorpe. When I meet a new dog, I don't lift up a hind leg and stick my face down there to check out the plumbing."

"This is just...oh, yuck."

"The garbage can is over there."

Thorpe removed his sock, and I wracked my brain to figure out how this could be salvaged.

"Any chance you want to keep this dog instead? You said she was a magnificent broad."

"Bitch, Mr. McGlade. It's what we call female dogs."

"I was trying to put a polite spin on it."

"I want Marcus. That was the deal."

"Okay, okay, let me think."

I thought.

Julia had her nose in the garbage can, sniffing Thorpe's sock. If I could only switch dogs somehow.

That was it.

"I'll switch dogs somehow," I said.

"What are you talking about?"

"Like a hostage trade. I'll call up Ms. Cummings, and trade Julia for Marcus."

"Do you think it'll work?"

"Only one way to find out."

I picked up the phone.

"Ms. Cummings? I have your dog."

"I know. I watched you steal him an hour ago."

For someone who looked like a mime, she was sure full of comments.

"If you'd like your dog back, we can make a deal."

"Is my little Poopsie okay? Are you taking care of her?"

"She's fine. I can see why you call her Poopsie."

"Does Miss Julia still have the trots? Poor thing."

I stared at the land mines dotting my floor. "Yeah. I'm all broken up about it."

"Make sure she eats well. Only braised liver and the leanest pork."

Julia was currently snacking on a tuna sandwich I'd dropped under the desk sometime last week.

"I'll do that. Look, I want to make a trade."

I had to play it cool here, if she knew I knew about Marcus, she'd know Thorpe was the one who hired me.

"What kind of trade?"

"I don't want a female dog. I want a male."

"Did Vincent Thorpe hire you?"

Dammit.

"Uh, never heard of him."

"Mr. Thorpe claims I have his dog, Marcus. But the last time I saw Marcus was at an AKC show last April. I have no idea where his dog is."

"That's not how he tells it."

Nice, Harry. I tried to regroup.

"Look, Cummings, you have twelve hours to come up with a male dog. I also want sixty dollars, cash."

Thorpe nudged me and mouthed, "Sixty dollars?"

I put my hand over the mouthpiece. "Carpet cleaning."

"I don't know if I can find a male dog in just 12 hours, Mr. Dognapper."

"Then I turn Julia into a set of luggage."

I heard her gasp. "You horrible man!"

"I'll do it, too. She's got enough hide on her to make two suitcases and a carry-on. The wrinkled look is hot this year."

I scratched Julia on the head, and she licked my chin. Her breath made me teary-eyed.

"Please don't hurt my dog."

"I'll call you tomorrow morning with the details. If you contact the police, I'll mail you Julia's tail."

"I…I already called the police. I called them right after you left."

Hell. "Well, don't call the police again. I have a friend at the Post Office who gives me a discount rate. I'm there twice a week, mailing doggie parts."

I hit the disconnect.

"Did it work?" Thorpe asked.

"Like a charm. Go home and get some rest. In about twelve hours, you'll have your dog back."

The trick was finding an exchange location where I wouldn't be conspicuous in a ski mask. Chicago had several ice rinks, but I didn't think any of them allowed dogs.

I decided on the alley behind the Congress Hotel, off of Michigan Avenue. I got there two hours early to check the place out.

Time crawled by. I kept track of it in my notepad.

9:02am—Arrive at scene. Don't see any cops. Pull on ski mask and wait.

9:11am—It sure is hot.

9:33am—Julia finds some rotting fruit behind the dumpster. Eats it.

10:01am—Boy, is it hot.

10:20am—I think I'm getting a heat rash in this mask. Am I allergic to wool?

10:38am—Julia finds a dead rat. Eats it.

10:40am—Sure is a hot one.

11:02am—Play fetch with the dog, using my pencil.

Julia ate the pencil. I was going to jot this down on the pad, but you can guess how that went.

"Julia!"

The dog jerked on the leash, tugging me to my feet. Abigail Cummings had arrived. She wore a pink linen pants suit, and more make-up than the Rockettes. All of them, combined. I fought the urge to carve my initials in her cheek with my fingernail.

Dog and dog owner had a happy little reunion, hugging and licking, and I was getting ready to sigh in relief when I noticed the pooch Abigail had brought with her.

"I'm no expert, but isn't that a Collie?"

"A Collie/Shepherd mix. I picked him up at the shelter."

"That's not Marcus."

Abigail frowned at me. "I told you before, Mr. Dognapper. I don't have Vincent Thorpe's dog."

Her bottom lip began to quiver, and her eyes went glassy. I realized, to my befuddlement, that I actually believed her.

"Fine. Give me the mutt."

Abigail handed me the leash. I stared down at the dog. It was a male, but I doubted I could fool Thorpe into thinking it was Marcus. Even if I shaved off all the fur and shortened the legs with a saw.

"What about my money?" I asked.

She dug into her purse and pulled out a check.

"I can't take a check."

"It's good. I swear."

"How am I supposed to remain incognito if I deposit a check?"

Abigail did the lip quiver thing again.

"Oh my goodness, I didn't even think of that. Please don't make Julia into baggage."

More tears.

"Calm down. Don't cry. You'll ruin your…uh…make-up."

I offered her a handkerchief. She dabbed at her eyes and handed it back to me.

It looked like it had been tie-dyed.

"I think I have two or three dollars in my purse," she rasped in her smoker voice. "Is that okay?"

What the hell. I took it.

"I'll take those Tic-Tacs, too."

She handed them over. Wint-O-Green.

"Can we go now?"

"Go ahead."

She turned to leave the alley, and a thought occurred to me.

"Ms. Cummings! When the police came to visit you to look for Marcus, did you have an alibi?"

She glanced over her shoulder and nodded vigorously.

"That's the point. The day Vincent said he brought the dog to my house, I wasn't home. I was enjoying the third day of an Alaskan Cruise."

Vincent Thorpe was waiting for me when I got back to my office. He carefully scanned the floor before approaching my desk.

"That's not Marcus! That's not even a Shar-pei!"

"We'll discuss that later."

"Where's Marcus?"

"There have been some complications."

"Complications?" Thorpe leaned in closer, raised an eyebrow. "What happened to your face?"

"I think I'm allergic to wool."

"It looks like you rubbed your cheeks with sandpaper."

I wrote, "I hate him" on my notepad.

"Look, Mr. Thorpe, Abigail Cummings doesn't have Marcus. But I may have an idea who does."

"Who?"

"First, I need to ask you a few questions…"

My face was too sore for the ski mask again, so I opted for a nylon stocking.

It was hot.

I shifted positions on the branch I was sitting on, and took another look through the binoculars.

Nothing. The backyard was quiet. But thirty feet away, next to a holly bush, was either a small, brown anthill, or evidence that there was a dog on the premises.

I took out my pencil and reviewed my stake-out sheet.

9:46pm—Climbed tree.

9:55pm—My face hurts.

10:07pm—It really hurts bad.

10:22pm—I think I'll go see a doctor.

10:45pm—Maybe the drug store has some kind of cream.

I added, "11:07pm—Spotted evidence in backyard. Remember to pick up some aloe vera on the way home."

Before I had a chance to cross my Ts, the patio door opened.

I didn't even need the binoculars. A man, mid-forties with short, brown hair, was walking a dog that was obviously a Shar-pei.

Though my track-team days were far behind me (okay, non-existent), I still managed to leap down from the tree without hurting myself.

The man yelped in surprise, but I had my gun out and in his face before he had a chance to move.

"Hi there, Mr. Ricketts. Kneel down."

"Who are you? What do…"

I cocked the gun.

"Kneel!"

He knelt.

"Good. Now lift up that dog's back leg."

"What?"

"Now!"

Glen Ricketts lifted. I checked.

It was Marcus.

"Leash," I ordered.

He handed me the leash. My third dog in two days, but this time it was the right one.

Now for Part Two of the Big Plan.

"Do you know who I am, Glen?"

He shook his head, terrified.

"Special Agent Phillip Pants, of the American Kennel Club. Do you know why I'm here?"

He shook his head again.

"Don't lie to me, Glen! Does the AKC allow dognapping?"

"No," he whimpered.

"Your dog show days are over, Ricketts. Consider your membership revoked. If I so much catch you in the pet food isle at the Piggly Wiggly, I'm going to take you in and have you neutered. Got it?"

He nodded, eager to please. I gave Marcus a pat on the head, and then turned to leave.

"Hold on!"

Glen's eyes were defeated, pleading.

"What?"

"You mean I can't own a dog, ever again?"

"Not ever."

"But...but...dogs are my life. I love dogs."

"And that's why you should have never stole someone else's."

He sniffled, loud and wet.

"What am I supposed to do now?"

I frowned. Grown men crying like babies weren't my favorite thing to watch. But this joker had brought it upon himself.

"Buy a cat," I told him.

Then I walked back to my car, Marcus in tow.

"Marcus!"

I watching, grinning, as Vincent Thorpe paid no mind to his expensive suit and rolled around on my floor with his dog, giggling like a caffeinated school boy.

"Mr. McGlade, how can I ever repay you?"

"Cash is good."

He disentangled himself from the pooch long enough to pull out his wallet and hand over a fat wad of bills.

"Tell me, how did you know it was Glen Rickets?"

"Simple. You said yourself that he was always one of your closest competitors, up until his dog died earlier this year."

"But what about Ms. Cummings? I talked to her on the phone. I even dropped the dog off at her house, and she took him from me. Wasn't she involved somehow?"

"The phone was easy—Ms. Cummings has a voice like a chainsaw. With practice, anyone can imitate a smoker's croak. But Glen really got clever for the meeting. He picked a time when Ms. Cummings was out of town, and then he spent a good hour or two with Max Factor."

"Excuse me?"

"Cosmetics. As you recall, Abigail Cummings wore enough make-up to cause back-problems. Who could tell what she looked like under all that gunk? Glen just slopped on enough to look like a circus clown, and then he impersonated her."

Thorpe shook his head, clucking his tongue.

"So it wasn't actually Abigail. It was Glen all along. Such a nice guy, too."

"It's the nice ones you have to watch."

"So, now what? Should I call the police?"

"No need. Glen won't be bothering you, or any dog owner, ever again."

I gave him the quick version of the backyard scene.

"He deserves it, taking Marcus from me. But now I have you back, don't I, boy?"

There was more wrestling, and he actually kissed Marcus on the mouth.

"Kind of unsanitary, isn't it?"

"Are you kidding? A dog's saliva is full of antiseptic properties."

"I was speaking for Marcus."

Thorpe laughed. "Friendship transcends species, Mr. McGlade. Speaking of which, where's that Collie/Shepherd mix that Abigail gave you?"

"At my apartment."

"See? You've made a new friend, yourself."

"Nope. I've got a six o'clock appointment at the animal shelter. I'm getting him gassed."

Thorpe shot me surprised look.

"Mr. McGlade! After this whole ordeal, don't you see what amazing companions canines are? A dog can enrich your life! All you have to do is give him a chance."

I mulled it over. How bad could it be, having a friend who never borrowed money, stole your girl, or talked behind your back?

"You know what, Mr. Thorpe? I may just give it a shot."

When I got home a few hours later, I discovered my new best friend had chewed the padding off of my leather couch.

I made it to the shelter an hour before my scheduled appointment.

The End

If you think dead pets aren't funny and want a different ending, go to page 130.

If you think dead pets can be funny, go to page 131.

To return to the previous section, go to page 113.

Through the magic of Write Your Own Damn Story technology, I went back in time a few sentences.

"Mr. McGlade! After this whole ordeal, don't you see what amazing companions canines are? A dog can enrich your life! All you have to do is give him a chance."

I mulled it over. How bad could it be, having a friend who never borrowed money, stole your girl, or talked behind your back?

"You know what, Mr. Thorpe? I may just give it a shot."

When I got home a few hours later, I discovered my new best friend had chewed the padding off of my leather couch. So I dropped him off at the cosmetics factory, where he was kept in a small cage, starved, and subjected to painful experiments. But he didn't die for a long time.

The End

If you think that ending still sucks, go to page 140.

If you want to start over, go to page 2.

To return to the previous section, go to page 113.

If your name is Maria, go to page 289.

There were a lot of Amish in the Amish settlement, and if I had to personally beat up every single one of them to find out who Lulu's husband was sleeping with, I'd do it. Even if it took weeks of non-stop beatings.

Walking though the corn, I stopped at a plain-looking house, which was in plain view. After knocking on the door, some plain chick answered.

"May I help you, Brother?"

"Yes. My name is Brother Karamazov. I'd like to speak to your husband."

"Amos?"

"Is every man in this village named Amos?"

"All the ones named Amos are."

"You going to let me in or what? Didn't God say be nice to strangers in one of those bible things?"

"Please come in, Brother Karamozov. But I must beseech you not to bother our son, Little Amos. His pet rabbit just passed away, and he's in a terrible state. He had that rabbit for six years."

I stuck my head in the door. "Is that rabbit stew I smell?"

"No, that's a chateau Briand. We wouldn't be so cruel as to eat Little Amos's pet. Instead, we chopped up the corpse, threw it in the compost heap, and will use it to fertilize our vegetable garden."

"Neat. You letting me in, or what?"

She opened the door, and I stepped into their plain little house. Little Amos was sitting at the dinner table, tears on his chubby red cheeks. Since nothing tugs at my heartstrings like a child in need, and since I'm a caring, consoling type, I sat next to him.

"Cheer up, little buckaroo. I heard about your bunny. But that's just part of God's master plan. See, God kills everything we love. One day He'll kill your mommy and your daddy. He'll even kill you."

Little Amos began to cry even harder.

"Christ, don't be a baby about it. What are you, seven years old? Time to thicken up that skin, Mr. Girlypants."

That pep talk didn't work, either. Neither did offering the kid the good luck charm on my keychain, a rabbit's foot. I tried slapping the sorrow out of him, but that seemed to have an adverse effect. Finally, with no other options left, I resorted to technology and pulled my ereader from my jacket pocket.

Yes, ereader is so small, it fits in your pocket. It also has 50% better contrast on the e-ink screen. What will those techno-geniuses think of next?

"Look, kid. Do you like to read?"

He sniffled and nodded. "I read my bible every day."

"Well this little device has a lot of fictional books on it, just like the bible. In fact, a lot of them are for children to help them cope with the loss of a pet. I bet they'll really help you get over your bunny rabbit's death."

"Can I see it?"

"No. This is mine. Use your own ereader."

"But I don't have an ereader."

"Sucks to be you. And you know what else you don't have? A bunny. Now tell me, is your dad snogging some ho name Lulu?"

"What's snogging?"

"It's flarching, without the gas."

He shook his little, tear-stained head. "No, Brother. My father was attacked by some mean men who want us to leave our homes so they can build strip malls."

"Cool," I said, imagining a mall full of strippers.

"So he's not snogging or flarching anyone, because they stomped on his junk and it swelled up to the size of a pumpkin."

"Must be tough for him to find slacks that fit."

"Can we help you with anything else, Brother Karamozov?" Little Amos's mother asked.

"No. I'll just be taking a plate of chateau Briand, and I'll be on my way."

Do you want to keep interrogating the Amish? Go to page 44.

Do you want to read a list of books that help children deal with the loss of a pet? If so, go to page 164.

"I need your help, McGlade."

I stared at the timecaster, Talon Avalon, standing in my doorway. Talon was a cop who could see into the past, thereby being able to solve any crimes. Except now he was on the run, having been framed. Or some convoluted shit like that. Read the book if you want the whole backstory.

"I figured you did," I said. "Can you pay?"

"Eventually. I'm having a little chip problem at the moment." Talon held up his arm, showing me the hole. In this current year of 2054, all money was extracted from bank accounts through implanted biochips. But apparently, someone had extracted Talon's chip by cutting open his arm. One helluva withdrawl.

"An IOU from a lifer ain't worth much," I said.

"I won't be a lifer. They'll kill me in prison. I'll make sure you're a beneficiary on my insurance."

I brightened at that. "Okay. C'mon in. Have a seat in my office. I'll get some P&P."

"Nothing too heavy. I have to keep my wits."

I snorted. "What wits?"

I was two steps away when Talon screamed after me. "McGlade! You have a pet?"

"Yeah. His name is Penis. Don't step on him."

"I stepped on something else."

"Smells awful, doesn't it? They don't tell you that at the genipet store."

Penis was a genetically modified African elephant. Brown and hairy and about the size of a raccoon. I grabbed the pills and pot and heard Penis trumpet as I walked back to the office.

"Hello, Peanuts," Talon said, giving the elephant a scratch on the head.

"Not *Peantus*," I corrected, scooping up the elephant and holding him at eye-level. "*Penis*. Check out the size of his junk."

My elephant did, indeed, have impressive junk.

"It's like a second trunk," I marveled. "You want to touch it?"

I shoved the elephant in Talon's face, its lengthy dong flopping around and threatening to take out one of his eyes.

"No thanks."

"He's a bonsai elephant." I set the pachyderm down. "That's as big as he gets."

"He's… very elephantish."

"Yeah. I gotta get him a mate. Problem is, they're so freakin' expensive. I tried a few non-elephant surrogates. A cat and a poodle. He killed them both."

"His tusks?"

"Naw. Slipping them the high, hard one."

"Nice."

"They both sounded like they died happy. The poodle especially. Vet said it was a heart attack."

"And the cat?"

"Internal bleeding. Here, take these." I handed him six pills.

"What are they?"

"Morphine, hash, and valium."

"There's enough here to kill me, McGlade."

"The other three are speed, so you don't lapse into a coma. Take them and go shower. There's a robe hanging in the bathroom."

"Is the robe clean?"

"No. But after the pills, you won't care."

While Talon was in the shower, I took a few pills myself. Just to relax a bit, before operating on him. I wasn't a doctor, but I knew my way around a scalpel. Basically, there was a sharp end, and a dull end. The sharp end was the one you cut with.

I placed my scalpel, and several other sharp tools, on the table.

"I'm in the office!" I yelled when I heard the water shut off.

"What's all that for, McGlade?" Talon asked when he trudged in. He looked pale.

"This is why you came to me, isn't it, Talon? They switched off your headphone, and you want it working again. Right?"

"Yeah."

"How do you think that'll happen? Hope and a head massage?"

"Have you done this before?"

"Four times. Two of them successful. I'm charging you five thousand credits for this, by the way. That includes patching up your arm and hand."

"I also have some broken ribs."

"We'll call it an even fifty-five hundred. Though tipping isn't discouraged."

"I dunno about this, McGlade."

"Don't worry. Penis is here to help."

Penis was standing on the table, holding a scalpel in his trunk. Talon giggled. The drugs were primo. And legal. All drugs were legal. What a wonderful future, wasn't it?

"Sit before you fall over," I told him. "Put you head on this semi-clean towel here."

I patted a rolled-up towel. Penis dropped the scalpel and walked up to it.

"Your pet is getting amorous with the towel," Talon said.

"Just the inside. You'll have your head on the outside."

Talon weaved over to the chair and managed to sit down without falling over. The elephant was really going at it, his tiny elephant hips a blur. After a few more thrusts he trumpeted and walked away.

"I want a new towel," Talon said.

"You're such a little girl." I tossed the towel over my shoulder and placed a pillow on the table. "Head down, princess."

Talon complied, resting his ear on the towel. Just a few inches away, Penis stared at him. It was a prurient stare. His trunk extended and he sniffed Talon's nostrils.

"Get him off the table," Talon said. "I don't trust him."

"He's fine. He won't hurt you."

"He looks like he's sizing me up."

"Don't worry. He's got a long refractory period."

"Off the table, McGlade."

"Fine. Sheesh. You're some kind of animal hater, you know that, Princess Talon?"

"I want my nose to remain a virgin."

I grabbed Penis (the elephant) and set him on the floor. Then I picked up a bottle of iodine.

"First I'm going to sterilize the area. Then it might get a little, um, uncomfortable."

Talon sat up, suddenly. "Hold on a second. This entire section… what was the point?"

"Whatever do you mean?"

"This excerpt. It seemed like nothing more than one big advertisement for the Joe Kimball novel, *Timecaster*."

I shook my head. "That's not true. This section was essential for solving the Amish mystery."

"No, it wasn't. It's just a lame attempt to sell more ebooks."

"Ereaders are the future, you know. But *Timecaster* will have a paperback release as well as an ebook release, in 2011. It will be followed by a sequel, *Timecaster Supersymmetry*. Both novels are filled with sex, laughs, sci-fi gadgetry, and me, Harry McGlade the Third."

"Now you've stepped over the line from product placement to blatant self-promotion."

"You're a timecaster. You should have seen this coming."

"Get out."

"It's my house. You get out."

"I mean get out of this excerpt."

"Konrath might also write a Timecaster children's book called *Timecaster Disaster*. It rhymes, like Dr. Seuss. Want to hear a verse?"

"No."

"He saw into the past, and a bad guy kicked his ast."

"That's terrible. And we're done here."

If you want to get back to the Amish adventure, go to page 44.

To put Harry in the middle of the ebook Endurance by Jack Kilborn, go to page 107.

To start over at the beginning, go to page 2.

To read some rejected Dr. Seuss titles, go to page 113.

So I jumped out the window.

Now I'm dead.

Thanks a lot, jackass. Way to bow to peer pressure.

To start the adventure over, go to page 2.

To return to the previous section, go to page 131.

Through the magic of *Write Your Own Damn Story* technology, I went back in time a few sentences. Again.

"Mr. McGlade! After this whole ordeal, don't you see what amazing companions canines are? A dog can enrich your life! All you have to do is give him a chance."

I mulled it over. How bad could it be, having a friend who never borrowed money, stole your girl, or talked behind your back?

"You know what, Mr. Thorpe? I may just give it a shot."

When I got home a few hours later, I discovered my new best friend had chewed the padding off of my leather couch. So I took him to a new home with a new family, who ate him.

The End

To interview some Amish people, go to page 44.

To go back to the beginning, go to page 2.

To return to the previous section, go to page 113.

Bored with that damn Amish case, I went back to my office and waited for another client to come in. One did.

"I want you to kill the man that my husband hired to kill the man that I hired to kill my husband."

If I had been paying attention, I still wouldn't have understood what she wanted me to do. But I was busy looking at her legs, which weren't adequately covered by her skirt. She had great legs, curvy without being heavy, tan and long, and she had them crossed in that sexy way that women cross their legs, knee over knee, not the ugly way that guys do it, with the ankle on the knee, though if she did cross her legs that way it would have been sexy too.

"Mr. McGlade, did you hear what I just said?"

"Hmm? Yeah, sure I did, baby. The man, the husband, I got it."

"So you'll do it?"

"Do what?"

"Kill the man that my husband—"

I held up my hand. "Whoa. Hold it right there. I'm just a plain old private eye. That's what is says on the door you just walked through. The door even has a big magnifying glass silhouette logo thingy painted on it, which I paid way too much money for, just so no one gets confused. I don't kill people for money. Absolutely, positively, no way." I leaned forward a little. "But, for the sake of argument, how much money are we talking about here?"

"I don't know where else to turn."

The tears came, and she buried her face in her hands, giving me the opportunity to look at her legs again. Marietta Garbonzo had found me through the ad I placed in the Chicago phone book. The ad used the expensive magnifying glass logo, along with the tagline, Harry McGlade Investigators: We'll Do Whatever it Takes. It brought in more customers than my last tagline: No Job Too Small, No Fee Too High, or the one prior to that, We'll Investigate Your Privates.

Mrs. Garbonzo had never been to a private eye before, and she was playing her role to the hilt. Besides the short skirt and tight blouse, she had gone to town with the hair and make-up; her blonde locks curled and sprayed, her lips painted deep, glossy red, her purple eye shadow so thick that she managed to get some on her collar.

"My husband beats me, Mr. McGlade. Do you know why?"

"Beats me," I said, shrugging. Her wailing kicked in again. I wondered where she worked out. Legs like that, she must work out.

"He's insane, Mr. McGlade. We've been married for a year, and Roy always had a temper. I once saw him attack another man with a tire iron. They were having an argument, Roy went out to the car, grabbed a crow bar from the trunk, then came back and practically killed him."

"Where do you work out?"

"Excuse me?"

"Exercise. Do you belong to a gym, or work out at home?"

"Mr. McGlade, I'm trying to tell you about my husband."

"I know, the insane guy who beats you. Probably shouldn't have married a guy who used a tire iron for anything other than changing tires."

"I married too young. But while we were dating, he treated me kindly. It was only after we married that the abuse began."

She turned her head away and unbuttoned her blouse. My gaze shifted from her legs to her chest. She had a nice chest, packed tight into a silky black bra with lace around the edges and an underwire that displayed things to a good effect, both lifting and separating.

"See these bruises?"

"Hmm?"

"It's humiliating to reveal them, but I don't know where else to go."

"Does he hit you anywhere else? You can show me, I'm a professional."

The tears returned. "I hired a man to kill him, Mr. McGlade. I hired a man to kill my husband. But somehow Roy found out about it, and he hired a man to kill the man I hired. So I'd like you to kill his man so my man can kill him."

I removed the bottle of whiskey from my desk that I keep there for medicinal purposes, like getting drunk. I unscrewed the cap, wiped off the bottle neck with my tie, and handed it to her.

"You're not making sense, Mrs. Garbonzo. Have a swig of this."

"I shouldn't. When I drink I lose my inhibitions."

"Keep the bottle."

She took a sip, coughing after it went down.

"I already paid the assassin. I paid him a lot of money, and he won't refund it. But I'm afraid he'll die before he kills my husband, so I need someone to kill the man who is after him."

"Shouldn't you tell the guy you hired that he's got a hit on him?"

"I called him. He says not to worry. But I am worried, Mr. McGlade."

"As I said before, I don't kill people for money."

"Even if you're killing someone who kills people for money?"

"But I'd be killing someone who is killing someone who kills people for money. What prevents that killer from hiring someone to kill me because he's killing someone who is killing someone that I…hand me that bottle."

I took a swig.

"Please, Mr. McGlade. I'm a desperate woman. I'll do anything."

She walked around the desk and stood before me, shivering in her bra, her breath coming out in short gasps through red, wet lips. Her hands rested on my shoulders, squeezing, and she bent forward.

"My laundry," I said.

"What?"

"Do my laundry."

"Mr. McGlade, I'm offering you my body."

"And it's a tempting offer, Mrs. Garbonzo. But that will take, what, five minutes? I've got about six loads of laundry back at my place, they take an hour for each cycle."

"Isn't there a dry cleaner in your neighborhood?"

"A hassle. I'd have to write my name on all the labels, on every sock, on the elastic band of my whitey tighties, plus haul six bags of clothes down the street. You want me to help you? I get five hundred a day, plus expenses. And you do my laundry."

"And you'll kill him?"

"No. I don't kill people for money. Or for laundry. But I'll protect your guy from getting whacked."

"Thank you, Mr. McGlade."

She leaned down to kiss me. Not wanting to appear rude, I let her. And so she didn't feel unwanted, I stuck my hand up her skirt.

"You won't tell the police, will you Mr. McGlade?"

"Look, baby, I'm not your priest and I'm not your lawyer and I'm not your shrink. I'm just a man. A man who will keep his mouth shut, except when I'm eating. Or talking, or sleeping, because sometimes I sleep with my mouth open because I have the apnea."

"Thank you, Mr. McGlade."

"I'll take the first week in advance, Visa and MasterCard are fine. Here are my spare keys."

"Your keys?"

"For my apartment. It's in Hyde Park. I don't have a hamper, so I leave my dirty clothes all over the floor. Do the bed sheets too—those haven't been washed since, well, ever. Washer and dryer are in the basement of the building, washer costs seventy-five cents, dryer costs fifty cents for each thirty minutes, and the heavy things like jeans and sweaters take about a buck fifty to dry. Make yourself at home, but don't touch anything, sit on anything, eat any of my food, or turn on the TV."

I gave her my address, and she gave me a check and all of her info. The info was surprising.

"You hired a killer from the personal ads in Famous Soldier Magazine?"

"I didn't know where else to go."

"How about the police? A divorce attorney?"

"My husband is a rich and powerful man, Mr. McGlade. You don't recognize his name?"

I flipped though my mental Rolodex. "Roy Garbonzo? Is he the Roy Garbonzo that owns Happy Roy's Chicken Shack?"

"Yes."

"He seems so happy on those commercials."

"He's a beast, Mr. McGlade."

"The guy is like a hundred and thirty years old. And on those commercials, he's always laughing and singing and dancing with that Claymation chicken. He's the guy that's abusing you?"

"Would you like to see the proof again?"

"If it isn't too much trouble."

She grabbed my face in one hand, squeezing my cheeks together.

"Happy Roy is a vicious psycho, Mr. McGlade. He's a brutal, misogynist pig who enjoys inflicting pain."

"He's probably rich too."

Mrs. Garbonzo narrowed her eyes. "He's wealthy, yes. What are you implying?"

"I like his extra spicy recipe. Do you get to take chicken home for free? You probably have a fridge stuffed full of it, am I right?"

She released my face and buttoned up her blouse.

"I have to go. My husband gets paranoid when I go out."

"Maybe because when you go out, you hire people to kill him."

She picked up her purse and headed for the door. "I expect you to call me when you've made some progress."

"That includes ironing," I called after her. "And hanging the stuff up. I don't have any hangers, so you'll have to buy some."

After she left, I turned off all the office lights and closed the blinds, because what I had to do next, I had to do in complete privacy.

I took a nap.

When I awoke a few hours later, I went to the bank, cashed Mrs. Garbonzo's check, and went to start earning my money.

My first instinct was to dive head-first into the belly of the beast and confront Mrs. Garbonzo's hired hitman help. My second instinct was to get some nachos, maybe a beer or two.

I went with my second instinct. The nachos were good, spicy but not so much that all you tasted was peppers. After the third beer I hopped in my ride and headed for the assassin's headquarters, which turned out to be in a well-to-do suburb of Chicago called Barrington. The development I pulled into boasted some amazingly huge houses, complete with big lawns and swimming pools and trimmed bushes that looked like corkscrews and lollipops. I double-checked the address I'd scribbled down, then pulled into a long circular driveway and up to a home that was bigger than the public school I attended, and I came from the city where they grew schools big.

The hitman biz must be booming.

I half expected some sort of maid or butler to answer the door, but instead I was greeted by a fifty-something woman, her facelift sporting a deep tan. I appraised her.

"If you stay out in the sun, the wrinkles will come back."

"Then I'll just have more work done." Her voice was steady, cultured.

"Are you here to clean the pool?"

"I'm here to speak to William Johansenn."

"Billy? Sure, he's in the basement."

She let me in. Perhaps all rich suburban women were fearless and let strange guys into their homes. Or perhaps this one simply didn't care. I didn't get a chance to ask, because she walked off just as I entered.

"Lady? Where's the basement?"

"Down the hall, stairs to the right," she said without turning around.

I took a long, tiled hallway past a powder room, a den, and a door that opened to a descending staircase. Heavy metal music blared up at me.

"Billy!" I called down.

My effort was fruitless—with the noise, I couldn't even hear myself. The lights were off, and squinting did nothing to penetrate the darkness.

Surprising a paid assassin in his own lair wasn't on the list of 100 things I longed to do before I die, but I didn't see much of a choice. I beer-belched, then went down the stairs.

The basement was furnished, though furnished didn't seem to be the right word. The floor had carpet, and the walls had paint, and there seemed to be furniture, but I couldn't really tell because everything was covered with food wrappers, pop cans, dirty clothing, and discarded magazines. It looked like a 7-Eleven exploded.

William "Billy" Johansenn was asleep on a waterbed, a copy of Creem open on his chest. He had a galaxy of pimples dotting his forehead and six curly hairs sprouting from his chin.

He couldn't have been a day over sixteen.

I killed the stereo. Billy continued to snore. Among the clutter on the floor were several issues of Famous Soldier, along with various gun and hunting magazines. I poked through his drawers and found a cheap Rambo knife, a CO_2 powered BB gun, and a dog-eared copy of the infamous How to be a Hitman book from Paladin Press.

I gave the kid a shake, then another. The third shake got him to open his eyes.

"Who the hell are you?" he said, defiant.

"I'm your wake-up call."

I slapped the kid, making his eyes cross.

"Hey! You hit me!"

"A woman hired you to kill her husband."

"I don't know what you're—"

He got another smack. "That's for lying."

"You can't hit me," he whined. "I'll sue you."

I hit him twice more; once because I didn't like being threatened by punk kids, and once because I didn't like lawyers. When I pulled my palm back for threesies, the kid broke.

"Please! Stop it! I admit it!"

I released his t-shirt and let him blubber for a minute. His blue eyes matched those of the woman upstairs. Not many professional killers lived in their mother's basement, and I wondered how Marietta Garbonzo could have been this naïve.

"I'm guessing you never met Mrs. Garbonzo in person."

"I only talked to her on the phone. She sent the money to a P.O. Box. That's how the pros do it."

"So how did she get your home address?"

"She wouldn't give me the money without my address. She said if I didn't trust her, why should she trust me?"

Here was my proof that each new generation of teenagers was stupider than the last. I blame MTV.

"How much did she give you?"

He smiled, showing me a mouth full of braces. "Fifty large."

"And how were you going to do it? With your BB gun?"

"I was going to follow him around and then…you know…shove him."

"Shove him?"

"He's an old guy. I was thinking I'd shove him down some stairs, or into traffic. I dunno."

"Have you shoved a lot of old people into traffic, Billy boy?"

He must not have liked the look in my eyes, because he shrunk two sizes.

"No! Never! I never killed anybody!"

"So why put an ad in the magazine?"

"I dunno. Something to do."

I considered hitting him again, but didn't know what purpose it would serve.

I hit him anyway.

"Ow! My lip's caught in my braces!"

"You pimple-faced little moron. Do you have any idea what kind of trouble you're in right now? Not only did you accept money to commit a felony, but now you've got a price on your head. Did Mrs. Garbonzo tell you about the guy her husband hired to kill you?"

He nodded, his Adam's apple wiggling like a fish.

"Are-are you here to kill me?"

"No."

"But you've got a gun." He pointed to the butt of my Magnum, jutting out of my shoulder holster.

"I'm a private detective."

"Is that a real gun?"

"Yes."

"Can I touch it?"

"No."

"Come on. Lemme touch it."

This is what happens when you spare the rod and spoil the child.

"Look kid, I know that you're a loser that nobody likes, and that you're a virgin and will probably stay one for the next ten years, but do you want to die?"

"Ten years?"

"Answer the question."

"No. I don't want to die."

I sighed. "That's a start. Where's the money?"

"I've got a secret place. In the wall."

He rolled off the bed, eager, and pried a piece of paneling away from the plaster in a less-cluttered corner of the room. His hand reached in, and came out with a brown paper shopping bag.

"Is it all there?"

Billy shook his head. "I spent three hundred on a wicked MP3 player."

"Hand over the money. And the MP3 player."

Billy showed a bit of reluctance, so I smacked him again to help with his motivation.

It helped. He also gave me fresh batteries for the player.

"Now what?" he sniffled.

"Now we tell your parents."

"Do we have to?"

"You'd prefer the cops?"

He shook his head. "No. No cops."

"That blonde upstairs with the face like a snare drum, that your mom?"

"Yeah."

"Let's go have a talk with her."

Mrs. Johansenn was perched in front of a sixty inch television, watching a soap.

"Nice TV. High definition?"

"Plasma."

"Nice. Billy has something he wants to tell you."

Billy stared at his shoes. "Mom, I bought an ad in the back of Famous Soldier Magazine, and some lady gave me fifty thousand dollars to kill her husband."

Mrs. Johansenn hit the mute button on the remote, shaking her head in obvious disappointment.

"Billy, dammit, this is too much. You're a hired killer?"

"Sorry," he mumbled.

"You're father is going to have a stroke when he hears this."

"Do we have to tell Dad?"

"Are you kidding?"

"I gave the money back."

"Who are you?" Billy's mom squinted at me.

"I'm Harry McGlade. I'm a private eye. I was hired to find Billy. Someone is trying to kill him."

Mrs. Johansenn rolled her eyes. "Oh, this gets better and better. I need to call Sal."

"You husband?"

"My lawyer."

"Ma'am, a lawyer isn't going to do much to save Billy's life, unless he's standing between him and a bullet."

"So what then, the police?"

"Not the cops, Mom! I don't want to go to jail!"

"He won't survive in prison," I said. "The lifers will pass him around like a bong at a college party. They'll trade him for candy bars and cigarettes."

"I don't want to be traded for candy bars, Mom!"

Mrs. Johansenn frowned, forming new wrinkles. "Then what should we do, Mr. McGlade?"

I paused for a moment, then I grinned.

"I get five-hundred a day, plus expenses."

I celebrated my recent windfall with a nice dinner at a nice restaurant. I was more of a burger and fries guy than a steak and lobster guy, but the steak and lobster went down easy, and after leaving a 17% tip I headed to Evanston to visit the Chicken King.

Roy Garbonzo's estate made the Johansenn's look like a third world mud hut. He had his own private access road, a giant wrought iron perimeter fence, and a uniformed guard posted at the gate. I was wondering how to play it when the aforementioned uniformed guard knocked on my window.

"I need to see Roy Garbonzo," I told him. "My son choked to death on a Sunny Meal toy."

"He's expecting you, Mr. McGlade."

The gate rolled back, and I drove up to the mansion. It looked like five mansions stuck together. I parked between two massive Doric columns and pressed the buzzer next to the giant double doors. Before anyone answered, a startling thought flashed through my head.

How did the guard know my name?

"It's a set up," I said aloud. I yanked the Magnum out of my shoulder holster and dove into one of the hydrangea bushes flanking the entryway just as the knob turned.

I peeked through the lavender blooms, finger on the trigger, watching the door swing open. A sinister-looking man wearing a tuxedo stepped out of the house and peered down his nose at me.

"Would Mr. McGlade care for a drink?"

"You're a butler," I said.

"Observant of you, sir."

"You work for Roy Garbonzo."

"An excellent deduction, sir. A drink?"

"Uh—whiskey, rocks."

"Would you care to have it in the parlor, sir, or would you prefer to remain squatting in the Neidersachen?"

"I thought it was a hydrangea."

"It's a hydrangea Neidersachen, sir."

"It's pretty," I said. "But I think I'll take that drink inside."

"Very good, sir."

I extricated myself from the Neidersachen, brushed off some clinging leaves, and followed Jeeves through the tiled foyer, through the carpeted library, and into the parlor, which had wood floors and an ornate Persian rug big enough to park a bus on.

"Please have a seat, sir. Mr. Garbonzo will be with your shortly. Were you planning on shooting him?"

"Excuse me?"

"You're holding a gun, sir."

I glanced down at my hand, still clenched around my Magnum.

"Sorry. Forgot."

I holstered the .44 and sat in a high-backed leather chair, which was so plush I sank four inches. Waddles returned with my whiskey, and I sipped it and stared at the paintings hanging on the walls. One in particular caught my interest, of a nude woman eating grapes.

"Admiring the Degas?" a familiar voice boomed from behind.

I turned and saw Happy Roy the vicious misogynist psycho, all five foot two inches of him, walking up to me. He wore an expensive silk suit, but like most old men the waist was too high, making him seem more hunched over than he actually was. On his feet were slippers, and his glasses had black plastic frames and looked thick enough to stop a bullet.

"Her name is Degas?" I asked. "Silly name for a chick."

He held out his hand and I shook it, noticing his knuckles were swollen and bruised.

"Degas is the painter, Mr. McGlade. My business advisors thought it was a good investment. Do you like it?"

"Not really. She's got too much in back, not enough up front, and her face is a double-bagger."

"A double-bagger?"

"I'd make her wear two bags over her head, in case one fell off."

The Chicken King laughed. "I always thought she was ugly too. Apparently, this little lady was the ideal beauty hundreds of years ago."

"Or maybe Degas just liked ugly, pear-shaped chicks. How did you know I was coming, Mr. Garbonzo?"

He sat in the chair across from me, sinking in so deep he had trouble seeing over his knees.

"Please, call me Happy Roy. I've been having my wife followed, Mr. McGlade. The man I hired tailed her to your office. Does that surprise you?"

"Why should I be surprised? I remember that she came to my office."

"What I meant was, are you surprised I'm having my wife followed?"

I considered it. "No. She's young, beautiful, and you look like a Caucasian version of one of the California Raisins."

"I remember those commercials. That's where I got the idea for the Claymation chicken in the Chicken Shack spots. Expensive to produce, those commercials."

"Enough of the small talk. I want you to call off your goon."

"My goon?"

"The person your wife hired to whack you, he's a teenage kid living in the suburbs. He's not a real threat."

"I'm aware of that."

"So you don't need to have that kid killed."

"Mr. McGlade, I'm not having anyone killed. I'm Happy Roy. I don't kill people. I promote world peace through deep fried poultry. I simply told my wife that I hired a killer, even though I didn't."

"You lied to her?"

Happy Roy let out a big, dramatic sigh. "When I found out she wanted me dead, I was justifiably annoyed. I confronted her, we got into an argument, and I told her that I'd have her assassin killed. I was trying to get her to call it off on her own."

I absorbed this information, drinking more whiskey. When the whiskey ran out, I sucked on an ice cube.

"Tho wmer mmmpt wooor—"

"Excuse me? I can't understand you with that ice in your mouth."

I spit out the ice. "She said you abuse her. That you're insane."

"The only thing insane about me is my upcoming promotion. Buy a box of chicken, get a second box for half price."

I wondered if I should tell him about the bruises she had, but chose to keep silent.

"What about divorce?"

"I love Marietta, Mr. McGlade. I know she's too young for me. I know she's a devious, back-stabbing maneater. That just makes her more adorable."

"She wants you dead."

"All spouses have their quirks."

I leaned forward, an effort because my butt was sunk so low in the chair.

"Happy Roy, I have no doubt that Marietta will kill you if she can. When this doesn't pan out, she'll try something else. Eventually, she'll hook up with a real assassin."

Happy Roy's eye became hooded, dark. "She's my wife, Mr. McGlade.

I'll deal with her my way."

"By beating her?"

"This conversation is over. I'll have my butler show you to the door."

I pried myself out of the chair. "You're disgustingly rich, powerful, and not a bad looking guy for someone older than God. Let Marietta go and find some other bimbo to play with."

"Good bye, Mr. McGlade. Feel free to keep working for my wife."

"Are you trying to pay me off, so I drop this case?"

"No. Not at all."

"If you were thinking about paying me off, how much money would we be talking?"

"I'm not trying to pay you off, Mr. McGlade."

I got in the smaller man's face. "You might be able to afford fat Degas and huge estates, but I'm a person, Happy Roy. And no matter how rich you get, you'll never be able to buy a human being. Because it's illegal, Happy Roy. Buying people is illegal."

"I'm not trying to buy you!"

"I'll find my own way out."

I stormed out of the parlor, through the library, into the dining room, into another parlor, or maybe it was a den, and then I wound up in the kitchen somehow. I tried to back track, wandered into the dining room, and then found myself back in one of the parlors, but I couldn't tell if it was the first parlor or the second parlor. I didn't see that painting of the naked heifer, but Happy Roy may have taken it down just to confuse me.

"Hello?" I called out. "I'm a little lost here."

No one answered.

I went back into the dining room, then the kitchen, and took another door which led down a hallway which led to a bathroom, which was fine because I needed to go to the bathroom anyway.

When the lizard had been adequately drained, I discovered some very interesting prescription drugs, just lying there, in the medicine cabinet.

And then it all made sense.

Forty minutes later I found the front door and headed back to my apartment.

Time to drop the truth on Little Miss Marietta.

At first, I thought I had the wrong place. Everything was so…clean. Not only were all of my clothes picked up, but the apartment had been vacuumed—a real feat since I didn't think I owned a vacuum cleaner.

"Mrs. Garbonzo? You here?"

I walked into the bedroom. The bed had been made, and the closet door was open, revealing over a dozen shirts on hangers.

In the kitchen, the sink was empty of dishes for the first time since I rented the place fifteen years ago. There was even a fresh smell of lilacs and orange zest in the air.

The door opened and I swung around, hand going to my gun. Mrs. Garbonzo entered, carrying a plastic laundry basket overflowing with my socks. She flinched when she saw me.

"Mr. McGlade. I didn't expect you back so soon."

"Surprised, Marietta? I thought you might be."

"Did you take care of the guy?"

"Sit down. We need to talk."

She set the basket down on my kitchen counter, and seductively perched herself on one of my breakfast bar stools. Her blouse had been untucked from her skirt, the shirt tails tied in a knot around her flat stomach.

"You lied to me, Marietta."

"Lied?" She batted her eyelashes. "How?"

There was a bottle of window cleaner next to the sink that I'd never seen before. I picked it up.

"How about opening up that shirt and letting me squirt you with this?"

"Is that what turns you on? Spraying women with glass cleaner?"

I grabbed her blouse and pulled, tearing buttons.

"I was thinking more along the lines of washing off those fake bruises. They're so fake, the purple has even rubbed off on your collar. See?"

I shot two quick streams at the marks, then used my sleeve to wipe them off.

They didn't wipe off.

I tried again, to similar effect.

Marietta sneered at me. "Are you finished?"

"So what's that purple stuff on your collar?"

"Eye shadow." She pointed at her eyes. "That's why it matches my eye shadow."

"Big deal. So you gave yourself those bruises. Or paid someone to give them to you. I met your husband today, Mrs. Garbonzo. All ninety pounds of him. He couldn't beat up a quadriplegic."

"My husband abuses me, Mr. McGlade."

"Yeah, I saw his swollen knuckles. At first, I thought they were swollen from hitting you. But he didn't hit you, did he Marietta? Roy has rheumatoid arthritis. I saw his medication. His knuckles are swollen because of his disease, and they undoubtedly cause him great pain. So much pain, he'd never be able to hit you."

Marietta put her hands on her hips.

"He beats me with a belt, Mr. McGlade."

"A belt?"

"These bruises are from the buckle. It also causes welts. See?"

She turned around, lifting her blouse. Angry, red scabs stretched across her back.

I gave them a spritz of the window cleaner, just to be sure.

"Ow!"

"Sorry. Had to check."

Marietta faced me. "I've paid you, I've done your laundry, and I've cleaned your apartment. Did you take care of the assassin for me?"

"Your husband didn't hire an assassin."

"Is that what he told you?"

"I know it for a fact. The guy you hired is a sixteen-year-old pimply-faced kid. He couldn't whack anyone. He couldn't even whack a mole."

I smiled at my pun.

Marietta made a face. "I thought he sounded young on the phone. He really won't do it?"

"He lives in his parent's basement."

The tears came. "I gave him a lot of money. Everything I've been able to hide from Roy during six years of marriage."

I thought about mentioning I got the money back, but decided against it.

"Look, Marietta, just divorce the guy."

"I can't. He threatened to kill me if I divorced him."

"You can run away. Hire a lawyer."

She sniffled. "Pre-nup."

"Pre-nup?"

"I signed a pre-nuptial agreement. If I divorce Roy, I don't get a penny. And after six years of abuse, I deserve more than that." She licked her lips. "But if he dies, I get it all."

"Don't you think killing the guy is a little extreme?"

She threw herself at me, teary-eyed and heaving. "Please, Harry. You have to help me. I'll give you half—half of the entire chicken empire. Help me kill the son of a bitch."

"Marietta…"

"I cleaned your place, you promised you'd help." She added a little grinding action to her hug. "Please kill him for me."

I looked around the kitchen. She did do a pretty good job. I wondered, briefly, if I'd make a decent Chicken King.

"I'll tell you what, Marietta. I don't do that kind of thing. But I know someone who can help. Do you want me to make a phone call?"

"Yes. Oh, yes."

I pried myself out of her grasp and picked up the phone, dialing the number from memory.

"Hi, partner. It's me. Look, I've got a woman here who wants to kill her husband. I told her I'm not interested, but I thought maybe you'd be able to set something up. Say, tomorrow, around noon? You can meet her at the Hilton. Rent a room under the name Lipshultz. No, schultz, with a U-L. Okay, she'll be there."

I hung up. "Got it all set for you, sugar."

She squeezed me tight and kissed my neck. "Thanks, Harry. Thank you so much. Is there anything I can do to repay you?" Her breath was hot in my ear. "Anything at all?"

"You can start by folding those socks. And maybe some dusting. Yeah, dusting would be good."

She smiled wickedly and caressed my cheek. "I was thinking of something a little more intimate."

"I was thinking about dinner."

"Dinner would be wonderful."

"I'm sure it will be. Have the place dusted by the time I get back."

Marietta Garbonzo called me the next night, around eight in the evening.

"You son of a bitch! You set me up! You didn't call a hitman! You called a cop!"

"You can't go around murdering people, sweetheart. It's wrong on so many levels."

"But what about all of the washing? The cleaning? The dusting? And what about after dinner? What we did? How could you betray me after that?"

"You expect me to throw away all of my principles because we spent five minutes doing the worm? It was fun, but not worth twenty to life."

"You bastard. When I get out of here I'll…"

I hung up and went back to the Sharper Image catalog I'd been thumbing through. I had my eye on one of those massaging easy chairs. That would set me back two grand. Earlier that day, I bought a sixty inch plasma TV. The money I took from William "Billy" Johansenn was being put to good use.

I plopped down in front of the TV, found the wrestling channel, and settled in to watch two hours of pay-per-view sports entertainment. The Iron Commie had Captain Frankenbeef in a suplex when I felt the gun press against the back of my head.

"Hello, Mr. McGlade."

"Happy Roy?"

"Yes. Stand up, slowly. Then turn around."

I followed instructions. Happy Roy held a four barreled COP .357, a nasty weapon that could do a lot of damage at close range.

"How'd you get in?" I asked.

"You gave a key to my wife, you moron. I took it from her last night, when she got home." His face got mean. "After you slept with her."

"Technically, we didn't do any sleeping."

The gun trembled in Happy Roy's hand.

"She's in jail now, Mr. McGlade. Because of you."

"She wanted to kill you, Happy Roy. You should thank me."

"You idiot!" Spittle flew from his lips. "I wanted to kill her myself. With my own two hands. Now I have to get her out of jail before I can do it.

Do you have any idea what Johnny Cochrane charges an hour?"

"Whatever it is, you can afford it."

Happy Roy's voice cracked. "I'm practically broke. Those damn Claymation commercials are costing me a fortune, and no one is buying the tie-in products. I've got ten thousand Happy Roy t-shirts, moldering away in a warehouse. Plus the burger chains with their processed chicken strips are forcing me into bankruptcy."

"Those new Wendy's strips are pretty good."

"Shut up! Put your hands over your head. No quick moves."

"What about your mansion? Can't you sell that?"

"It's a rental."

"Really? Do you mind if I ask what you pay a month?"

"Enough! We're going for a ride, Mr. McGlade. I'm going to introduce you to one of our extra large deep fryers, up close and personal."

"You told me I could keep working with your wife."

"I said you could work with her, not set her up!"

"Six of one, half a dozen of…"

"I'm the Chicken King, goddammit! I'm an American icon! Nobody crosses me and gets away with it!

I'd had enough of the Chicken King's crazy ranting, so I reached for the gun. Happy Roy tried to squeeze the trigger, but I easily yanked it away before he had the chance.

"Let me give you a little lesson in firearms, Happy Roy. A COP .357 has a twenty pound trigger pull. Much too hard to fire for a guy with arthritis."

Happy Roy reached for his belt, fighting with the buckle. "You bastard! I'll beat the fear of Happy Roy into you, you son of a bitch! No one crosses…"

I tapped him on the head with his gun, and the Chicken King collapsed.

After checking for a pulse, I went for the phone and dialed my Lieutenant friend.

"Hi, Jack. Me again. Marietta Garbonzo's husband just broke into my place, tried to kill me. Yeah, Happy Roy himself. No, he doesn't look so happy right now. Can you send someone by? And can you make it quick? He's bleeding all over my carpet, and I just had it cleaned. Thanks."

I hung up and stared down at the Chicken King, who was mumbling something into the carpet.

"You say something, Happy Roy?"

"I should have stayed single."

"No kidding," I said. "Relationships can be murder."

The End

To go back to the beginning, go to page 2.

To return to the previous section, go to page 38.

Harry's List of Books to Help Children Cope with the Loss of a Pet

IT'S EUTHANASIA, CHARLIE BROWN! by Charles M. Schultz

RIBSY AND THE DRUNK DRIVER by Beverly Cleary

GARFIELD'S MYOCARDIAL INFARCTION by Jim Davis

THE CAT IN THE HAT DROPS DEAD by Dr. Seuss

ARE YOU THERE GOD? WHY DID YOU KILL CUDDLES? by Judy Blume

FUN FACTS ABOUT DECOMPOSITION by Bill Nye the Science Guy

WHERE'S WALDO'S DOG? by Martin Handford

THE BLACK STALLION: FATAL MALNOURISHMENT! by Walter Farley

ONE FISH, TWO FISH, DEAD FISH, YOUR FAULT by Dr. Seuss

WHERE THE BREATHING ENDS by Shel Silverstein

THE VELVETEEN RABBIT STEW by Margery Williams

SEE SPOT DIE (DICK AND JANE DIG A GRAVE) by Unknown

WHERE THE WILD THINGS ROT by Maurice Sendak

PARVO THE PUPPY: A MATTER OF TIME by Ken L. Coff

YOU SAID CUDDLES WAS IN HEAVEN AND I FOUND HER IN THE TRASH by Erma Bombeck

HAROLD AND THE PURPLE DECOMPOSING GERBIL by Crockett Johnson

POLLY WANT A EULOGY? by Nina Laden

THE BERENSTAIN BEAR RUG by Jan and Stan Berenstain

ALL DOGS TASTE LIKE CHICKEN a Walt Disney Reader

WHY WON'T HUCKLE CAT WAKE UP? by Richard Scarry

THE VERY HUNGRY HAMSTER ATE HER BABIES by Eric Carle

A.S.P.C.D.O.A. by Sandra Boynton

BABE THE PORK LOIN by Dick King-Smith

To skip to another ebook that features one of Harry's pets, go to page 166.

To return to the beginning for the gazillionth time, go to page 2.

Someone knocked on the door of my Winnebago. I'd been expecting Jack, so I told her to come in. She was with Phin, and I could tell by looking at them they were knocking boots. In fact, *Cherry Bomb* by J.A. Konrath, which this scene was taken from, has some pretty explicit sex in it. You should go buy a copy. In fact, but two. Get one for your mom. She likes sex. She had you, didn't she?

"Jesus, Harry, it stinks in here," Jack said.

"I'm working on that."

I dangled a handful of those cardboard pine-scented car-fresheners shaped like Christmas trees. Unfortunately, they didn't do much to mask the zoo smell, which was courtesy of my new pet.

There was a scream to our left, and Jack dropped to one knee and reached for the gun in her purse. I quickly grabbed her wrist.

"Jack, don't shoot Slappy!"

Another screech, coming from the wire cage. Inside the cage was my monkey. It was light brown, perhaps eight or nine pounds, with large brown eyes and the cutest little monkey face.

Jack put her gun away.

"This is the extra help you recruited?" she asked.

I nodded, grinning. "He's a pig-tailed macaque." I took care to pronounce it correctly, as *mack-a-cue*.

"I think it's pronounced ma-keek," Phin said.

"That's not what Al told me."

"Al?"

"Al at *Al's Exotic Pets*, in Deer Park. He sold him to me this morning."

"He's adorable," Jack said. "Why'd you name him Slappy?"

On cue, the monkey slapped himself on the side of the head. He did this over and over, increasing in speed and force. The sound wasn't unlike applause.

I frowned. "There wasn't much of a selection down at Al's. It was either him or another primate I would have named Gassy. He also had some sort of gibbon, missing an arm and both legs."

"Stumpy?" Phin said.

"More like Sitty. I've seen turtles that moved faster. I wonder if he was dead."

"I think you chose perfectly," Jack said.

Slappy screeched again, baring sharp yellow teeth.

"You sure he's tame?"

"Most of the time. But don't put your fingers near the cage."

Jack knelt down on the carpet to get a closer look. "Hello, Slappy. I'm Jack."

Something wet hit me in the cheek. Something wet and brown and horribly stinky.

"Your monkey threw poop at me."

"He does that. There are baby wipes next to his cage."

Jack reached for one, and Slappy managed to pitch another slider, which hit Jack in the nose.

"I think he's aiming for my mouth," Jack said, mopping her face with baby wipes.

"Are you wearing make-up? He was rescued from a research lab. They tested cosmetics on him. Don't let him see your lipstick—he gets a little agitated."

"I'm not wearing—" I dodged left, a monkey turd zinging by my face. He was definitely aiming for my mouth.

"I like him," Phin said. "He's spunky."

Slappy aimed and Phin ducked, dung splattering on the wall.

"Remind me again why you bought this thing," Jack said.

"I wanted to train him to get me beer and watch sports. But all he does is throw feces, hit himself in the face, and scream. He's kind of a downer."

Slappy screamed in agreement. Then pressed his pelvis against the side of the cage and urinated on the floor. The smell was pee times a hundred, and made me cover my nose.

"He does that too," I said. "A lot. Al said he knows how to use the toilet."

The stream arced through the air, landing on my sofa. I picked up a coffee mug that said *Don't Worry Be Happy* and tried to catch the stream. Jack stepped away.

"I think maybe Al lied to you."

Slappy screeched, then began banging his little monkey head into the side of his cage.

"You should buy him a helmet," Phin said.

"He came with one. I took it off, because I thought it was cruel. Now I'm afraid to get close enough to put it back on."

Jack crouched down again, warily. "I think you just need to learn some manners, and then you'll be fine," she said, her voice soft. "You're probably just scared. I would be too, living with Harry. But I bet with a few days of training, you'll be a perfect gentlemen.

Slappy stopped banging his head and made an adorable cooing sound. Then he grabbed his little monkey ding-dong and began to beat off with frightening intensity, keeping his eyes on Jack the whole time.

"What does he eat?" Phin asked.

"It's called monkey chow. It's not that bad. Sort of tastes like meat-flavored charcoal briquettes."

"You tried it?"

"Yeah. Want some?"

"I'm gonna pass on that one."

"Slappy hates them. See?"

I bent over and handed Slappy a tan square object the size of a mini candy bar. Slappy took it, screeched, and bounced the food off of my forehead.

"There's something I don't understand," Phin said. "You keep jumping into other J.A. Konrath books, but what's the point?"

"I like to think of it as a Harry McGlade Greatest Hits collection," I replied.

"But Konrath fans have already read these scenes. Like this monkey scene from *Cherry Bomb*"

"Sure, but in that book, it was Jack's point of view. Now we're in my point of view."

"It looks pretty similar," Phin said, taking out his Ereader and paging through *Cherry Bomb*

"Trust me. It's vastly different."

"I dunno. Seems like a lazy way to write a book. All of Konrath's fans are expecting new content, and he's just giving them rehashed old stuff."

"Hey!" I said. "Don't knock Konrath. Without him, none of us would be here."

"Actually," Jack said, "This would qualify as metafiction."

"What's that?" I asked.

"Use your Ereader dictionary."

I whipped out my Ereader and read the definition. "Yeah, I guess this is metafiction. We're really breaking the fourth wall here by acknowledging we're in a story and directly addressing the reader."

"More like directly ripping off the reader," Phin said. "How much of this $2.99 epic is actually new material?"

"A lot, probably," I said. "But you have to read through it sixty or seventy times just to find it all."

"Fuck that," Phin said. "I'm just going to read the whole thing, page by page."

"It won't make sense that way."

"Who cares? This is nothing but an endless parade of jokes anyway. It's not like structure is important here."

"Exactly!" Slappy said. "I've been thinking the exact same thing!"

We all stared at him.

"You can talk?" I asked.

"No," Slappy answered.

None of us had a reply to that.

"So what next?" Jack said, crossing her arms.

"I'm going back to the Amish story," I said. "I want to see how it ends."

"Or if it ends," Phin said.

To return to the Amish adventure, go to page 45.

To start over, go to page 2.

I opted for the sex.

"I will make love like an Olympian!" I declared. "In record time!"

I wondered about the chicks they had in heaven. Was Marilyn Monroe here? Or Lynn Redgrave? I loved Lynn Redgrave in the movie *The Happy Hooker*. But I didn't want to nail the old one, who died of cancer. I wanted the young Lynn, when she was still pretty and had both of her boobs.

"The human has chosen sex!" the angel bellowed. "Bring forth his mate!"

The gate opened. Imagine my surprise, when instead of Marilyn or Lynn, a fat old man waddled out.

"Is that Mickey Rooney?" I asked.

The fat guy was wearing a thong, which clung to his junk like an Italian family reunion.

"You want to sex him up?" The angel nudged me with his shoulder.

"I think my penis just got smaller," I said. "What's the opposite of a hard-on? Because that's what's happening with me, biologically."

"You will not need an erection, puny human. You'll be catching, not batting."

The fat guy stood next to me, clapping his hands in front of him. "Let's do this!"

My eyes were irrepressibly drawn to his thong. I believe the current term for it was *banana hammock*. For an old, fat guy, his banana was formidable.

"Look," I said. "I'm really not into guys. I mean, I experimented a bit when I was younger, for ten or twelve years. But that was just curiosity. We're all guilty of that. These days, I dig the ladies."

"Me too," said the fat old guy. "Which is why I want you to moan in falsetto. Also, I'm using this black marker to draw breasts on your back."

He held up a black marker. I held up my sword.

"I don't think so, pal," I told him. "I think I'm getting out of here instead."

If Harry should fight, go to page 174.

If Harry should just let it happen, go to page 176.

If Harry should play Combville, go to page 6.

To return to the previous section, go to page 100.

Naturally, I picked the bananas.

Well, I didn't *actually* pick them. They were already picked. But few hundred pounds of them were brought out, in a big cloth sack that looked like a hammock, strung up between two stegosauruseses. Stegosuari. Dinosaurs with spiny tails.

"Eat it, Bitch Tits!" goaded the angel. "Eat it all!"

Seeing so many bananas in one place reminded me of my former pet monkey, Slappy. He loved bananas. He also loved malt liquor and pissing on my floor. Currently, he was loose in the suburbs, sexually preying on small dogs.

I missed him.

As the banana hammock was set down in front of me, I formulated a plan. If I quickly ate five hundred bananas, I could throw the peels all around me, and then escape while my captors humorously slipped and fell during their attempts to chase me.

Or I could use my sword to slash my way out of there.

But which was the better plan?

To eat five hundred bananas, go to page 177.

To fight, go to page 174.

To return to the previous section, go to page 100.

Clearly, the only way to get out of heaven was the same way you got into heaven—by slaughtering as many of your enemies as possible.

One, two! One, two! And through and through: The vorpal blade went snicker-snack!

And then, with verve, I pinched a nerve, in my galumphing back.

Immobilized by pain, I dropped the sword after only killing a few big-headed green angels. Then I curled up into a ball like a hero and triumphantly whimpered for mercy.

"I am Callooh Callay, leader of the Reptiloids!" said someone named Callooh Callay. "You have fought valiantly, Bitch Tits! As a reward, you shall be returned to earth."

This green angel had a bigger head than most. He also had a crown on his head.

Could this be God? Was the true name of God really Callooh Callay? If so, couldn't He have picked a better name for himself? Like Steve? Or Rick?

"I hurt my back in my frenzy to kill in your name, oh mighty one. Can you heal me?"

"Don't be such a mimsy," he burbled. "Quit your jabber and walk out of my coliseum, my beamish boy."

So, like Alice through the rabbit hole, I walked out of heaven and back to the cornfield. Once safely back on terra firma, I made a vow to never drop acid again. Especially in Indiana.

And let that be a lesson to all of you. On the surface, drugs may be a lot of fun and transport you to magical places like heaven. But under the surface, they're illegal because the government wants control over your body. Who do you think you are, believing you should be able to make your own decisions on what you consume?

Once I was feeling suitably beamish again, I decided to go forward with the Amish adventure. But what should I do next? How could I get to the bottom of this perplexing mystery, the very nature of which I'd forgotten?

Should Harry call a town meeting? If so, go to page 178.

Should Harry hop into another ebook? One with vampires?

If so, go to page 179.

If you enjoyed the Jabberwocky reference, and would like to read more poems, go to page 185.

To return to the previous section, go to page 171.

"Okay, we'll get busy," I said, unzipping my pants. "But no rusty trombones, or donkey punches, or Cleveland steamers."

"How about a brass clown?" the fat guy asked.

I considered it. "Yeah, I'm fine with that. Do you have a name, by the way?"

"Does it matter?"

"No, not really."

The unnamed fat guy pulled off his banana hammock, and the crowd cheered. That's when I realized this was all a dream. It had to be. Nothing else made sense.

"It's not a dream," the green angel said, reading my mind.

"How do I know?" I asked, wide-eyed and innocent.

"You'll know in about eight seconds, when he starts violating you. He's going to tear you open like a Christmas present."

That was an image I didn't need in my head. Like imagining the *Golden Girls* naked.

"Look, you're an angel, right?"

"No. I'm a Reptiloid from—"

"Yeah, yeah, blah blah blah. But if you are really an angel, would I be able to do this?"

Swinging my sword, I neatly cut off the angel's bald, round head. If I were really in heaven, that would probably be a sin, and God would crucify me or something. But the only thing that happened was the crowd screaming and running out of the stands, trampling over each other in their hurry to exit. I hadn't seen so many people running out of a theatre since the premier of *Gigli*.

"See?" I said to the old naked fat guy. "It's only a dream. Watch."

I turned the sword on myself, stuck it into my belly, and promptly died.

To start over at the beginning, go to page 2.

To return to the previous section, got to page 171.

At 7:35 that evening, they gave me a lot of bananas.

Then I began.

I liked bananas, but not a bunch.

By 8:15 I couldn't eat any more.

By 9:28 I was finally dead.

The End

To restart the adventure, go to page 2.

To return to the previous section, go to page 173.

"I've called this town meeting to get to the bottom of the mystery of who is screwing Lulu's husband," I said. "After carefully following the many clever clues seeded throughout this ebook, I'm ready to make a startling accusation."

The Amish people gathered around me in the cornfield murmured to each other. Then the unholy Stephen King monster that lived in the corn came out and ate everyone.

The End

Start the adventure over, go to page 2.

To contact Stephen King and inform him of a possible copyright violation, go to page 6.

To return to the previous section, go to page 174.

The problem with having so many naked women trying to hump me senseless was…

Actually, there was no problem with it at all.

While I can't admit to being in the peak of physical condition (I get winded tying my shoes, which I can't see unless I suck in my gut), I've got a spring-loaded pelvis and can crack walnuts with my butt cheeks. In fact, I've done the walnut thing on a bet before. Watching the guy eat them afterwards was priceless.

That said, I was in good form when the Olympic Copulation began. I'm not quite porn star material, but what I lack in size I make up for in speed.

I figured out early on that not much was required from me in the reciprocation department. Everyone wanted a Bit-O-Harry, and I was happy to oblige. I just laid back, closed my eyes, and let the ladies take what they wanted.

There was a bad moment, when I felt someone with a mustache kissing me, but it turned out not to be a mustache.

Yes, there was sucking. And groping. And fondling. And pulling. And thrusting. And lots of other *ing* words. And by the time it was finally over, I had to admit that it was indeed the greatest thirty seconds of my life.

"That's enough, baby." I forced back an overzealous Harry fan. "No use trying to prime a dry pump."

I disentangled my legs, pulled my fingers out from wherever they'd been, and shoved away some tattooed vixen writhing on the floor, because she was writhing on my pants.

"Any of you ladies know where the back door is?" I slapped away an intrusive hand. "Not that one. The exit."

"Aren't you enjoying yourself, Mr. McGlade?"

It was Vlad. He'd taken off his leather ensemble, and stood naked in the doorway. The last time I'd seen anything that small, it was stuck in a *hors d'oeuvre.*

"I'm having a blast, Vladdy old boy. But all good things must end, and frankly, you're all a bunch of psycho freaks. So I'm afraid that—*Jesus!*"

The vixen nearest to me had sunk her bridgework into my ankle, and it hurt like…well…getting bitten on the ankle.

I pulled back, then felt a similar pain on my left hand. And then on my right arm. I kicked away my attackers and limped over to an empty corner of the room to finish pulling up my pants.

"Blood is the elixir of life, Mr. McGlade."

Vlad bared his own fangs, and I noticed Little Vlad waking up to see what all the excitement was about. Even turgid, it was more appropriate for picking locks than satisfying the ladies.

"You've got a real tiny rodney there, Vlad. No wonder you're a power-mad sadist. The shrinkological term is 'overcompensation'."

Vlad squeaked his squeaky squeak-laugh.

"You're to be the ultimate sacrifice, Mr. McGlade. We're going to eat you alive, then deliver your corpse to the president of the network."

"I've met him. He'd prefer tranny hookers."

I zipped up and glanced around the room. Naked, drooling vampires were closing in from all directions. There were at least a dozen. The only door to the room was the one Vlad stood in front of. The wall behind me felt solid, final.

"They didn't listen to our letter writing campaign," Vlad whined. "Or our Internet petition. So maybe your drained, lifeless corpse will show them we aren't fooling around."

I raised an eyebrow.

"What the hell are you talking about, dinky?"

"*Fatal Autonomy.* We want it back on the air."

I had enough bravado left to fake a belly laugh.

"You've got to be kidding! You lured me here, humped me dry, and now want to kill me, all to get my show renewed?"

Vlad got a crazy look in his eye. Well, a *more* crazy look.

"The whole warren loved the show. We watched it every Thursday night." His voice became school-teachery. "What is your favorite TV show, children?"

"*Fatal Autonomy*," they droned in unison.

I pinched myself. I'd had this dream before. Usually, though, there were a few recognizable actresses in the orgy pile. Like the chicks from *Friends*. Or the *Golden Girls*. And no fat naked vampire guy who was hung like a Smurf.

"Look, Vlad, we're all upset when our favorite shows get cancelled. I had to see a therapist for a while after *Xena* ended. But killing me won't…"

"We have a script," Vlad said. I half expected him to pull a sheaf of papers out of his ass and show me. "It's called *Fatal Autonomy, The Rise of the Vlad Pires.*"

Everyone thinks they're a writer.

"In the script, do you have a bigger Johnson?"

"Get your jokes in now, Mr. McGlade. When your body is found, the media frenzy will ignite a resurgence of interest in your series. The public will demand to know what really happened to Harry McGlade. And next season, they'll find out—in the first half of a two-parter."

"You're crazy. Television doesn't work like that."

Actually, it kinda did. But I didn't want to encourage the fruit loop.

"Children of the night…*ATTACK!*"

Even though they'd sexed me up, I'd had enough of Vlad and the Snuggle Bunch. Two Pires with lunging fangs got a Moe-style head-crunch, which sounded more like a dull thud than two coconuts hitting. I planted a heel onto the nose of a some nude skinny guy, drilled an elbow into the cheek of a chick who moments ago was making me sing soprano, and then sprinted right at Vlad, stepping on legs and spines and necks, and giving him a swift kick in the peanuts.

Vlad cradled his delicates like a child holding two raisins and a bran flake, and I pushed past and ran into Crazy Chainsaw Goon, just as he was yanking the cord.

I couldn't hear my screams above the roar of the saw, but I could guess they oozed machismo and self-confidence. I took a quick left through a doorway, another left down a hall, yanked open another door, and flew into a room filled with Vlad and a dozen angry, naked vampires.

I hugged my knees and Crazy Chainsaw Goon toppled over me, falling face first onto his appliance. He must have pinned down his trigger finger, because the saw revved and came up through his shoulder blades like a shark fin, misting me with blood.

I pushed backwards, bare feet sliding in the gore, and scrambled back down the hall with a flock of Pires on my heels.

Which is where I met up with Crazy Knife Goon and his Big Ass Knife.

He slashed. I ducked. But I didn't duck far enough, and the blade dinged off my scalp. The pain was painful. I fell onto my butt, and he raised the blade for the *coup de grace*.

"Hold on!" I said, showing him my palm. "You're not really a vampire! You're just a freak with fake fangs!"

He shrugged. "No shit."

"Well, when readers clicked on the link to come here, they were expecting real vampires. This is just an excerpt from *Suckers*, where the vampires are decidedly not real."

"Wasn't *Suckers* co-written by Jeff Strand?" Crazy Knife Goon asked.

"He wrote the adjectives."

"Did you get his permission to use this excerpt?"

"Nope," I said. "I doubt he even knows about it."

"What about giving him royalties?"

His face was serious when he said it, but after a moment we both started cracking up.

"Royalties!" I howled. "You kill me!"

Crazy Knife Goon raised his blade again.

"Wait!" I said. "I meant figuratively! I was talking about royalties. As far as Strand knows, <u>Suckers</u> has only sold six copies."

"What sold six copies?"

I turned and saw a man standing next to us. It was Andrew Mayhem, star of *Graverobbers Wanted (No Experience Necessary)*, *Single White Psychopath Seeks Same*, and *Casket For Sale (Only Used Once)*, all by Jeff Strand.

"I thought you were in the Pit, being horribly murdered," I said to Mayhem.

"Does Konrath owe Strand money?" he asked.

"Of course not. And anytime Strand wants, he can check the doctored spreadsheet which was falsified to make it seem like there haven't been any sales."

"Oh, he'll check it, alright," Mayhem said. "I'll make sure of it. Especially since he did that other project with Konrath."

"That one isn't earning anything either," I said.

"What other project?" asked Crazy Knife Goon.

"It's cool," Mayhem said. "And unlike the epic bag of fail that is <u>Suckers</u>, it actually has real vampires in it."

"What's it called?" queried CKG.

"*Draculas*," I chimed in. "A full length horror novel. Konrath and Strand co-wrote it with F. Paul Wilson and Blake Crouch."

"Wow!" exclaimed CKG. "F. Paul Wilson? I thought he was dead."

"Nope. He's just like ninety-six years old."

"Who's Blake Crouch?" asked CKG.

I shrugged. "No idea. You want to see an excerpt from *Draculas*? Or would you rather hack up Andrew Mayhem into little pieces while I escape?"

CKG scratched his chin. "I dunno. I'm going to have to ask the readers for help on this one."

Should you check out *Draculas*? If so, go to page 205.

Should CKG kill Andrew Mayhem? If so, go to page 209.

To read a bonus short story by J.A. Konrath and Jeff Strand, go to page 276.

To return to the previous section, go to page 174.

I'm a sucker for poignant, heartfelt poetry. Here are some of my favorites from the book Dumb Jokes and Vulgar Poems by J. Andrew Haknort. Enjoy...

Why the Floor is Wet

I pissed,

And I missed.

Anal Sex

I had anal sex,

With my girl Gidget,

She got knocked up,

The kid looked like shit.

My Dog Shag

I have a dog with no legs,

His name is Shag,

I can't take him for a walk,

I take him for a drag.

Data

Data, data,

Dis and data,

I can't go out,

Without my hata,

The baby's crying,

What's the matta?

Data, data,

Dis and data.

Hot Dog

You sure this is a hot dog?

What's with all the veins?

Is this a foreskin?

I'll trade you for your chips.

Auntie Shirley

I have an Auntie Shirley,

Her hair is very curly,

Especially around her vagina.

Vegetable Crimes

I had sex

With a melon

Now I'm wanted

As a felon.

My Candles

I made some candles,

Out of my ear wax,

What?

You say something?

Hair On My Balls

There's hair on my balls!

There's hair on my balls!

And now there's hair on my tongue!

Daughter

I sewed gills on my daughter,

So she could breathe underwater,

It worked really great,

Now she can't get a date.

I Lost My Squirrel

I lost my squirrel!

I lost my squirrel!

It just fell off now I'm a girl!

Subway

I rode the subway naked,

Just to see people react,

It was really quite exciting,

Up until I got attacked.

Crime

A bunch of banditios!

Stole all my Fritos!

I'm mad because now

I have nothing to eatos!

Dinah

Dinah was a lizard,

Dinah was a whore,

She fucked a pterodactyl,

And boy was Dinah sore.

Jack in the Box

Hey!
Let me out!

Salmon

Salmon spawn,
On my lawn,
It turned brown,
And now it's gone.

Obese Bat

Obese bat!
Obese bat!
It can't fly
'Cause it's too fat!

Being Frivolous

I ran through a preschool nude,
And now I'm being sued.

I'm Afraid to Flush My Toilet

I'm afraid to flush my toilet,
I'm afraid I'll get sucked down,
So I just refuse to flush it,
And it's getting very brown.

Fishing

Merv can bait a hook,
But I'm the master baiter.

Boom!

Boom boom boom!

Boom boom boom!

Catch little Timmy!

He's falling down the stairs!

Penguin

Penguin! Penguin!

Silly little penguin!

Look at him waddle!

Look at him swim!

Look at the walrus!

It's eating him!

To start the adventure over, go to page 2.

To read a Harry McGlade adventure about zombies, go to page 100.

To read a Harry McGlade adventure about private schools, go to page 21.

To read a Harry McGlade adventure about dogs, go to page 114.

To read a Harry McGlade adventure about assassination go to page 141.

To read Harry McGlade's very first adventure, go to page 255.

To read about books J.A. Konrath might write someday, go to page 190.

To return to the previous section, go to page 174.

A note from the author...

I've figured out the secret to becoming a bestseller. All you have to do is sell a whole bunch of books.

These are some books that I'm currently working on or just finished:

I'm writing a book about prison. It will be released in three to five years.

I'm writing a book about acne. I think it will be my breakout book.

I'm writing a book about massage techniques. It has a happy ending.

I wrote a book about bees. It's generating a lot of buzz. But a lot of the reviews have really stung.

I wrote a book about assassination. It will be a hit. They're selling it exclusively at Target. The reviews have been killer.

I wrote a book on snakes, and was bitten eight times. Next time, I'll write the book on paper instead.

I'm writing a book about my car. It's an autobiography.

I'm writing a book called The Locked Door. But I just can't get into it.

I wrote a book called The 144 Murders. It's gross.

I wrote a book called The Paraplegic Murders. It'll keep you glued to the chair. You'll read it in one sitting. But the ending is lame.

I wrote a book called The Elephant Murders. It's a trunk novel.

I wrote book called The Chickadee Murders. Buy it. It's cheep.

I'm writing a book about drug use. I'm calling it Addictionary.

I wrote book called The Elevator Murders. It has its ups and downs.

I wrote a book called The Viagra Murders. It's a pop-up book.

I wrote a book called The Caffeine Murders. It's guaranteed to keep you up all night.

I'm writing a book about a man who buys a cemetery, but it isn't a good plot.

I wrote a book about menopause, but it is hard to understand because it doesn't have any periods.

I'm writing a book about elderly dinosaurs. It's called Geriassic Park. The T-Rex hero breaks a hip, and his children never call.

I wrote a book about potty training. It was a number two bestseller.

If you want to know J.A. Konrath's favorite banned books, go to page 192.

If you'd rather get back to the Amish adventure, go to page 44.

To return to the previous section, go to page 185.

Joe's List of Favorite Banned Books

Huckleberry Taint

The Cat in the Hat Eats His Young

Dora the Explorer — Boots Gets Neutered

The DaVinci Chode

Tales of a Fourth Grade Pedophile

The Lion, The Witch, And The Whoremonger

Where the Wild Things Hump

Horton Has a Colostomy!

Lemony Snicket and a Series of Unfortunate Open Sores

Charlie and the Chocolate Highway

Diary of a Wimpy Kid — I'll Get a Gun and Show Them All

How the Grinch Stole My Virginity

Are You There, God? It's Me, Anne Frank

The Hardy Boys and the Mystery of the Bad Touch

One Fish, Two Fish, Two Girls, One Cup

Harry Potter and the Nocturnal Emission

To restart the adventure, go to page 2.

To return to the previous section, go to page 190.

I raised my fist, ready to go all Guantánamo on this God-fearing pacifist. But before I could throw the punch, Amos had karate-kicked me right in the chest.

I staggered backwards, rubbing my ribs.

"Hey!" I said. "You're supposed to be non-violent!"

"I know who put you up to this," Amos said, sneering. "It was my wife, Lulu. Lulu! Get out here!"

The bedroom door opened. Lulu stepped out, her head hanging low. She wore only a g-string and pasties. But, befitting her religion, both items were very plain.

"Yes, Husband?" she meekly asked. "How may I serve you?"

Amos rushed over to Lulu, taking her roughly by the upper arm. "I wondered where the horse and buggy went. You took them to the big city to hire some jackass!"

"You also hired someone else?" I said.

Lulu looked terrified. "I swear, Amos. I didn't do anything."

"The bible says to honor your husband, woman," Amos declared. "Haven't I given you everything? A plain house to live in. A stripper pole in our bedroom. All those piercings. Everything a good Amish woman needs."

Lulu pulled away, her face becoming venomous. "You treat me like I'm your property, Amos Coleslaw!"

"Technically, you are. I traded a horse and two mules for you."

"You beat me!"

"That's a lie!"

She turned around, showing us her damn-near perfect ass.

"What about this?" she said, pointing to a tiny red mark on her left cheek.

"That's a birthmark!" Amos said.

"Is not!"

"Is so!"

I whipped out the magnifying class I keep in my pocket for opportunities like this, and knelt next to Lulu.

"This appears to be a nevus flammeus, also known as a port-wine stain. Port-wine stains are present at birth and range from a pale pink in color, to a deep wine-red. They're caused by a deficiency or absence in the nerve supply to blood vessels. This forces the blood vessels to dilate, and blood to collect in the affected area. Over time, port-wine stains may become thick or develop small ridges or bumps, and do not fade with age."

I switched off Wikipedia and put away my iPhone.

"Well, maybe it is a birthmark," Lulu said, "But you're still cheating on me!"

Amos patted his own chest. "I'm too much Amish for just one woman. The Mormons get a lot of cootchie. Why should I have to suffer just because I was born into the wrong, backasswards, repressive, fundamentalist religion?"

He had a point.

"Kick his Amish ass, Harry," Lulu said. "And stomp on his balls until they swell up to the size of Kirstie Alley."

I raised my fists, and one of my feet. Amos tore off his plain shirt, revealing a six pack. While he drank one, I couldn't help but notice he was also heavily muscled.

"They have a gym in Plaintown?" I asked.

"It opened up last year, next to the Blockbuster Video."

"Yeah? Well, I prefer Netflix."

I actually didn't prefer Netflix. Two years ago, I rented *Showgirls* and misplaced the DVD. So far it has cost me three hundred and eighty seven dollars.

"I must warn you," Amos said. "I'm a master at karate, tae kwon do, jujitsu, judo, capoeira, muy thai boxing, monkey style Shaolin kung fu, Australian dick wrestling, charades, bowling, *Sorry* by Parker Brothers, *Hungry Hungry Hippos* by Galoob, and Pokemon."

I was out the door right after he said *karate*. But as I ran into the Amish village, screaming for help at the top of my lungs, no mob of torch-wielding, angry villagers came to my aid. I tried yelling, "Frankenstein! We must destroy the monster!" but got similar, unimpressive results. Apparently, real life wasn't like a Universal horror movie from the 1930s. I wish someone had warned me.

Shaolin Amos was right on my heels, jogging methodically after me. Finally, after twenty yards of frenzied sprinting, I was too tired to go on. I had no choice but to face him.

I turned around, gasping in air, and realized I had two options. I could draw my gun and shoot him, or fight him man-to-man with my bare hands and hope that one yoga class I took in high school was enough martial arts training to help me win.

But which should I choose? If only there were some magical, all-knowing force to guide my direction and make that decision for me…

Should Harry fight Amos with his fists? If so, go to page 197.

Should Harry just shoot him? If so, go to page 198.

To return to the previous section, go to page 44.

"You can beat me all you want to, Brother," said Amos. "But look at all the clues. Amish women don't wear make-up, or perfume, or have fake nails. When you went into the costume shop, Clandestine Westin called Lulu by a different name and said she'd rented a costume there. And Amish women don't have cell phones."

He was right. I *could* beat him all I wanted to. So even though you, the reader, wanted me to try common sense, I vetoed that lame decision and punched this gentle, tolerant man right in the jaw.

"Confess!" I ordered, kicking him in the procreation stick. "Are you cheating on your wife? Have you ever been a member of the Communist Party? What role did you play in 9/11? How long have you practiced witchcraft, and danced naked in satanic orgies while eating newborn babies? What is the average annual rainfall in the Amazon basin? Answer me!"

He answered all of them, except the rainfall one. Which was okay, because I didn't know the answer either. And though he didn't actually cheat on his wife, or have anything to do with the destruction of the World Trade Center, he did admit to eating a newborn child.

"Only its leg," he said. "And it was too chewy and salty, so when the other Satanists weren't looking, I spit it out."

After giving him a stern lecture about joining cults without fully committing to their insane practices, I left his home and found my way back to my car. This case was like an onion—an herbaceous perennial monocot from the order asparagales. The only choice I had left was to quit and not refund Lulu's money.

So common sense won out after all.

The End

To start over, go to page 2.
To return to the previous section, go to page 44.

I put up my fists, hoping this ebook was almost over. Then Lulu threw herself at me, wrapping her arms around my neck.

"Don't hurt him, Amos!" she cried. "I love him!"

"Do you love her?" Amos asked me.

I shrugged. "Sure. At this point, why the hell not?"

"Then by the power vested in me, I now pronounce you man and wife."

I raised an eyebrow. "Excuse me?"

Lulu snuggled against my cheek. "I love you, Harry McGlade. This was all an elaborate ruse to get us together. Amos isn't really my husband. He's a minister."

"Excuse me?"

"And this isn't really an Amish settlement. This is the back lot at Warner Brothers Studios. Everyone you've seen is actually an actor."

"Excuse me?"

"We're married now, Harry! Kiss me!"

If Harry should kiss her, go to page 214.

If Harry is dreaming because Amos has beaten him unconscious, go to page 215.

To return to the previous section, go to page 193.

Tired of playing around, I took out my .44 Magnum and aimed it at Amos's bearded face.

"I'm tired of playing around. So I'm sticking my .44 Magnum in your bearded face, Amos."

"I know. I can read."

"Are you going to tell me the truth about your affair? Or do I have to kill you, and then you'll tell me the truth?"

Amos held up his palms. "How about instead of killing me, we have some ice cream?"

"No way. You think you can bribe me with ice cream? What flavor?"

"Times New Roman."

"That's not a flavor. That's a font."

"So you're saying you don't like that type?"

I cocked my gun. "Just let me know what flavor ice cream you've got."

"I've got many flavors, Brother. How about chocolate?"

"Never heard of it. Try something familiar."

"How about Booger?"

"Booger ice cream? Who came up with that?"

"I picked it myself."

I winced.

"How about jumbo jet?" he asked.

"Jumbo jet ice cream?"

He shrugged. "We Amish are a plane folk."

I shot him in the face.

I went to prison for life. But I still felt justified.

The End

To restart the adventure, go to page 2.

To look at other bad ice cream flavors Amos had, go to page 210.

Harry's List of Amputee Jokes

What do you call a person with no arms and no legs…

…in a cooking pot?
Stu.

…in a fireplace?
Bernie.

…in a hole?
Phil.

…in a pile of leaves?
Russel.

…on a BBQ grill?
Frank. Or Chuck. Or Patty.

…in a spice rack?
Herb. Or Basil.

…in a mailbox?
Bill.

…on your wall?
Art.

…in a bag?

Carry.

…in a lingerie drawer?
Teddy.

…in a vase?
Rose. Or Lily.

…covered in sauerkraut?
Reuben.

…is offended by these jokes and wants to hire a lawyer to file a class-action suit against Konrath?
Sue.

Start the adventure over, go to page 2.
Read how Harry lost his hand in *Rusty Nail*, go to page 201.
To return to the previous section, go to page 107.

"How you doing, Harry?" Phin asks me.

How was I doing? I was tied to a chair with wire, and some psycho just cut off all my fingers and used a blowtorch to stop the bleeding.

What the hell was wrong with that Konrath guy? Where did he come up with this stuff? His book covers are so bright and cheerful, and he's always talking about how funny they are. Nowhere on the book jacket does it talk about psychos cutting off fingers.

"Got any aspirin?" I asked Phin. He was also tied up, but he still had all of his fingers. Lucky bastard.

"Other pair of pants," he said.

"Nuts."

"How's the hand, Harry?"

"Doesn't hurt much, because there's not much left to hurt. Hope my screaming didn't disturb you."

"Actually, you interrupted my nap. Try to keep it down next time."

"I'll try. Sorry about that."

I frowned, wondering how I was going to ever be able to count to ten again.

"So your full name is Harrison Harold McGlade?" Phin asked.

"Yeah."

"Your parents named you Harry Harry?"

"Yeah."

"That's pretty funny, don't you think?"

"This from a guy named Phineas Troutt."

I took a deep breath, let it out slow, and tried to focus on the positive. Though my hand was horribly mangled, and both Phin and I were going to be killed, I was happy I no longer had to go to the bathroom. It's the little triumphs that help you get by.

"At least I don't have to piss anymore," I said. "When my thumb was cut off, I wet my pants."

"Nothing to be ashamed of, Harry Harry."

"All you dry pants guys say that."

A minute passed.

"I can see my fingers," I said.

"How's that?"

"They're on the floor in front of me. Think a doctor can reattach them?"

"Sure."

"Assuming we get out of here."

"I'm working on it."

"What are you doing?" I asked. "Using your psychic powers to call the other members of the Justice League?"

"I'm going to break this wire."

"It's too strong. You'll cut your hands off first."

"Either way I'll be free."

"Good plan. If it doesn't work, I've got a plan too."

"What's your plan?" Phin asked.

"When the psycho comes back, I'm going to swallow my own tongue and choke to death."

"Good plan."

"Yeah. That'll show 'em."

I stared at my fingers again, which looked so strange now that they were no longer attached to me. Then something happened that made me kind of freak out.

"GODDAMIT! GET AWAY FROM THAT, YOU SON OF A BITCH!"

"Harry? You okay?"

"YOU BASTARD! I'LL HUNT YOU DOWN AND ROAST YOU!"

"Harry, what's up? Who are you screaming at?"

"Goddamn rat. Ran off with one of my fingers."

Damn rat bastard.

"It was my middle finger, I think."

"I'm sorry, Harry."

"That was my favorite finger."

It was, too. I used it all the time, to communicate my displeasure with society.

"Maybe we can get it back," Phin says.

"Ah shit. I can see it, in the corner, holding it up."

Phin began to laugh. "The rat is giving you the finger?"

"Kiss my ass, Phin. It's not funny."

"What's it doing now, Harry? Using your finger to pick its nose?"

"It's eating it. Corn on the cob style."

If I hadn't been a fictitious character in a novel, I would have been pissed.

"Could be worse," Phin said. "Did you read that bear trap scene in *Afraid* by Jack Kilborn?"

"I did read it, and it scared me shitless."

"That one gave me nightmares. Or the gridiron in *Trapped*. That was even more disturbing."

"I haven't gotten to that one yet," I said.

"You should. Scary stuff."

"After we break out of here and save the day, I'll buy it for my new ereader."

"Is that the one with the enhanced contrast and longer battery life?" Phin asked.

"Yeah. It's also 21% smaller and 17% lighter than the ereader."

"I love Smashwords."

"Me too. Ereader users are confident and sexy and all-around better people than non-ereader users," I said, truthfully. "They're also so smart and hip that they get the joke when they download a $2.99 ebook which is filled with scenes stolen from other novels."

"Ereader readers are indeed lovely," Phin agreed.

I sighed. "I can't wait to get my hands on my Ereader and download some Konrath and Kilborn ebooks."

"Hand," Phin said.

"Huh?"

"You said *hands*. Plural. You only have one hand now."

"Did I say hands? Really?"

I began to laugh. So did Phin. We laughed and laughed and laughed until the psycho returned for the dramatic, heart-pounding finale.

Start the adventure over, go to page 2.

To return to the previous section, go to page 199.

The ER was frantic with activity, most of it focused around the gurney where her elderly employer had stopped breathing. Nurse Jenny only turned her eyes away for a second, trying to gather herself, not ready to see Mortimer die. She forced herself to look back, to say a final, silent goodbye.

Mortimer was *standing,* on top of the gurney, restraints broken off and dangling from his ankles and wrists, his mouth wide and—

Is he hissing?

The sound came from deep in Mortimer's throat, less like a threatened cat, more like a tea kettle coming to boil. It kept rising in pitch until it became a shrill whistle, the noise unlike anything Jenny had ever heard. Inhuman.

"Oh my God."

Mortimer's teeth. Something was happening to them. They were falling out—no—he was spitting them out, spitting them at the doctor and the nurses who were frantically trying to coax him off the gurney.

She started toward Mortimer. The old man abruptly stopped hissing, and Jenny could hear that prick Dr. Lanz ordering him down off the gurney.

Stiff as a plank, Mortimer fell face-first onto the floor.

Jenny rushed to him. She didn't care anymore about hospital protocol, or Lanz having her thrown out. *Mortimer needs me.* Jenny had never seen anything like this in twenty-five years of health care.

She pushed her way through the nurses surrounding Mortimer and knelt at his prone body.

"Jenny? What the hell are you doing in my hospital?" Dr. Lanz demanded.

"This is my patient," she said, touching Mortimer's neck and seeking out the pulse of his carotid. To her surprise, she didn't have to press hard. His entire neck was vibrating, his artery jolting beneath her fingers like a heavy metal drum solo.

The only thing she could compare this to was a crystal meth OD, the heartbeat raging out of control.

Jenny patted the old man's back, checking to see if he was conscious.

"Mortimer, can you hear me? It's Jenny. I'm right here. We're gonna help—"

"*I'm* going to help him. Somebody get me security."

She felt Dr. Lanz's hands grip her shoulders, dragging her away from Mortimer just as her patient grabbed her hip.

Jenny felt instant pain, and not only from the pressure of Mortimer's grip. Something sharp was digging into her skin through her nurse's uniform.

That can't be Mortimer's hand.

It was more like a claw. A bloody, ragged claw. Jenny stared, mouth agape. Mortimer's finger bones—the phalanges—were extending out through his fingertips, splitting the skin and coming to five sharp points.

The old man hissed again, a high-pitched keen, and when he turned his head to look at Jenny, calm, stoic Nurse Duthie said, "Oh, sweet Jesus."

His cheeks exploded like a grenade had gone off inside his mouth, white points bursting through his lips, shearing flesh, digging rents into his face.

Oh my God. Fangs.

He's growing fangs.

His new teeth began to elongate—an inch, two inches, bursting through his bleeding gums in rows that ended in wicked, dagger-like tips. They shredded his mouth into jagged strips, and he began to snap his jaws, chewing through the inside of his mouth, grinding off his cheeks all the way back to his earlobes, making room for his monstrous new dentata.

Then Mortimer's lower jaw unhinged, thrusting forward and hanging open like some perversion of an angler fish. He stared at Jenny, his eyes wide, pupils dilating beyond anything human, spreading until they eclipsed the whites.

For the first time in her life, Jenny screamed a scream of abject, primordial terror.

She jerked back, trying to pull away from Mortimer's grip, but his sharp, bony fingers had embedded themselves into the meat of her hip. She watched her skin stretch through the holes in her clothing—stretch, but not tear—and realized that the bones protruding from Mortimer's finger tips were barbed like fish hooks.

Then he jerked his hand back, taking Jenny with it, knocking her onto her butt, her face inches from his snapping jaws.

Mortimer rolled on top of her, like a lover, blood and saliva dripping onto Jenny's face and neck. She reached up to push him away, but even as terror-stricken as she was, Jenny couldn't bring herself to touch him. It was like willingly sticking your hand into a box of angry rattlesnakes. Even as his jaws drew near, Jenny's revulsion wouldn't allow her to fight back. She stretched out her hand—her face imploring—to Dr. Lanz, who stood within reach. But he shrank away from her beckoning fingers, retreating into the safety of the nurse's station.

This is it, Jenny thought. *I'm going to die.*

"Cool," Crazy Knife Goon said.

I nodded. "*Draculas* is a real roller coaster ride. Soon the whole hospital is overrun, with a few remaining survivors fighting for their lives."

"Which parts did Jeff Strand write?" Andrew Mayhem asked.

I gave CKG a knowing nod, and then we both shoved Mayhem at the creature, who tore into Mayhem's throat like a fatty ripping open a bag of potato chips, except blood came out, not chips, and it wasn't a fatty, it was a dracula. There was babyish squealing and some unmanly cries for help from Mayhem, who was probably a bed wetter, and then the dracula ate him all up and we all gave each other high-fives.

Also, despite the very reasonable $2.99 ebook price, *Draculas* never sold a single copy, so Strand never got any royalties.

To start this never-ending ebook all over again, go to page 2.

"I gotta go with killing Andrew Mayhem," Crazy Knife Goon said. "While I dig his witty combination of horror and comedy, I'm a bloodthirsty bastard at heart, and really want to stick this Big Ass Knife into somebody."

"Be my guest," I told him.

Mayhem died screaming like a little baby.

"There's your royalties, buddy!" I told him.

"There's your royalties, buddy!" I told him.

"There's your royalties, buddy!" I told him.

CKG stopped his hack and slash long enough to look at me. "You said that three times."

"I did?"

"Yeah. I thought it was a ereader formatting error. But you actually repeated yourself."

"Hmm. Could be déjà vu. What do you think?"

If you think it's déjà vu go to page 6.

If you can't believe Andrew Mayhem is really dead, go to page 254.

To return to the previous section, go to page 174.

Amos's List of Bad Ice Cream Flavors

Squirrel

Windex

Corn

Chris Farley

Smegma

Fire Ant

Acne

KY Jelly

Polyester

Salmon

Kidney Stone

Possum

Lint

Cactus

WD40

Prostate

Fishing Hooks

Pee Pee

Corduroy

To read some jokes that Konrath wanted to put in this ebook but didn't, go to page 211.

To start over, go to page 2.

Jokes That Didn't Make It Into This Ebook

I broke my ereader. In retrospect it was really stupid to save my place by folding over the corner.

I'm pretty sure I'm allergic to tequila. After seventeen shots I get really sick and throw up.

It's not fun watching a grown man cry. Unless you have a comfy chair to sit in, and maybe some snacks.

I don't believe in ghosts, or bigfoot, or ESP, or any of that nonsense, because that's what Galnok, my Martian friend, told me.

Don't you hate waking up and stepping barefoot on a big pile of dog shit after a night of drinking, then remembering you don't own a dog?

I never pulled the wings off flies or stuck firecrackers in frogs when I was a child. That didn't happen until I was in my twenties.

The universe is expanding, which is incredible, especially in this economy.

If you took all the snakes in the world, and laid them end to end, it would probably take a lot of time.

You shouldn't throw out the baby with the bathwater. Unless you really don't like being a parent that much. Or your baby is butt ugly.

I would like sushi more if it were breaded and fried in a square shape, then put on a bun with some American cheese. And served by a clown.

Birthday wishes are nice. But nobody gave me what I really wanted; a robot stripper filled with gummy bears and cocaine. Maybe next year...

If someone cut off my leg, I'd be mad. Hopping mad.

You have to watch out for bad cholesterol. The other day, I was eating a pizza, and some bad cholesterol stole my car.

I'm free of inherited disorders. Except for sprinting. That runs in my family.

I'm embarrassed by my bed-wetting problem. Especially because I'm awake when it happens.

The hardest thing about killing zombies is convincing the cops they were already dead when you shot them.

Some say you should love your enemy. I say, love his wife. That'll really piss him off.

The things that come out of the mouths of babes. Like this toaster. How'd he fit that whole thing in there?

To go back to the very beginning and start this awful ebook all over again, go to page 2.

To kill yourself because you can't take the bad jokes anymore, go to page 213.

You kill yourself, and now you're dead.

Lots of cool people attend your funeral. In heaven, you have a ménage à troi with Marilyn Monroe and Elvis. It was awesome. You should have killed yourself years ago.

The End

To start over, go to page 2.

I kissed her. Then we went into the fake cornfield and made furious love.

Lulu may have been lying about almost everything, but she'd been telling the truth about her flarching problem.

After a quickie divorce in Mexico, I got half of her stuff, and lived happily ever after.

The End

To start over, go to page 2.

To pop into another Konrath ebook, go to page 216.

To return to the previous section, go to page 197.

I opened my eyes, and saw Amos was still kicking my ass. Which didn't make sense, because Amish folks were supposed to have that *Thou Shalt Not Kick Ass* commandment.

But then, a lot about this case didn't make sense. Rather than try to understand it, I chose instead to ignore it all and concentrate on not getting beaten to death. To accomplish this, I had to use one of Chuck Norris's patented self-defense moves—curling up in a ball with my hands protecting my face.

Unfortunately, Amos knew the counter-move—kicking me over and over really hard. As my life drained away, I couldn't help but wonder where I would be if I had made different choices.

Then I remembered it wasn't my choices that brought me this fate. It was your damn choices.

You suck.

The End

To return to the previous section, go to page 215.

To restart the Amish adventure, go to page 2.

To try a different Harry adventure, go to page 227.

Bub was crouching before Andy, his black wings billowing out behind him like a rubber parachute.

Andy's mouth went dry. The demon was the most amazing and horrifying thing he'd ever seen.

Hoofs big as washtubs.

Massively muscled black legs, with knees that bent backwards like the hindquarters of a goat.

Claws the size of manhole covers, ending in talons that looked capable of disemboweling an elephant.

Bub approached the Plexiglas and cocked his head to the side, as if contemplating the new arrival. It was a bear's head, with black ram horns, and rows of jagged triangular teeth.

Shark's teeth.

His snout was flat and piggish, and he snorted, fogging up the glass. His elliptical eyes—black bifurcated pupils set into corneas the color of bloody urine—locked on Andy with an intensity that only intelligent beings could manage.

He was so close, Andy could count the coarse red hairs on the demon's broad chest. The animal smell swirled up the linguist's nostrils, mixed with odors of offal and fecal matter.

Bub raised a claw and placed it on the Plexiglas.

"Hach wi' hew," Bub said.

Andy yelled again, crab-walking backwards and bumping into the sheep. The sheep bleated in alarm.

Bub, as if commanded, backed away from the window. His giant, rubbery wings folded over once, twice, and then tucked neatly away behind his massive back. He walked over to a large tree and squatted there, waiting.

Sun led the sheep past the Plexiglas and to a doorway on the other side of the room. They entered, and a minute later a small hatch opened inside the habitat, off to Bub's left.

Andy mentally screamed at Sun, *"Don't open that door!"* even though the opening was far too narrow for Bub to fit through.

Bub watched as the sheep walked into his domain. The door closed behind it.

The sheep shook off its blindfold and looked around its new environment. Upon seeing Bub it let forth a very human-sounding scream.

In an instant, less than an instant, Bub had sprung from his spot by the tree and sailed through the air almost twenty feet, his wings fully outstretched. He snatched up the sheep in his claws, an obscene imitation of a bat grabbing a moth.

Andy turned away, expecting to hear chomping and bleating. When none came, he ventured another look.

Bub was back by the tree, sitting on his haunches. The sheep was cradled in his enormous hands, as a child might hold a gerbil. But it was unharmed. In fact, Bub was stroking it along its back, and making soft sounds.

Sheep sounds.

"He's talking to the sheep," Dr. Belgium said. "He's going to do it. Here comes the miracle."

Andy watched as the sheep ceased in its struggle. Bub continued to pet the animal, his hideous face taking on a solemn cast. There was silence in the room. Andy realized he'd been holding his breath.

The movement was sudden. One moment Bub was rubbing the sheep's head, the next moment he twisted it backwards like a jar top.

There was a sickening crunch, the sound of wet kindling snapping. The sheep's head lolled off to the side at a crazy angle, rubbery and twitching. Andy felt an adrenaline surge and had to fight not to run away.

"Now here it comes," Dr. Belgium said, his voice a whisper.

Bub held the sheep close to his chest and closed his elliptical eyes. A minute of absolute stillness passed.

Then one of the sheep's legs jerked.

"What is that?" Andy asked. "A reflex?"

"No," Sun answered. "It's not a reflex."

The leg jerked again. And again. Bub set down the sheep, which shook itself and then got to its feet.

"Jesus," Andy gasped.

The sheep took two steps and blinked. What made the whole resurrection even more unsettling was the fact that the sheep's head hung limply between its front legs, turned completely around so it looked at them upside down.

Andy's fear changed to awe. "But it's dead. Isn't it dead?"

"We're not sure," Sun said. "The lungs weren't moving a minute ago, but now they are."

"But he broke its neck. Even if it was alive, could it move with a broken neck?"

The sheep attempted to nibble at some grass with his head backwards.

"I guess it can," Sun said.

"Amazing," Dr. Belgium said. "Amazing amazing amazing."

"Shouldn't you get the sheep?" Andy asked. "Run some tests?"

"Go right ahead," Sun said. "The door's over there."

"Probably not a good idea to go in there before Bub's eaten." Dr. Belgium said.

"What the fuck is that ugly ass thing?" I asked.

Andy, Sun, and Dr. Belgium turned to look at me.

"Who are you and how did you get in here?" Sun demanded.

"I'm Harry McGlade. I got sick of the ebook I was in and popped into this one. Is that Satan?"

"We don't know yet," Andy said.

"What ebook is this?"

Sun answered, "*Origin*, by J.A. Konrath."

"That Konrath sure writes a lot," I said. "Is this one scary, or funny?"

"A little little little of both," said Dr. Belgium.

"Nice stammer there, Doc. Makes you sound as stupid as you look."

"Who are you, puny human?" Bub was standing in front of the Plexiglas, staring at me.

"I'm the President of Shut The Hell Up, you ugly ass demon thing." I glanced at Andy. "Why is he called *Bub*?"

"Short for Beelzebub."

"Clever. I suggest you kill him now, while he's still locked up. Supporting characters don't usually end well in Konrath thrillers."

"I'm the main character," Andy said.

I patted his shoulder. "Sure you are, chief."

"How about me me me?" Dr. Belgium asked. "Do I live?"

"Are you serious? Dr. Stammer Stupid? I'm surprised you're not dead already."

"Hey!" Bub bellowed. "I'm talking to you!"

"Talk to the hand," I told him, giving him the finger. Then I cozied up to Sun. "You want to get out of here before the shit hits the fan? You know Bub is going to get out of that cage and wreak havoc. You'd have to be retarded not to see that coming."

Sun took a quick glance at Andy, then nodded. "Okay. Let's go."

"Hey!" Andy said. "She and I were going to hook up in a later chapter!"

"In your dreams, demon chow."

"Can I I I come?" Dr. Belgium asked.

"No you can't can't can't. I'm taking Sun to one of my old adventures. Have fun fighting for your lives."

Should Harry take Sun into *Fuzzy Navel* by J.A. Konrath? If so, go to page 221.

Should Harry take Sun into *Dirty Martini* by J.A. Konrath? If so, go to page 224.

To return to the previous section, go to page 214.

They drove in silence for a mile, Donaldson glancing between the girl and the road.

"Highway's packed this time of day. I bet we'd make better time on the county roads. Less traffic. If that's okay with you, of course."

"I was actually just going to suggest that," Lucy said. "Weird."

"Well, I wouldn't want to do anything to make you feel uncomfortable." Donaldson glanced down at Lucy's pocket. "Pretty young thing like yourself might get nervous driving off the main drag. In fact, you don't see many young lady hitchers these days. I think horror movies scared them all away. Everyone's worried about climbing into the car with a maniac."

Donaldson chuckled.

"I love county roads," Lucy said. "Much prettier scenery, don't you think?"

He nodded, taking the next exit, and Lucy leaned over, almost into his lap, and glanced at the gas gauge.

"You're running pretty low there. Your reserve light's on. Why don't we stop at this gas station up ahead. I'll put twenty in the tank. I also need something to drink. This mountain air is making my throat dry."

Donaldson shifted in his seat. "Oh, that light just came on, and I can get fifty miles on reserve. This is a Honda, you know."

"But why push our luck? And I'm really thirsty, Donaldson."

"Here." He lifted his Big Gulp. "It's still half full."

"No offense, but I don't drink after strangers, and I um...this is embarrassing...I have a cold sore in my mouth."

The gas station was coming up fast, and by all accounts it appeared to be the last stop before the county road started its climb into the mountains, into darkness.

"Who am I to say no to a lady?" Donaldson said.

He tapped the brakes and coasted into the station. It had probably been there for forty years, and hadn't updated since then. Donaldson sidled up to an old-school pump—one with a meter where the numbers actually scrolled up, built way back when closed-circuit cameras were something out of a science fiction magazine.

Donaldson peered over Lucy, into the small store. A bored female clerk sat behind the counter, apparently asleep. White trash punching the minimum wage clock, not one to pay much attention.

"The tank's on your side," Donaldson said. "I don't think these old ones take credit cards."

"I can pay cash inside. I buy, you fly."

Donaldson nodded. "Okay. I'm fine with doin' the pumpin'. Twenty, you said?"

I frowned from the back seat. "Hey. This isn't *Fuzzy Navel.*"

Donaldson and Lucy both turned around to look at me and Sun.

"Who the hell are you both?" Donaldson demanded.

"I'm Harry. This is Sun. What ebook is this?"

"*Serial Killers Uncut*," said Lucy. "By J.A. Konrath, Jack Kilborn, and Blake Crouch."

"Blake who?" I asked.

Lucy looked at Donaldson. "Is it Crouch? Or Couch?"

Donaldson scratched his double chin. "I think it's Crouch."

"Never heard of him," I said.

Sun leaned forward, putting her arms on the front seats. "So… you guys are serial killers trying to kill each other?"

"We were, until you showed up," Donaldson said.

"What do you mean, *were*?" Lucy asked, pulling out a knife.

Donaldson also pulled out a knife, and they both began to stab each other in earnest. The blood slopped all over the place, like a warm, wet rainstorm. I even got some in my mouth. Yuck.

"Nice first date, Harry," Sun said. But her dour expression told me she didn't really mean it.

"Hey, at least I saved you from that demon," I said.

"No. You didn't."

Sun and I turned around, and there was another backseat. Sitting there, behind us, was Bub.

"Wow. Twist ending," I said.

Then Bub ate all of us.

The End

To go to the beginning, go to page 2.

To return to the previous section, go to page 216.

Jack Daniels grabbed the rookie, Officer Buchbinder.

"How would you like a temporary promotion to Homicide/Gangs/Sex?" she asked.

Buchbinder frowned. "My Sergeant will bust my balls if I leave my post."

"What's your post?"

"Parking enforcement."

"I'll smooth it over. You got a car?"

"A bike."

"Even better. Let's go."

That cheered Jack up a bit. She liked bikes. Her ex-husband had a 1982 Harley-Davidson Sportster, and they'd go riding whenever Jack had free time. Which, as far as she could remember, was twice.

Jack worked a lot back then.

Unfortunately, when Buchbinder said *bike*, he meant *scooter*. The tiny little electric moped barely had room for two, and had a top speed of slow. A five-minute walk took them ten minutes on the bike, because Officer Buchbinder stopped for all traffic signals, pedestrians, strong breezes, and optical illusions. He also pulled behind a horse and buggy giving six geriatrics a tour of the Magnificent Mile—a tour so excruciatingly sluggish that Jack doubted all of them would live long enough to see its conclusion.

"Go faster," she said.

"If I follow too closely, there could be an accident."

As it turned out, there was an accident. Buchbinder couldn't brake in time, and coasted right through the largest pile of horseshit Jack had ever seen.

"Apparently they can do that while trotting," she said.

"Did you see that? It came out of nowhere."

Actually, Jack did see it, along with where it came out of. But she chose not to mention it.

"Some got in the spokes," Buchbinder whined. "I just cleaned the spokes."

"Pay attention to the road."

"My God, my bike is trashed. What was that horse eating?"

"Let's get off this topic."

"What's that on the fender... peanuts?"

"Pass the damn horse or I'm firing you."

He made a hand signal and thankfully got around the horse and cart. But getting past it and getting past it were two different things.

"I gotta clean this quick, before it hardens. Don't want to have to chisel it off."

"Let's talk about something else," Jack said. She didn't say, "Like your non-future in the Homicide division."

Buchbinder, however, was fixated.

"I can smell it. Can you smell it?"

"Don't you have an off button?"

"I got some on my pants."

"Buchbinder, shut the hell up about the horse already."

"Okay. But I never saw Mr. Ed do that, no sir. That manure pile was the size of a small child. Lucky we weren't both killed."

Jack didn't feel lucky. Not even a little bit.

"Do you smell peanuts?"

They got to Willoughby's shortly thereafter. Jack instructed the Horseshit Whisperer to take witness statements after he cleaned his pants. Then she spoke with the bartender.

"Hiya, Jackie," I said. "What's up?"

Jack narrowed her eyes. "Harry? You're not in the scene."

"Thanks to the magic of ereaders, yes I am. This is Sun, from the book

Origin. Sun, this is Jack Daniels."

"You smell like horse poo," Sun said, her nose wrinkling.

"Look, I've got a lot of work to do," Jack said. "Can you guys leave? Like right now?"

"Boy, you're bitchy," I said. "You need to chillax."

"Don't you need to finish your stupid Amish adventure?" Jack countered.

"It's not stupid," I told her.

Sun folded her arms. "It is pretty stupid, Harry. I mean, it jumps all over the place. None of it makes sense. And you're constantly stopping the narrative to make these stupid lists."

I giggled. "Hehe. Did you read the banned book list? That was my favorite."

"I'm outie," Sun said, walking away.

I frowned. "Damn. I never even saw her naked."

"Go back to your ebook, Harry, and stay out of *Dirty Martini* until you're supposed to be in it."

"Wow. Double rejection. But FYI, Jackie, you don't decide what I do and don't do. That's up to the reader."

Should Harry go back to the Amish adventure? If so, go to page 215.

To return to the previous section, go to page 216.

My name is Harry McGlade. I'm a private eye. But I'm not a stereo-type. In fact, I haven't used my stereo since getting an iPod. Those things were off the hook. I've also got a rotary phone. It's also off the hook. Which explains why not too many people call.

I was in my office, waiting for a client to arrive. He'd called earlier, promising he'd be there by one o'clock. It was four minutes to one. And I was starving.

I'd missed breakfast, having slept until 12:15, so I really needed to nosh on something. Luckily, I kept a tiny refrigerator in my office, which I kept stocked with edibles.

I opened the refrigerator door, my nose wrinkling at an otherworldly smell, accompanied by a faint, greenish gas. The entire contents of the fridge were a takeout box from Ling's Mandarin, and a small yellowish object on a plate that might have been an old lemon, a lump of butter, or some kind of cake.

I took out both items and set them on my desk. The yellow thing had cracks in it, and a shiny film on one side. Opening the takeout box, I was assaulted by an acrid odor that curled my nostril hairs. But the half order of General Tsao's chicken still looked edible, even though I honestly couldn't remember when I had actually bought it. Far as I could recall, I hadn't eaten Chinese food in five months. But perhaps the food elves who lived in my vents had put it in the fridge for me.

Both items were questionable, but my stomach was growling so loud it hurt my ears. I knew it was inevitable I'd eat one of them. And then I'd also eat the other one when you returned to this section on your ereader.

But which one should I eat now?

Harry should eat the yellow thing, go to page 228.

Harry should eat the General Tsao chicken, go to page 231.

Harry should eat them both, go to page 234.

To return to the previous section, go to page 215.

I went with the yellow thing. I prodded it with my finger, finding it to be sticky and spongy. I picked off a few curly hairs, then popped the whole thing in my mouth.

It was porous, chewy, and filled with cool, bitter liquid.

Sponge cake?

No. Just a sponge. I remembered a month ago, when I threw it in the fridge to inhibit bacteria growth, after cleaning my toilet.

I spit out half of it, having already swallowed the other half. I knew I didn't worry too much about it, because I knew I'd see it again later, one way or another. Then the office door opened and a woman walked in. She wore a stylish business suit, heels, and a pearl necklace with matching earrings. Everything about her said *class*. Especially her shirt, which had CLASS written on it in big letter.

"Mr. McGlade, I need your help."

"Have a seat, Miss…?"

"Reader. Avid Reader. Call me Avid."

"How can I help you, Avid?"

She opened up her stylish, classy purse and took out a ereader. One of the new models, with the 50% improved contrast.

"I just bought this ereader, and I'm overwhelmed with choices. There are thousands of ebooks on Smashwords store, and more than a million free ebooks on the Internet. Where can I even begin?"

I pursed my lips and nodded. Hers was a common problem. The sheer number of ebooks available was daunting.

"What kind of books do you like to read?" I asked.

"Thrillers. Mysteries. Horror."

"Have you heard of the Jack Daniels series by J.A. Konrath? Jack is a woman, a Homicide lieutenant in Chicago, and she chases some pretty nasty criminals. The books are funny, laugh out loud, but also have some scary parts."

"How many are there?"

"Seven so far. The eighth will come out in 2011. And best of all, I'm in every single one of them."

She smiled. "They sound fabulous. What order should I read them in?"

"They can be read out of order. But if you're a bit anal—"

"I am."

"Good. I like anal. So I'd read them in the order they were written. They go:

Shot of Tequila

Whiskey Sour

Bloody Mary

Rusty Nail

Dirty Martini

Fuzzy Navel

Cherry Bomb

Shaken

Stirred

You can also read about me and Jack Daniels in various short stories and novellas, including:

Jack Daniels Stories

Floaters

Planter's Punch

Suckers

Serial Killers Uncut

Flee

Jack also has a cameo in *The List*. All of these ebooks are under $5. Most are $2.99."

Avid batted her eyelashes. "Those all sound wonderful. Do you have any scary books you can recommend?"

I nodded. "J.A. Konrath also writes horror novels under the name Jack Kilborn. If you like to be frightened, check out:

Disturb

Origin

Afraid

Trapped

Endurance

Horror Stories."

Avid Reader stood up, offering her hand. "Thank you, Mr. McGlade. Now I'll have dozens of hours of inexpensive, delightful reading enjoyment on the best ereader on the market. You're my hero."

"Yes. Yes I am. I'm all things to all people. And to show you how cool I am, I'll let you read an exclusive excerpt from Shaken, the latest Jack Daniels ebook, coming out October 26, 2010."

"I'd love to read that. But I'd also love to show my gratitude for your help." She leaned over my desk, her lips almost touching mine. "Are you man enough to handle me, Harry McGlade?"

Should Harry kiss Avid Reader? If so, go to page 237.

Would you rather read an excerpt from Shaken? If so, go to page 238.

To return to the previous section, go to page 227.

"It's just me and you, General Tsao. But I think I'm man enough to handle you."

I dug in.

The first two bites were putrid.

The next two bites were absolutely fucking revolting. It tasted like someone crapped a dead rat onto a rotten cabbage and then puked on it.

My eyes were watering. My stomach was turning flip-flops. My tongue wanted to kill me, then itself. I had the dry heaves, and the shakes, and my sphincter puckered.

I could barely finish the last three bites. Then my door opened, and a man walked in. An old, bearded, frail-looking man who had one of those old person humps on his back, making him look like a question mark.

"Are you Harry McGlade? I'm Haknort. J. Andrew Haknort."

"The poet," I said.

He raised a bushy old eyebrow. "You've heard of me?"

"Of course. You're the most famous poet in the room right now. But I thought you were dead."

"You're thinking of William Shakespeare."

"Oh yeah. Of course I am. Have a seat, Mr. Haknort."

He sat across from my desk, his vertebrae crackling like a bag of chips. "I hear you know a thing or two about the ereader, Mr. McGlade."

"I know lots of things. What have you got in mind?"

He reached into a tattered old satchel and took out a sheaf of papers, tossing them ontp my desk. "I just wrote a children's book. I want to make it available for ereading. But I need help creating the cover art, and I need someone to format it and assist me in uploading it to pubit.barnesandnoble.com."

"Carl Graves does all the cover art for J.A. Konrath. You can reach him at cgdouble2@sbcglobal.net. He charges about $300 per cover."

"I've seen his covers. They're terrific. But how about formatting?" the old man asked.

"I use a guy named Rob Siders. He can do the formatting, and also help you upload the document."

"What does he charge?"

"I'll let him answer. Rob?"

Rob came out of my broom closet, where he waited 9-to-5 everyday in the hopes someone would come to me asking an ebook formatting question.

"Pleased to meet you, Mr. Haknort. Thinking about adding your book to the Smashwords store but don't know how to start? Frustrated with converting your Microsoft Word file or PDF to a Smashwords-friendly format by yourself? I can help. My name is Rob Siders and I've been designing and creating ebooks for the better part of a decade. I can save you time and hassle by getting your source document to play nice with ereader formats. Less time plus less hassle equals more time for you to focus on marketing and selling your ebook. Reasonable rates. Thorough work. Satisfied when you're satisfied. Visit my webiste at www.52novels.com and let's talk about your project."

"Thanks, Rob. Back into the closet with you. And don't touch anything while you're in there. I paid eight bucks for that broom."

Rob nodded, then headed back to his hidey-hole.

"Well, Mr. McGlade, I'm certainly impressed. Thank you for your help. Would you like to take a look at my children's ebook? You'd be the first one to see it."

"What's it called?"

"*Ninnie-the-Poop Visits His Friend Jiglet.*"

"Ninnie-the-Poop? That sounds a lot like—"

"It's nothing like that at all," Haknort interrupted. "It's a completely different name, and it qualifies as a parody, which is fair use under international copyright law."

"I see," I said, somewhat dubious.

"You wanna read it, or not? It's pretty offensive, and not for everyone."

I wasn't sure. On one hand, I liked offensive children's book parodies. On the other hand, my stomach wasn't feeling so hot and I needed to make a thunder-box deposit.

If Harry should read Ninnie-the-Poop, go to page 242.

If Harry should run to the bathroom, go to page 253.

I was hungry. Damn hungry. So I plunked the weird yellow thing onto the old Chinese food and gobbled the whole mess up, holding my nose so I didn't have to smell it or taste it. Even so, it was like eating a sweaty gym sock stuffed with maggots, rotten meat, and pig dung, with a hint of sesame oil.

When I finished licking the box clean, I logged onto Facebook to get some quality Combville time. Then she walked into my office.

This woman had it all. Legs. Eyes. Elbows. A big head of blond hair that for some reason I wanted to comb. She wore a plain blue dress, and had a white bonnet on her head, which was unusual for Chicago. Actually, it was unusual for pretty much everywhere.

"Are you Harry McGlade? The private investigator?"

I nodded, still tapping the COMB button on my screen. Fifty-six thousand more strokes and I'd get a virtual gold coin. When I earned ten coins, I'd be able to buy a different color comb.

"My name is Lula. Lula Coleslaw. I need your help."

I looked up from my computer screen and scratched my neck. This all seemed very familiar.

"Let me guess," I said. "You ask me to take your case, but I keep playing Combville. Isn't that how it works?"

"What are you talking about?"

"You're Amish. You want me to prove your husband is cheating. I get abducted by aliens, your husband kicks my ass, I pop into a lot of J.A. Konrath and Jack Kilborn books, cracking bad jokes, and then I wind up dead several times. Right?"

"It's a hallucination," said General Tsao. "You have sever food poisoning, and you're hallucinating."

"Prove it," I challenged.

"A moment ago I was an Amish woman, and now I'm a Chinese

General with chicken feet."

He wiggled his chicken feet.

"So this whole *Choose Your Own Damn Story* thing was a hallucination due to eating spoiled food?" I asked.

"Pretty much," he said. Then he began scratching and pecking at the floor.

"Huh. How about that." It made as much sense as anything else. "So what happens next?"

General Tsao laid an egg, then sat on it. "You throw up, pass out, crap your pants, and the cleaning lady discovers you wallowing in your own mess and calls 911."

"That doesn't sound too bad."

"I'm lying. You die."

"Oh. Well, that sucks. I never even solved the mystery, though."

"There was no mystery," Lulu said. Apparently General Tsao could morph back into Lulu at will. "I was working for a land development country. I pretended to be Amish, then I hired you to disrupt a peaceful community of God-fearing pacifists, knowing that with your inept fumbling around you'd probably destroy their entire settlement within a few days."

"Yeah. That sounds like something I'd do."

"So you'll do it?"

"Do what?"

I burped, and a piece of my stomach lining came up in my mouth. I swallowed the piece, figuring I needed it.

"Will you help me, Mr. McGlade?"

"Hmm?"

Combville had once again captured my attention. Damn these repetitive, boring, addictive Facebook games. Why did I even bother with Facebook? And why did I only have five Facebook friends? And why were they all jerks?

I kept combing.

"Will you help me?" she asked, apparently still in my office.

"What? Oh. No. No I won't. I've got too much to do right now. But check back in a few days."

Sadness fell across her face and she stood up, turning to leave.

"Wait," I said. "Are you on Facebook?"

"No. We shun modern technology, Mr. McGlade. My ereader doesn't even have 3G."

"You mean it's only WiFi?"

She nodded, sadly. I felt for her, but I had to be firm on this. "Sorry, tastycakes. I'm really busy."

"Please, Mr. McGlade. I really need your help."

"Let me think about it again."

Should Harry take the case? If so, go to page 5.

If he should keep playing Combville, go to page 7.

"I'm man enough, baby," I whispered. "I've got so much testosterone, I have to shave the bottoms of my feet. You might get pregnant simply by standing so close."

Her soft lips parted. So did mine.

Then I puked bathroom sponge all over her face.

Avid Reader politely ran off, gagging and swearing. But I knew, as soon as she showered, she'd be back.

Five hours later, she hadn't come back.

It didn't matter, though. I had my ereader and my ebooks to read. Who needed anything more?

The End

To return to the previous section, go to page 228.

To restart the adventure, go to page 2.

Phin showed Herb Benedict and me the mud lines on the carpeting in the hallway.

"He must have wheeled in a gas canister on a hand truck," Phin said. "Stuck the tube under the door and filled the bedroom. That's why he didn't wake us up when he abducted Jack."

"So he's a doctor?" Herb asked. Herb was Jack's partner, a fat guy with a fat head. He was jotting things down in his notebook. "He has access to anesthetics?"

"Not necessarily," Phin said. "You can get nitrous oxide—laughing gas—at any welding supply store. When I woke up, I had a metallic taste in my mouth that could have been nitrous."

Herb blinked at me. "What?" he asked.

"Every time I see you, you have another chin," I told him.

Herb scowled. "Have you taken your pill today?" he asked.

"What pill?"

"Your *shut the fuck up* pill."

"Funny," I said. I thought about asking him if he took his appetite suppressant pill, but I already knew the answer.

"Guys, stay focused," Phin said.

Herb gave me a lame glare, then turned back to Phin. "How did he know when you went to sleep?"

"He was watching the house. Or maybe a listening device."

"I'll check for bugs," I said. "I brought my spy gear."

I set a metal suitcase on the floor and opened it up, spilling contents all over the carpet. One of the items that rolled away was a sex toy.

"That's spy gear?" Herb said, pointing at the pink dildo.

"It's got a listening device in it. I swapped it with a woman's vibrator and put it in her desk drawer, trying to catch her cheating on her husband."

"Did it work?" Phin asked.

I frowned. "I got the switches mixed up. All I recorded was three hours of *bzzzz-zzzz...oh god...bzzzz...oh my god...bzzzz*. I should have put a camera in it, too."

"You're an idiot," Herb said.

"And you're a miracle of evolution," I replied. "Somehow a sea cow grew limbs and learned how to talk."

Phin stepped between us. "Harry, put away the dildo microphone. Herb, unclench your fists. Do either of you have any idea who could have Jack?"

Herb let out a slow breath, then shook his head. "Not so far. We normally get alerts when someone we put away gets out. All the major ones are still in there. Got a few baddies who were up for parole recently, but they were all denied."

"Were there any cases Jack was working on before she quit? Any open cases?"

Herb's brow crinkled. "Only one. But it couldn't be him."

"Harry? Were you and Jack working on anything?"

"Nothing big." I picked up a slim black case with an antenna sticking out of it. "Bug detector," I said. Then I held it next to Herb, said, "Beep beep beep! Crab lice alert!"

Herb shoved the device away, then got behind me and roughly pressed me up against the wall. "You keep it up, and the next thing your magic dildo is going to record is you going *pbbthhhh* when I shove it up your—"

"Enough," Phin said, pulling Herb off of me. "I will personally kick both your asses if you don't cut this shit out and focus. Harry, have you noticed anything weird lately? Strange phone calls? Emails?"

"There is the one guy, keeps emailing me, telling me I won the Nigerian lottery. I'm thirty percent sure it isn't legit."

"Seen anyone hanging around the office? Anyone following you or Jack?"

I had a flash of memory. "Actually, there was this one guy. A few days ago. Spooky looking mother. Black, greasy hair. Pale as the sickly, white underbelly of a morbidly obese sea cow."

"Where did you see him?"

"Outside the office. Just standing on the corner, staring up at our window."

"Did Jack see him?" Phin asked.

I closed my eyes, thinking. "No. She was on the phone with a client. I was playing *Farmville*—I just earned enough from my turnip patch to buy a tractor—and I noticed him down there. Checked again a few minutes later, and he was still there."

"What did you do then?"

"I plowed my field in like one tenth of the time. That tractor is epic."

Farmville was fun, but it wasn't as cool as Combville.

"Did you go down and talk to him?" Phin asked me.

"Naw. When I checked again, he was gone. Hey, how come we aren't *Facebook* friends?"

"Because I'm not on *Facebook*," Phin said. "I actually have a life."

"You should get on there, and friend me, and then send me fuel for my new tractor."

Phin backed me up against the wall, much like Herb had a moment ago.

Hey, easy buddy," I said.

"If you kill him," Herb said, "I'll call it suicide in the police report."

"You're not taking this seriously, McGlade." Phin spoke softly. "Someone has Jack. We need to stop screwing around."

"Relax, Phin. How many times have we been in this situation? So many times, we already know how it's going to end. It'll be a close call, but me, or you, or Tubby the Talking Manatee here will save her at the last possible second. That's what always happens."

"Strangle him," Herb said. "We'll make it look like auto-erotic asphyxiation."

"Check the house for bugs, Harry," Phin ordered. "And don't say another goddamn word."

Phin released me. I smoothed out my rumpled suit and said, "When I win the Nigerian lottery, I'm not giving either of you a penny." Then I turned on his bug detector and walked into the bedroom.

To return to the previous section, go to page 228.

To start the Amish adventure over, go to page 2.

Ninnie-the-Poop Visits His Friend Jiglet by J. Andrew Haknort

(with apologies to Milne)

One fine day, Ninnie-the-Poop, or Poop for short, was walking through the Thirty-Eight Acre Wood to visit his friend Jiglet, who lived beneath the Big Ash Tree. Poop was singing a song to himself that went like this:

Oh how nice to be a bear!

Without a worry or a care!

The sun is out, the sky is blue!

So little time, so much to do!

Poop sang this song to himself, over and over and over again, when all of the sudden he realized he'd walked much farther than he'd intended.

"Oh bother," said Poop. "I really fucked up this time."

So he (he being Poop) sat down under a small elm tree to contemplate his position while he smoked some crack cocaine.

That shit fucked him up, but good.

He was about to light another rock when he saw his good friend Eyesore, the old gray donkey, walk by.

"Hallo, Eyesore," said Poop.

"Blow it out your ass, faggot," was Eyesore's reply.

Poop frowned.

"Did you lose your tail again, Eyesore?" asked Poop.

"No," said Eyesore. "I just found out I have prostate cancer."

Poop laughed and laughed at his silly friend.

"Don't worry, Eyesore. I can fix you."

Eyesore spit out a big loogie and gave Poop the finger.

"That rock has fucked up your very small brain, Poop," said Eyesore. "You can't fix me. I've got a tumor up my ass the size of a casaba melon."

So Poop pulled out his 9mm and shot the old gray donkey between the ears.

Poop wasn't walking for very long when he ran into his friend, Winchester Probin.

"Hallo, Winchester Probin," said Poop. "What are you doing there?"

Winchester Probin had a hammer and some nails.

"Hallo, Poop! I'm nailing Bunny's ears to this tree."

"Oh, hallo Bunny!" said Poop. "I didn't know that was you under all that blood. How are you?"

Bunny didn't answer. His mouth was stapled shut.

"So what are you up to, you silly old Bear?" asked Winchester Probin.

"I was going to Jiglet's house, but I got lost. I'm so angry I could fuck broken glass."

"That's too bad." Winchester Probin said. The small boy picked his nose. "Would you like to stay here and play with Bunny and me?"

"No thank you," said Poop, rubbing his ass in recollection of the last time he had played with Winchester Probin.

"Can you watch Bunny for me while I go get my propane torch?" asked Winchester Probin.

"Sorry, no," said Poop. "I must be going."

"I never loved you, you fucked-up little cocksucker!" cried Winchester Probin, reaching out to grab Poop.

But Poop was faster. He pulled out his 9mm and shot the small boy four times in the chest.

Winchester Probin fell to the ground with a sucking chest wound. His belly looked like hamburger.

Finally, after puking up a lot of blood and part of his intestinal tract, Winchester Probin died.

Poop stopped playing with himself and turned his attention to Bunny.

"Would you like me to let you go, Bunny?" Poop asked.

Bunny nodded, his big eyes wet with tears.

Poop spent the next hour sodomizing Bunny.

When Poop was finished, he poked Bunny repeatedly with a very sharp stick.

After Bunny died, Poop raped his eye socket, and then he continued on his journey to Jiglet's house.

He was halfway there when he ran into his dealer, Trigger. As usual, Trigger was bouncing up and down on his tail.

"Hallo, Trigger!" said Poop.

"Hallo, Poop!" answered Trigger. "Need some meth? That's why Trigger's are so bouncy, don't you know."

And Trigger began to sing his song:

The wonderful thing about Triggers!
Is they love to smoke dat rock!
I'm so goddamned bouncy!
I just bounced on my cock!

Poop waited patiently while Trigger sang his song about eight thousand fucking times, jumping up and down like he'd been given a caffeine enema.

Finally, Poop had had enough. He pulled out his 9mm and blew off Trigger's tail.

"Take your Ritalin, you ADHD freak," said Poop.

"My bounce!" Trigger cried, picking up his bloody tail.

"Hurry the fuck up with that crack," chided Poop. "Or I'm killing your parents."

Trigger dug out some crack vials, and Poop threw a twenty at him.

"You had better see a doctor, Trigger, and get that looked at," said Poop.

Then Poop continued on his way to Jiglet's house.

He was almost there when he saw Rooga the kangaroo standing next to the trail.

"Bitch, where's my money?" Poop asked.

He slapped Rooga in the face.

"I'll get it, Mack Ninnie," said Rooga . "It's been slow! I swear to Christ!"

Poop grabbed one of Rooga's tiny arms. He stared at the track marks.

"Don't lie to me, ho! You've been shooting smack again!"

Poop kicked her in the pouch.

"I'll make some cheddar, Ninnie! I promise!"

"Damn straight you will!" Poop forced Rooga to her knees. "Now nibble on this furry bear hotdog."

Rooga made a face. "Poop—it smells like Bunny shit."

"Suck the poop off the Poop. Get to it, or I'll pimp stick you up the stank."

So Rooga got to it.

When she finished swallowing, Poop gave her a friendly slap across the face.

"You know I love you, bitch," cooed Poop. "Now get that sweet marsupial ass back on the street and make Daddy some money. And tell the same to your bratty kid. If he don't earn, the child will burn. Dig?"

Then Poop once again continued on his journey to Jiglet's house. But being a Bear of Very Little Intelligence, Poop got lost again.

"Oh, bother," said Poop.

Poop logged onto the Internet with his iPhone and tried to use MapQuest.com. He followed the directions closely, but came to a dead end.

MapQuest had fucked him, like it had so many others.

"Cock sucking monkey fucker," said Poop.

Poop finally arrived at his destination by pure luck, several hours later.

"It's about fucking time," Poop thought.

He knocked on the door.

"Hallo, Jiglet!" Poop yelled. "Are you home?"

"I'm taking a shit! Fuck off!" Jiglet yelled back.

Poop picked the lock and let himself in.

Jiglet appeared behind the corner. He was naked, brandishing a stiff six-shooter. He also had a gun.

"Oh, Poop! It's only you!"

Jiglet put down the gun and leaned against the counter, leaving a brown smear because he didn't wipe his ass.

"Who were you expecting, Jiglet?" Poop asked.

"My bookie, Guido. He told me he'd hammer my nuts flat if I didn't pay him."

Poop squinted. "He wouldn't need a very large hammer."

Jiglet farted.

"Fuck you, Poop. What the fuck do you want, you fat fuck?"

Poop smacked his lips. "I was wondering, perchance, did you have a smackeral of honey?"

Jiglet sat down, leaving another brown smear.

"Sorry, you freeloading fat ass. I don't have a thing to eat."

Poop took out his gun. "Maybe I'll just eat you instead."

Jiglet tried to get up, but his sticky poo-butt was stuck to the chair.

"You don't want to eat me, Poop! I'm just a little animal, small and stringy!"

But Poop wasn't listening. He was thinking about pork chops and bacon strips.

Poop preheated the oven to 350 degrees.

"Poop, please!" pleaded Jiglet. "We're friends! Friends don't eat each other!"

"We aren't eating each other," said Poop. "I'm eating you."

Poop yanked Jiglet out of the chair and shoved him into the hot oven. While Jiglet screamed and screamed, Poop sang this song to himself:

I'm cooking my best friend!

I'm cooking my best friend!

See what happens when

You don't wipe your rear end!

Then Poop pulled out his crack pipe and lit up a rock.

Unfortunately for Poop, he was careless with his Zippo, and accidentally set himself on fire. Within seconds, the fur had burned off of his arms.

Poop tried to beat out the flames, but soon his whole body was ablaze.

"Oh bother," said Poop, as his face burned away. "I really fucked up this time."

The End

To start the Amish adventure over, go to page 2.

To return to the previous section, go to page 231.

To reread Ninnie-the-Poop, go to page 242.

To return to playing Combville, go to page 6. Or 7. Or 8. Or just randomly flip to a page, it'll probably be Combville.

To stay on this page, go to page 252.

To reread this sentence, go back to the begining of this sentence.

To stop reading this and try a different book, put this one down and pick up something else, then begin reading.

To make a rum and Coke, mix some rum in some Coke.

To make pyroelecrtic fusion, use pyroelectric crystals to generate high strength electrostatic fields to accelerate deuterium ions into a metal hydride target also containing deuterium with sufficient kinetic energy to cause these ions to undergo nuclear fusion.

This space for rent.

"Excuse me," I said, putting a hand over my mouth and rushing past Haknort. But before I could even get out of my chair, I bazooka-vomited all over the elderly man.

"Blah! I got some in my mouth!" complained Haknort.

I hurled again, and let me tell you, it tasted even worse coming out.

"Damn you, General Tsao!" I cursed. "Damn you and your funky, spoiled chicken!"

Then I threw up my lungs through my nose, and died.

To start the Amish adventure over, go to page 2.

To return to the previous section, go to page 231.

Andrew Mayhem is really dead.

Unless Strand gets uppity and wants to sue. If so, this section was all just a dream.

To start over, go to page 2.

Author's Note: *This is the very first Harry McGlade story. It began at my friend Jim Coursey's house, when we both were fifteen years old. We wrote the first few pages on his Apple IIe, parodying private eye fiction, giggling like fools at the dumb puns and crude sexual references. I wound up finishing it three years later, and naïvely sent the story to Playboy Magazine to see if they'd publish it. Playboy wisely declined, sending me my very first rejection letter. But I eventually wrote several dozen Harry McGlade stories, similar to this one, and eventually used a toned-down version of him in Whiskey Sour over fifteen years later.*

Besides a few decent jokes, this story isn't good. Harry is too much of a jerk, the parody is too unreal and over-the-top, and a lot of the lines sound like they came from the movie Airplane!

But I can say this is the first thing I ever wrote that I was proud of, and it was the start of my love affair with the written word. I've included this story here as a bonus, with minimal changes. Feel free to skip it—you won't be missing much. This is for completists only. Since Banana Hammock is basically a 'Harry McGlade Greatest Hits' collection, I thought it would be fun to show people how he got started, way back in 1985, when I was a naïve teenager thinking about someday writing for a living...

The Case of the Husband Who Wasn't There Because He Was Missing

Chapter 1

It was a misty Saturday night. Misty like a dame who just lost her line of credit at Macy's. I was sitting at my desk in my simulated-leather swivel chair, crumpling up bills and tossing them into the wastepaper basket on the other side of my office. Then there was a knock at the door. Silhouetted through the frosted glass window was the profile of a woman with really big boobs.

"Can I come in?"

"I don't know if there's room."

"What?"

"Come in, please."

She opened the door and stepped in.

Wow.

If beauty were stock, she could have cornered the market. Painted on her over-abundant body was a low-cut black sequined dress, and I sat up in my chair and strained my neck to try to get a glimpse of her tatas. Incredibly high-heeled pumps hugged her feet, and a pair of black nylons licked at her calves. She had a nice ass, too.

The black mascara around her emerald eyes was smeared, meaning she either had been crying, or didn't know how to put on mascara. She forced a smile. I wanted to bring her back to my apartment, take off all of her clothes, and wear them myself.

"Are you Harry McGlade?" she asked.

"That's what it says on the door, lady."

"I need your help."

"Can't get out of that dress, huh? Hold on, I've got some scissors in my desk."

"No, that's not it. I'm looking for my husband."

"Have you checked your cleavage?"

She turned her head to the side and started to cry. I felt like a jerk, but that's okay, because I am a jerk.

"Hey, lady, I'm sorry. Just because you got huge jumblies doesn't mean I should make fun of you."

She sniffled. "It's just that I'm always being treated like a sex object instead of a person."

I zipped my fly back up. "Please have a seat."

She sat down in the chair across from my desk. I opened my top drawer to see if I had any Kleenex, but only found a pair of boxer shorts, stained from my last trip to the peep show. I offered them to her, and she dabbed her eyes lightly. Then she pulled a small photograph out of her handbag and handed it to me.

"This is my husband."

The picture was of an old, fat, balding man who resembled Pugsly from "The Addams Family."

"I'm sorry," I said.

"Don't be, he's got money coming out of his asshole."

I love a dame who's got a way with words. "So, what's the problem?"

"I want you to find him."

"He's missing then?"

"You're quick."

"It's my job, babe."

I grinned nonchalantly. She was obviously impressed.

"Can you do it?"

"Huh? I wasn't paying attention."

"Can you find my husband?"

"Honey, I can find a plumber on a Sunday."

Her eyes widened. "Really?"

"I wouldn't dick you around, babe."

"Oh," she said disappointedly.

I stood up, for no real reason besides the dramatic implication of the scene. "I get two hundred dollars a day plus free reign over my client's estate and personal assets. Any questions?"

"How long is your penis?"

"Let's just say I scare female elephants. Anything else?"

"No, that's all I need to know. You'll take the case then?"

"Yes, now if you'll excuse me."

"You're starting already?"

"No, I just farted."

She walked out before I realized I knew nothing about her husband.

Chapter 2

I went over to "Fred's Place" to find my informant, Sneaky Earl. Sneaky was at the bar, drowning his sorrows in a watered down pint of Jack Daniels. He was obviously happy to see me, because when I walked in he got so excited he jumped through the window and started running down the alley. Too bad it was a dead end. Sneaky Earl never did have much luck.

I found him trying to get into a half-open apartment window by standing on a Dumpster.

"How you doin', Earl?"

"Leave me alone, Harry. I don't want nothing to do with you."

"You're not still upset about the bomb, are you Earl? I tell you, I didn't know it was armed."

"Go away, Harry. Just go away."

I grabbed him by the leg and pulled him down, just as he got his upper body in the window.

"I said I was sorry, Earl. C'mon, give a guy a break. The scars are healed. Now I need your help."

"Whenever I help you I always get in trouble, Harry."

"Don't worry, Earl. This one's real easy."

I went for my pocket to get the picture and Sneaky took off down the alley again. I pulled my .44 Magnum from its nest inside my trench coat and fired, hitting Sneaky Earl in the back of the head, painting a garbage can with his face. I've got such lousy aim. I only wanted to fire a warning shot.

I reholstered my heater and exited the alley. My horoscope said I shouldn't have gone out today.

Chapter 3

I dusted myself off and walked over to my '67 Mustang, which was parked in front of a fire hydrant. I decided my next move was to go home and drink until I passed out. I live in a thirty-first floor apartment two blocks away from my office. It's in the high rent district. I'm just mentioning that because I like to flaunt it in front of people's faces.

As I drove, I couldn't stop thinking about Mrs. Tatas, and how stupid I was not to ask for her name. But I soon realized it didn't matter, because as I parked my car there she was, standing in front of my building, gyrating her hips. She had a saxophone with her. She was obviously horny.

I got out of my Stang and walked over to her. What I needed was a really great line to impress the hell out of this dame. Something that would make her melt like butter in the microwave.

"Hi," I said.

"Hi," she said.

We were off to a good start.

"Were you just in the neighborhood?" I asked.

"No. I purposely stopped by because I wanted to sleep with you."

I love a girl who doesn't beat around the bush. Especially one with tatas like Volkswagons. She wrapped her lips around the mouthpiece of the saxophone and coyly blew "Alexander's Ragtime Band."

I hoped she could blow other things better. She was terrible. She should have read "Dr. Ruth's Guide to Good Sax." I was expecting a water buffalo to come running down the street and jump her. Luckily, I had a grapefruit, so I shoved it in the instrument.

"Listen lady, I usually make it a rule not to get involved with my clients. But in your case, I'll make an exception."

I couldn't name all the dames I've fed that line to. But she ate it up just like the rest of them. She was practically taking off her clothes right there when a black Buick came careening around the corner, spraying bullets. I pushed the broad out of the way and drew my gun, emptying the clip as the car flew past. I missed it completely, and killed seven Japanese tourists across the street. Then I heard the wailing of a police siren in the distance and knew I would have to spend the night talking to some stupid cop who has trouble wiping his own ass as opposed to having an intimate and tender night of hide the salami.

I thought about giving the dame the gun, then running away, but I knew each one of the Japanese tourists had a Nikon chocked full of photographic evidence proving yours truly was to blame. At times like this, I wished I had listened to my mother and become a male stripper.

Chapter 4

So there I was, talking to Fitzmoron, Detective ninth class, explaining what had happened for the sixth time while he tried to type it up at three words a minute.

"And then you fired your weapon?"

"Yes. Then I fired my weapon. At the same time I fired it the other six times you asked me. Were you born incompetent or is it something you work at? No, don't write that down."

Fitzmoron pulled the paper out of the typewriter and crumpled it up. This guy was stupid enough to be twins. He inserted a new piece and began again.

"Name?"

"The same name as before, dumbo. I thought finishing junior high was mandatory to become a cop."

In the meantime, Fitzmoron was retrieving the old statement from the garbage to try and figure out my name. Every second the mental giant here wasted was a second I wasn't joined in coital bliss with Mrs. Tatas. Then the Captain walked in.

"How are we doing?" he asked.

Fitzmoron spoke. "He's highly uncooperative, Captain."

"McGlade is always uncooperative. It's part of his irresistible charm. Right, McGlade?"

"Blow it out your ass."

He did. It was gross.

Chapter 5

I got out of the station at six in the morning. Captain Krunch finally came to the conclusion it was self-defense. That, coupled with the fact that the good Captain hates Japanese tourists was enough to get me off. I drove back to my apartment and wasn't surprised to find that Mrs. Tatas was gone. The dizzy broad didn't even know the danger she was in. Great tatas, though.

I parked and walked up to my room while thinking about my situation. What I needed was a shot of whiskey and a good night's sleep. I also needed a new blender. I broke the old one mixing concrete. But I couldn't worry about that now.

I had to find Mrs. Tatas before somebody knocked her off. Or up.

I opened my door and walked into my humble abode, inhaling deeply the smell of a messy lifestyle. Which, coincidentally, smelled very much like moldy socks. I tried to turn on a light but all my bulbs were burned out. As I walked through the apartment in the dark, I bumped into my aquarium, and saw the fish were all dead. I must have forgotten to feed them a couple of times. In fact, I don't ever remember feeding them at all. Thinking about food made me hungry, so I went to the kitchen to eat.

I opened the refrigerator, only to stare at a single rotten cabbage. An old girlfriend had left it there two months ago, and never came back for it. Besides the cabbage, the only other things my fridge contained were ketchup, pickle relish, and half a beer, which had been there since 1983. A ketchup sandwich would have been okay, if I had had some bread. But I didn't.

My thoughts drifted to the fish, and how fresh they were. But a quick sniff of the tank made me want to yak, so I decided against it.

At this point I was really hungry, probably because I was dwelling on the fact. So I went back to the fridge and looked at the cabbage. It was kind of brown, with purple fuzz on one side. I took it out and peeled off a leaf without fuzz on it. Closing my eyes, I stuffed the leaf into my mouth and chewed. Then I passed out.

Chapter 6

I awoke as there was a knock at the door. My face was completely frost-bitten, and my lower lip was stuck to the metal handle of the drawer marked "Crisper" in the refrigerator.

"Jusss a minute!" I yelled, trying to remove my lip and only succeeding in pulling out the drawer with my face.

"Harry? Are you in there?"

It was Mrs. Tatas. I tried to yank the drawer off but instead stretched my lower lip down to my navel.

"I'm in da bafroom! Ow ve wight out!"

I stumbled over to the utensil drawer and took out a steak knife.

"I can come back later…"

"No, juss waid a shecond!"

I scraped the knife across my lip, causing the drawer to fall and land on my foot, corner first. I screamed.

"Are you okay, Harry?"

"I'm fine! Just fine! I'll be right there!"

I grabbed a greasy napkin and pressed it to my bleeding lip, then ran to the door.

"Hi," I said, trying to stop the blood and look nonchalant at the same time.

"What happened?"

"Cut myself shaving."

"You shave your lips?"

"Would you like to come in?"

She was wearing a pink dress, but with a dame like her, you rarely pay attention to the clothing. You pay attention to what's in it. And inside this dress was the most irresistible thing I've ever seen, next to Inflatable Debbie with the vibrating grip. I held her in the doorway, tightly, like I was trying to crush a beer can between our bodies.

She said she wanted my body. I told her I was still using it, but she could have it on loan. I pressed my lips to hers and she gagged on the greasy napkin stuck to my face. I pulled the napkin off and began to bleed on her dress. She stepped on my injured foot with her spiked heel, and I jerked my leg up and kneed her in the stomach. As she doubled over in pain, she hit her head on the doorway and collapsed in a pile on the floor, digging her nails into my chest on the way down. I bit my lip to control the pain, only to scream as my teeth sank into my open wound.

You could probably say the whole scene was not very romantic.

But the situation wasn't a total loss. Here I had a gorgeously well-endowed dame unconscious in my room. This was what I used to pray for in college. I dragged her inside and was just about ready to pull out Jack the Fun Machine when a cop appeared in the doorway.

"Harry McGlade?"

"Yeah?"

"Do you know this man?" He handed me a picture of the late Sneaky Earl.

"No," I said, and slammed the door.

But the cop knocked again. I hated dedicated cops. In fact, I hated all cops. I opened the door.

"Mr. McGlade, I'm afraid you'll have to come with me."

"I'd much rather stay here and come with her."

"That will have to wait, Mr. McGlade. Let's go."

I left the apartment realizing I still didn't know the broad's name.

Chapter 7

They charged me with seventeen counts of first degree murder, and jay-walking. My lawyer said I could beat the jay-walking charge but I'd be serving two hundred and fifty years to life for the murder rap. So there I sat there, locked in the slammer with a bunch of hardcore criminals, trying to make sure my pooper stayed a virgin. Then good old Detective ninth class Fitzmoron appeared and removed me from my cell. He took me to my lawyer, who was in the prison chapel, praying.

"How do things look, Sal?" I asked.

"Not good, Harry. I'm going to try to plea bargain for only three life sentences."

"But it's only a hearing, Sal."

"Trust me, Harry."

I trusted Sal about as much as I liked him. And I hated Sal. But I didn't really have a choice, unless I represented myself. And I've only been dressing myself for two months.

I would just have to hope for the best. Sal genuflected and we left the chapel.

Chapter 8

To make a long story short, I was acquitted. Sal had a nervous breakdown in court and the judge decided to just drop the whole matter and break for lunch. I took a cab back to my apartment and wasn't surprised to find Mrs. Tatas gone.

But she did leave a note. It told me to meet her at Chez Guevara for a six o'clock dinner reservation. And it was signed Mrs. Bertram P. Niss. So I finally found out who I was looking for. That was the break I needed.

I looked up Bertram's name in the phone book and called up his house to see if he was home. He wasn't. This was going to be harder than I thought.

I had a few hours before dinner so I decided to try and get some leads. So I left my apartment and went over to "Fat Louie's" to see... Fat Louie. He was in the back, eating a Fat Louie Burger. If anyone knew the streets, it was Fat Louie. If anyone knew fresh produce, it was Fat Louie. We went back a long way, and were like brothers.

"How you doin', Fat?"

"Fuck you."

"You know where Bertram P. Niss is?"

"No. Get out."

"Nice talking to you, Fat."

"Keep in touch."

I left "Fat Louie's" feeling optimistic. I wasn't any closer to finding

Bertram P. Niss, but at least I wasn't Fat Louie. I decided to approach the situation differently, and went to sleep.

Unfortunately, I was driving at the time, and I ran over a Cub Scout Troop practicing CPR in a parking lot. Rather than be sent to jail again, I dumped their bodies into the retention pond and spread towels and suntan oil along the shore to make it look like a swimming accident. Then I began tracking down leads again, though my spirits were considerably dampened for the next two hours.

Chapter 9

Seven years ago, I had a minor crisis when I thought I was the reincarnation of Fatty Arbuckle. That flashed back into my mind as I sat at a table in Chez Guevara, watching some fat broad stuck in the revolving door. How fat was she? She was so fat, she got stuck in the revolving door. But I wasn't there for the entertainment. I was waiting for Mrs. Niss and her big tatas to join me for dinner to discuss my recent developments. Since we had last met, I discovered some startling evidence that would conclusively prove Jimmy Carter was an alien from the planet Bonzo. Unfortunately, I had learned nothing concerning her missing husband. But she didn't have to know that.

She arrived a fashionable six hours late, wearing a slinky pink silk wrap that hugged her curvaceous body, along with a smile. She obviously expected good news. Oh well. She sat down on the mashed potatoes I had left on her chair.

"Oh. How stupid of me to leave those mashed potatoes on your chair. We better go to my place and soak that dress."

She was noticeably impressed by my clever ploy to remove her from her clothing. Now all I had to do was wait for the Mickey I slipped in her drink to take effect. Unfortunately, she noticed it, and ordered another drink without a mouse.

So the only way I was going to get her unconscious was to match her drink for drink, or hit her with a ball-peen hammer. And I left my hammer at home.

Fourteen drinks later, when the welders were almost done removing the fat broad, I had discovered that trying to Mrs. Niss drunk was like trying to get Mr. Rogers hard. I gave up and decided to lay my cards on the table.

"Want to play elevator?"

"How do you play?"

So I showed her my shaft. Then I asked her if she was going up.

"I'm not that kind of woman."

"Why? Do you have a penis?"

"No. I'm married."

Then it hit me. Why she had gone from coy to prude in less than twelve hours. I should have known it right away. It was the old *hire a private investigator then set him up for the murder of the husband and collect the insurance* scam. When all the while, she was the one that killed him.

"Where did you hide the body?"

"What are you talking about?"

"Don't play innocent with me. You killed him. Right? Am I right? You did it. Right?"

She laughed villainously. "Yes, I killed him. He had a life insurance policy worth more than the merchandising rights to Star Wars. And you're going to take the fall for it. While you were here waiting for me, I put his body in your apartment along with some revealing pictures of him and Jim Bakker. It will look like you tried to blackmail him, he didn't go for it, and you killed him with your gun."

"My gun?"

"Yes. I took a slug out of one of the Japanese tourists you shot when you were trying to protect me from the car I hired to shoot blanks at us in front of your apartment. Then I just substituted your bullet for the one I used to kill my husband. That's the one in his chest right now."

"You won't get away with this."

"Oh no? By now, the police are probably at your apartment and they've got all the evidence they need to put you away for life."

Boy, did I feel stupid. She set me up perfectly. I should have known, especially after seeing Body Heat. I was always a sucker for the ones with big cans. Worst of all, even though I solved the case, I knew I probably wouldn't get paid. At times like this, I wish I had gotten that sex change operation.

"So what happens now?" I asked.

"Now, we say goodbye. If you hurry, maybe you can make it to the border. I've got a date with an insurance company."

She got up to leave, but I unsheathed my .44 and yelled after her. "Me making it to the border has nothing to do with you being alive or not."

She turned around and laughed. "You couldn't hit a legless elephant from ten feet away."

Then she looked at my gun and froze.

"How do you like my new telescopic sight?" I asked.

And with that, I blew her head off. It was a shame. I never even got a chance to feel her up.

A waiter looked at me inquisitively.

"The lady will get the check," I said, and then left.

Chapter 10

I never did get arrested for killing her husband. The bimbo made one mistake. When she was putting the slug from my gun into her husband's body, she lost her wedding ring in the bullet hole. So I didn't really need to kill her, but it felt good. Besides, she was a tease. And that was the defense I used when I stood trial for her murder. The judge understood, and I only got sentenced to twenty hours of community service. Now, every Friday, I become troop leader for a group of Boy Scouts. This week I'm going to teach them how to cop a feel and pretend it was an accident.

Sometimes private investigation isn't pretty.

The End

To restart the Amish adventure, go to page 2.
To read Cub Scout Gore Feast, turn the page.

Cub Scout Gore Feast

A Bonus Short Story by J.A. Konrath & Jeff Strand

"Isn't this when you start telling scary stories, Mr. Hollis?"

Hollis grinned, staring at the boys around the campfire. Cub Scouts, none of them older than ten. For some, the first night they'd ever spent away from their families.

"Are you scouts sure you want to hear a scary story?"

"Yes!" they chorused.

"Even though it's dark and we're all alone in the spooky, menacing forest?"

"Yes! Yes! Yes!"

Hollis sat down on his haunches. His face became serious.

"Okay, I'll tell you a scary story. Scary because it's the absolute, hand-on-my-heart truth. You've all heard rumors about Troop 192, how they disappeared without a trace not too far from here, right?"

Several of the boys nodded.

"Well, the rumors were wrong. There were *lots* of traces of Troop 192. There were traces all over the place...on the ground, up in the trees, by the lake, maybe even under where you're sitting right now. Imagine if you took a blender, like the kind your mothers use to make smoothies, but it was a *giant* blender, maybe...I dunno, eighteen feet high. And then you dropped the entire Troop 192 into it, and accidentally left the lid off, so that when you pressed the 'blend' button they sprayed all over the place. That's what it looked like."

"I heard it was just one kid who went missing," said Anthony.

Hollis shrugged. "If you think one little kid has that many guts inside of his body, more power to you, but I was here. I saw it. It was *gross*."

"My mom said they found him the next morning. He was playing Nintendo."

"Oh, well, I guess your mom is in a position where she was allowed to accompany the law enforcement agencies on their search, huh? Did she somehow become deputized without anybody hearing about it? Do Hooters waitresses typically get to tag along on searches for missing children?"

"She works at Olive Garden."

"Whatever. She wasn't there on the night of the investigation. I'm telling you that it was the entire troop, and their insides were strewn as far as the eye can see." Hollis made a grand gesture with both arms to emphasize the extent of the carnage. "And do you know who got blamed for it?"

Several of the scouts shook their heads.

"Madman Charlie. Oh, they arrested him, and sent him to the electric chair the next morning. But it wasn't Madman Charlie. When Troop 192 was massacred, he was off murdering a young woman in a completely different county. No, Troop 192 wasn't slaughtered by Madman Charlie. They weren't even slaughtered by something...human."

One of the youngest scouts, Billy somebody, raised his hand. No doubt because he was too terrified to hear more.

"Billy, are you too terrified to hear more?" Hollis asked. "Because that's okay. Nobody here will judge you."

"No, Mr. Hollis. I have to go to the bathroom."

Hollis sighed again. "Go ahead, Billy. But don't go too far away. Anyway, there's something inhuman in these woods. Something that hungers for human flesh."

Theolonious raised his hand. Probably wet himself he was so scared.

"Do we have any more hot dogs?" Theolonious asked.

"You already had three."

"Jimmy ate the one I dropped on the ground."

"Jimmy didn't come with us on this trip."

"Well, okay, I ate it, but it wasn't as good as the two that didn't get dropped on the ground. Can I please have another one?"

"This inhuman creature," Hollis said, ignoring him and raising his voice, "slaughtered Troop 192 on a night very much like tonight. It cracked open their bones and sucked out the marrow, and slurped up their intestines like spaghetti, then flossed its sharp fangs with their muscle fibers. And rumor has it this insatiable monster still hunts in these very woods, on the night of..." Hollis paused for dramatic effect, "the *full moon*."

"Was it a Dracula?" Cecil asked.

"Draculas don't rip people up," said Anthony. "Draculas just look unhappy a lot, and kiss girls like in that movie my sister watched seventeen gazillion hundred times."

"Those were dumb Draculas," said Cecil. "But there are cool Draculas, like in *Lord of the Rings*."

"Those were orcs."

"Not those! The other ones!"

"That was a Kraken!"

"The horrible creature," Hollis said, standing tall and raising his arms over his head, "was a werewolf!"

"I thought werewolves just took off their shirts a lot like in that movie with the Draculas."

Hollis shook his head. "In real life, werewolves like to crack open the rib cages of little boys with their sharp claws and bite their still-beating hearts right from their chests. That's what happened to Troop 192."

"If they were attacked by a werewolf," said Anthony, "wouldn't they become werewolves?"

"Not if their bodies were shredded and thrown around all over the trees and lake and ground. If you'd been paying attention when I started telling the story you could have caught that little detail."

"What if a werewolf bit a skunk?" Theolonious asked. "Would it become a werewolfskunk?"

"A werewolf wouldn't bite a skunk," Hollis said.

"Why not?"

"Why *would* it bite a skunk? Would *you* bite a skunk?"

"I wouldn't bite a skunk today," said Mortimer, "but if I was a werewolf, I think I'd bite a skunk if there was one sitting there. You'd have to bite it gently, y'know, so that its whole head doesn't come off, but I think, y'know, werewolves can bite gently when they want to, even though they usually don't. They couldn't use their whole jaw or, y'know, anything like that, but if they just used their front teeth and didn't close them all the way, I think they could bite a skunk without its head coming off."

The other cub scouts murmured their agreement.

"Y'know," Mortimer added.

"And what if the werewolfskunk bit a deer?" asked Theolonious. "Would it turn into a werewolfskunkdeer?"

"I want to know how one werewolf ate all of Troop 192," said Cecil. "How big is a werewolf's stomach?"

"Haven't I already explained that twice?" asked Hollis. "The werewolf didn't eat their whole bodies. He ate the best parts, then scattered the rest of them all over the place so that the kids couldn't turn into little werewolves. Do you want a demerit? Do you?"

"I need toilet paper!" Billy yelled from the woods.

"Use leaves!" Hollis hollered back.

"I tried! They're all stuck to me!"

Fredrick raised his hand. "Would a werewolfskunkdeer try to eat people? Or would it just forage for nuts and berries?"

"You don't even know what 'forage' means," said Silas.

"It means to search for provisions."

"Well, you don't know what 'tourniquet' means!"

"Yes, I do. We learned about them last week. It's that thing you twist around your arm or leg to stop bleeding."

"Well, you don't know what 'hypothesis' means!"

"*Silas*! Enough!" Hollis clenched and unclenched his fists a few times. "Anyway..."

Theolonious frowned. "So is a werewolfskunkdeer a person who changes into something that's a wolf, skunk, and deer all at once, like it has fur and Bambi eyes and sprays skunk spray, or is it a person who can change into a wolf *or* a skunk *or* a deer?"

"I have no idea," Hollis said.

"I think he changes into one of them, but he can't control which one it is. So he'll be fighting Bigfoot and he'll want to change into a wolf because wolves are better at fighting Bigfoot, but he'll change into a skunk instead and Bigfoot just steps on him. That's probably why you don't see many werewolfskunkdeers around anymore."

"What if a werewolf bit a Dracula who bit a zombie who then bit the werewolf?" asked Cecil.

"My baby brother bit the babysitter, but she didn't turn into a baby."

"Shut up!" said Theolonious. "That's not what we're talking about!"

"But what if a werewolfskunkdeer bit a wolf? Is it a werewolfskunkdeerwolf, or does the wolf part just not matter because it was already a wolf?"

"Werewolfwolfskunkdeer sounds better," said Anthony.

"Soon the full moon will rise," Hollis said, raising his arms theatrically. "And then the werewolf takes its supernatural form and..."

"You mean the werewolfwolfskunkdeer."

"No. I mean the werewolf. There's no such thing as a werewolfskunkdeer."

"You forgot the extra wolf. It's werewolf*wolf*skunkdeer."

"I did not forget the extra wolf. We aren't talking about the werewolfskunk deer."

"The werewolf*wolf*skunkdeer."

"We're talking about a werewolf! A regular old werewolf! That's it. Just a man who turns into a goddamn wolf, okay?"

The scouts went silent. Hollis knew he'd gone too far by using the g.d. word, but the punchline to his story was *so* amazing and they were ruining it.

"Mr. Hollis, is this poison oak?" Billy asked, walking back to the campfire holding some leaves.

"Yes, Billy. Put that down."

"I wish I'd picked different leaves. Can I go home?"

"No. There's some baking soda in the tent. Let me finish my story and I'll get it for you."

"Could a werewolf eat a baby whole, in one bite?" asked Anthony.

"I suppose one could," Hollis said. Actually, he *knew* that one could. Firsthand. Heh heh.

"So when it pooped out the baby, would the baby be a werepoopwolf?"

"What if a werepoopwolf bit a werewolfwolfskunkdeer?"

"It would be a werewolfwolfwolfpoopskunkdeer."

"Enough," Hollis said. "The next person who says something gets a bad report to their parents and they won't get to come on any more of these trips. Got it? See that full moon up there? That ties into our little story, doesn't it?

Do you see the connection between what happened to Troop 192 and the lunar cycle of today? You get it, right? Do you know what Troop 192 was doing on that fateful night? They were—*irony alert*—sitting around listening to scary stories from their scoutmaster! Do you get where this is going?"

The scouts remained silent.

Hollis stood up.

"That's riiiiiiiiight! The story I was trying to tell you is foreshadowing what's going to happen tonight! Ha! How about that, you little brats? The reason there are so many similarities in the fate of Troop 192 and our situation at this very moment is because *I* am a werewolf!"

He stood there, facing the moonlight, waiting for the inevitable transformation.

"What story did you tell the other kids?" Cecil asked.

"Excuse me?"

"Were you telling them about another werewolf attack before that one?"

"Yes. That's right. It's all a vicious cycle. Each story I tell the scouts is about the previous massacre. I'll tell the next troop about you guys."

"If you killed all of those Cub Scout Troops, who keeps hiring you as a scoutmaster?"

He adjusted his angle. *Change, dammit, change!*

Theolonious raised his hand. "So if you bit a mummy—?"

Screw it, Hollis thought. He'd brought an axe.

Frederick was first, right in the middle of another stupid question when the axe caught him under the chin. It cleaved his jaw in half, his tongue waggling through the gap, blood spurting like a lawn sprinkler.

Hollis pinned Billy under his foot and hacked his arm off, then dangled it above his face, teasing him.

"Stop hitting yourself!" he yelled in Billy's face, slapping him with his own hand. It was good fun until shock set in and Billy stopped screaming.

Cecil got a straight chop to the throat, but the axe wasn't sharp enough to decapitate him fully, and his head flopped backward, still attached to some sinew.

As he'd warned earlier, Hollis drove the axe head into Anthony's ribcage, cracking it open, then diving in the feast on the child's still-beating heart with his razor-sharp werewolf fangs that seemed rather flat and dull for the job. He did manage to bite off a piece of something that could have been a ventricle, but might have been an atrium. Hollis always got those confused.

Theolonius watched, eyes wide, hugging his knees. He was covered in blood that wasn't his own. Hollis raised the axe, ready to make a lupine feast of the boy's small brain, when Theolonious began to scream.

No, not a scream.

That's more like a howl.

First the boy's nose extended, becoming hairy and snoutish.

Then claws burst from his fingertips, curving into the shape of scythes.

Hollis dropped the axe, dumbfounded, as the miniature werewolf then grew...

Antlers?

Theolonious quickly spun around, lifting his giant black tail, one that had a white stripe running down it ala Pepé Le Pew.

"Oh no..."

The werewolfskunkdeer sprayed Hollis with its anal scent glands while the scoutmaster was screaming, and some of the spray got into Hollis's mouth. The smell...the taste...was so bad, Hollis had no choice but to whip out his Swiss Army Knife, thumb open the mini scissors, and immediately begin snipping away at his own nose and tongue, *snip snip snipping* until...

"Mr. Hollis? Is this the baking soda?"

Hollis blinked away the daydream and stared at Billy.

Hollis sighed. "That's it, Billy."

Theolonious raised his hand. "Mr. Hollis? Will we get our fishing merit badges tomorrow?"

"Yes, Theolonious."

"Is storytime over?" Cecil asked.

"I guess."

Silas raised his hand.

"What, Silas? Do you want to ask me what 'transitory' means?"

"I want to know what's wrong with your ears. They're getting longer."

Hollis slapped his hands against the sides of his head. Indeed, his ears were getting longer. Longer and hairier.

He jammed a finger into his mouth, tapping the quick growing fangs.

It's about time.

Hollis leapt onto Silas, taking the boys whole head in his mouth. He squeezed his mighty werewolf jaws closed, feeling the skull bend inward, then crack suddenly, popping open like a walnut, squirting hot brains through Silas's nasal cavity.

With Cecil, he dug his snout into the boy's belly, clenching his teeth down on a length of intestines, holding tight as Cecil ran for the trees. Cecil managed to pull out his intestines, both large and small, his colon, his stomach, and something that might have been a spleen, before keeling over.

With Billy, Hollis dug one of his claws through the child's eye socket, then dug it through his skull and out the other eye, holding him like a six-pack. Then he pulled, tearing off the bridge of Billy's nose.

Theolonious cried out in horror, and Hollis ripped his lungs out of his chest, squeezing them like an accordion, making the scream go on and on and...

"Mr. Hollis? Is that a werewolfskunkdeer?" Cecil asked, pointing at something in the woods.

Hollis shook his head to clear it. The fantasies were getting more and more real. The medication wasn't working like it should.

"It's not?" Cecil asked.

"What are you pointing at, Cecil?"

"That thing, with the horns."

"You mean the tree?"

"No, the…oh, yeah. The branches looked like horns."

And then the transformation began. For real this time? Hollis bit down on the inside of his mouth as hard as he could. It hurt like hell—this was definitely real. Those little bastards were about to see what a *true* werewolf could do.

The scouts stared at him. Their jaws dropped as one.

The inside of his cheek was bleeding pretty badly. He shouldn't have bit so hard.

"That's right," he said. "Just like I've been hinting over and over, I am a werewolf! And on this night of the full moon, I shall enjoy a Cub Scout gore feast!"

Cecil screamed. Hollis laughed and then, transformation complete, let out the howl of the beast he had become.

"That's it?" asked Billy.

"What?"

"You're not very furry."

"My arms are hairy!"

"Not *that* hairy. My dad's arms are hairier."

"Look at my ears! Those aren't normal ears anymore. Look at my fingernails! And my nose sort of looks like a snout now!"

"I thought werewolves were supposed to be a lot scarier," said Theolonious.

"You know what? You kids *suck*! It's not my fault that the werewolf who bit me didn't break the skin all the way, and that I don't do a complete change! You should still be terrified! When's the last time you saw somebody's fingernails grow a full half-inch within ten seconds? Never, that's when? You've never seen somebody's nose change shape like that!"

"My sister got hit in the face with a basketball and—"

"Shut the hell up! I have killed hundreds of Cub Scouts, and if you think your ridiculous werewolfwolfskunkdeermoosepygmy fucker is the height of terror, then you can all just...just..." *No, no, no, I promised myself I wasn't going to do this again. Please, not again. Don't let it happen again...*

It happened again. Hollis succumbed to tears.

There was a long, uncomfortable silence.

"Mr. Hollis, can we go home and play Nintendo?"

"Yes." Mr. Hollis wiped the tears from his eyes. "Yes, we can."

The End

To return to the previous section, go to page 174.

To start over, go to page 2.

To read Harry McGlade's very first story, go to page 255.

"At the end of *Whiskey Sour* I killed the cyborg from the future, ensuring that there would be no nuclear war against the machines."

"That was end of *The Terminator*," Jack said.

"Was not."

Jack folded her arms. "Yes it was."

"Okay. At the end of *Whiskey Sour* I blow up the Death Star."

"Try again."

"I throw my precious into the lava pool at Mount Doom."

"*Lord of the Rings*."

"I shoot Liberty Valance."

"That's *The Man Who Shot Liberty Valance*."

"I sink the putt that wins the caddy tournament."

"*Caddyshack*. You aren't even trying."

"We all go to jail for being jerks?"

"The series finale of *Seinfeld*."

"That's all I got. Unless—"

"Be still my beating heart."

"—it turns out Bugs Bunny was drawing the cartoon all along."

"*Duck Amuck*."

"That's my favorite Loony Tunes. It was even cooler than that time I killed the Gingerbread Man at the end of *Whiskey Sour*."

Jack frowned. "Why don't I ever kill the bad guys?"

"You did, in one of them," I said. "Didn't you?"

Her face scrunched up in thought. "Which one?" she asked.

"The one named after the drink."

"Doesn't sound familiar."

"With the drink on the cover. Two word title."

"I don't remember that one."

"Which was the one where we turned out to be brother and sister?" I asked.

"None of them."

"Was there one where we ever…" I gave Jack a bit of bump and grind.

"No! Hell, no! Hell fuck no!"

"I think the books need more sex. Did you know J.A. Konrath also writes a science fiction series under the name Joe Kimball? The first book, *Timecaster*, has plenty of sex in it. And I'm in it, too."

"Are not," Jack said.

"Am too."

"Prove it. Or better yet, go jump out of the window."

To read a Harry McGlade scene from *Timecaster*, go to page 134.

To make Harry jump out of a window, go to page 139.

To return to the previous section, go to page 104.

Hi, Maria!

To restart the adventure, go to page 2.
To return to the previous section, go to page 113.

Other Books by J.A. Konrath

Jack Daniels Thrillers
Whiskey Sour
Bloody Mary
Rusty Nail
Dirty Martini
Fuzzy Navel
Cherry Bomb
Shaken
Stirred
Shot of Tequila
Banana Hammock
Jack Daniels Stories (collected stories)
Serial Killers Uncut (with Blake Crouch)
Suckers (with Jeff Strand)
Planter's Punch (with Tom Schreck)
Floaters (with Henry Perez)
Truck Stop
Flee (with Ann Voss Peterson)
Babe on Board (with Ann Voss Peterson)
With a Twist
Street Music

Other Books
Symbios (writing as Joe Kimball)
Timecaster (writing as Joe Kimball)
Wild Night is Calling (with Ann Voss Peterson)
Shapeshifters Anonymous
The Screaming
Afraid (writing as Jack Kilborn)
Endurance (writing as Jack Kilborn)
Trapped (writing as Jack Kilborn)
Draculas (with Blake Crouch, Jeff Strand, and F. Paul Wilson)
Origin
The List
Disturb
65 Proof (short story omnibus)
Crime Stories (collected stories)
Horror Stories (collected stories)
Dumb Jokes & Vulgar Poems
A Newbie's Guide to Publishing
Be the Monkey (with Barry Eisler)

Made in the USA
Lexington, KY
07 October 2012